JANISSARIES

JERRY POURNELLE

BAEN

JANISSARIES

A Baen Book

Baen Publishing Enterprises
P.O. Box 1403
Riverdale, NY 10471

ISBN: 0-671-87709-1

Cover art by John Pound

First Baen printing, March 1996

Distributed by Simon & Schuster
1230 Avenue of the Americas
New York, NY 10020

Printed in the United States of America

To Tom Doherty

CONTENTS

PART ONE:

THE MERCENARIES

1

The mortar fire was nearer.

Rick Galloway heard the sharp *crump!* of at least five mortars. Then there was silence for a moment. It was just twilight, and twilight does not last in the tropics. Night came fast, and with it the sound of the African tropic highlands: birds, crickets, unidentifiable creatures calling each other in the sudden dark. A warm breeze rustled the dry grass on the hilltop.

There was a rattle of distant machine-gun fire. It sounded much too close.

"I think the roadblock has gone," Lieutenant Parsons said. His voice was surprisingly calm. "They will be here within the hour."

"Yeah." Captain Galloway swept his night glasses along the southern slope of the hill, down toward the crossroad where he had left Major Hendrix with the wounded. There was nothing to see. He turned carefully, letting the glasses sweep the perimeter of the hill that for the moment was his entire world. He saw nothing at all except the tiny remnant of his command. The men were digging in and had done a good job with the little they had.

"Where the hell are those choppers?" Galloway demanded. He felt sweat drip from his forehead despite the cooling breeze that sprang up after sundown. "Elliot."

"Sir." Sergeant Elliot was at the other end of the trench where Galloway stood. The trench had not been bunkered, but there was no time to construct better defenses for the command post.

"Can't you raise headquarters?" Galloway demanded.

"No, sir. Warner's trying." The big sergeant turned back to the radio.

"Perhaps we should let the men run for it," Parsons suggested. "Some may escape."

Rick shook his head. "What's to run to?" he asked.

Parsons shrugged. "We sell our lives to no purpose—"

"We're giving our employers another hour," Galloway said. His voice was as bitter as he felt, although he had tried to hide his feelings. "There's no point, André," Galloway said. "We don't speak the language, we're the wrong color, and we're surrounded. I expect half the troops have run anyway. They know the score. Elliot!"

"Sir."

"How many effectives do we have?"

"Maybe fifty, Captain."

"So there you are," Rick said. "About half the number we brought up this silly hill. The rest have run." He knew he was talking too much, saying too many words; but he was young and inexperienced, and afraid.

Parsons nodded in the darkness. He took a plastic bottle from his belt. "Wine?"

"Sure." Rick took the liter bottle and drank a couple of swallows of the cheap local wine. Parsons always carried a bottle. Rick was certain that "Parsons" wasn't the lieutenant's real name. Parsons spoke French and German and sometimes let slip a few words about Legion experience.

It hardly mattered. Rick wasn't a real captain, either. The operation was CIA, and the Agency had borrowed men from anywhere they could get them.

Galloway handed the bottle back to Parsons, who raised it in a mock toast. "Here's to us. There are damned few left."

"They're taking their own sweet time about coming," Rick said.

"Afraid of us." Parsons' voice was a mocking lilt in the dark.

"Sure," Galloway said. But they well might be, he thought. We've broken more than one Cuban mercenary outfit. With any help at all from the politicians who put us out here in Sainte Marie, we'd have won. At that it was a near thing. What was it Wellington said about Waterloo? A near-run thing—as near a thing as you'd ever hope to see. Well so was this, but the difference is it's us who lost it.

Officially they were volunteers, and received no direct support from the United States at all; but most of the men were veterans of the US Army, and the CIA had brought them in. The Cubans and Russians had made no secret at all of their aid to the other side.

"I got headquarters," Sergeant Elliot announced.

"*Mirabile dictu,*" Parsons muttered.

Rick crawled over to the radio. Perhaps prayers are answered after all, he thought. There was more automatic weapon fire from the south, and a mortar bomb dropped in fifty yards downhill. Rick estimated the enemy at less than a mile. It wouldn't be long now.

"Galloway here," he told the microphone. "Can you get us the hell out of here?"

"Negative."

The single word was a death sentence. Rick started to say that, then thought better of it. They knew. "Why not?"

"I'm sorry, Rick." Galloway recognized Colonel Blumfeld's voice. Blumfeld was one of the men who'd talked him into volunteering for this mission. "Washington has canceled all support. Highest level. I'd send the choppers anyway and to hell with my career, but I don't have any to send. They came and took them away."

"They?"

"Higher command." Blumfeld sounded unhappy. Rick thought he damned well ought to be unhappy. "Your orders are to surrender," Blumfeld said.

"Bat puckey. The Cubans will have us in a show trial as mercenaries," Rick said. "Then they'll shoot us."

"They say they won't."

"Sure. Colonel, are you sending me any support? Anything at all?"

"No."

"Then go to hell." Galloway handed the mike to Sergeant Elliot, then went back to where Parsons stood.

Parsons listened with a half-smile that barely showed in the starlight. Then he took out his wine bottle. "We had a good run," he said.

Rick reached for the bottle. "I'll drink to that."

"And now what?"

Rick shrugged. There were few choices. They were white men in a black country. Rick had always been quick to learn languages, but even he hadn't enough of the local patois to do more than buy groceries. They would be spotted easily wherever they went.

Major Jefferson had taken all the black troops on an infiltration raid. Rick hoped they'd escape, but without the black troops, there wasn't even the pretense of an integrated army. No blacks to speak and front for them. Rick wondered if that would matter. It might, depending on who captured them.

It was his first command, and very likely the only one he'd ever have. He wasn't experienced. He'd begun as a junior lieutenant, just out of ROTC from the state university, and his promotion to brevet captain was due to being in the right place and time; he knew better than to think it meant more.

Rick thought it didn't mean very much at all. Parsons was a career man, but the military wasn't Galloway's career. ROTC had been an easy way to pay for the college education he couldn't afford.

The other alternative was football. Rick was quick and wiry. Had he gone out for football, he could have got a scholarship, with all the other perquisites of a star. But he didn't like the game. It required too much commitment.

Instead, he had joined the track team and won his letter. Track didn't have the glamour of football; the football jocks got first choice of the girls. On the other hand, they often couldn't enjoy their opportunities because of injuries or training rules. Being a runner was definitely superior in Rick Galloway's view. He told himself that quite often. But track hadn't been important enough to the alumni; there weren't all those easy jobs available. ROTC had provided Rick's spending money.

When he graduated, Rick realized that he'd never committed himself to anything. He had neither joined a fraternity nor opposed them. He had few political opinions. He was a professional neutral, and he wasn't sure he liked the image.

A classmate, John Henry Carter, had been a career military man and had volunteered for the CIA operation in Africa. He had talked Rick into coming along; an adventure, something to do while he was young before he settled into a dull job and duller life. He'd known there was a possibility of being killed, but he'd never been seriously threatened in his life. He could outrun any danger.

Carter was the only black man Rick had ever known well, and the only friend he'd had in the outfit. Now Carter was off with Major Jefferson. Major Hendrix was missing a leg and had stayed behind to hold the roadblock south of them. Parsons and Galloway were the only officers left.

The plan had been for Galloway to take the hilltop and hold it until the helicopters came; then they could go back for the wounded. Rick hadn't liked the idea, but Hendrix made it an order. Someone had to hold the roadblock and someone else had to capture a landing area; Hendrix couldn't move, which left the hilltop to Galloway.

But Hendrix hadn't held the roadblock very long—and now there wouldn't be any helicopters.

And that's that, Rick thought. He had no choices left. For the first time, he couldn't even run . . .

Something caught his attention. Rick looked up. "What the hell?" He pointed toward the ink-black sky. A bright light moved among the stars. It seemed to come closer, and it made no sound at all. "Where did Labon get aircraft?" Rick demanded.

Parsons shrugged. "From the Cubans, I suppose—Rick, that is no aircraft."

He was right. The silent light moved closer, and in strange patterns like no airplane Rick had ever seen before. There was only the one light; it was impossible to make out the size or shape of the craft, but it blotted out stars. Too many stars. He realized with a shiver that it was *big*. It moved too fast and turned in weird patterns, and it moved in total silence. He felt the hair rising on the back of his neck.

It came lower, and a bright light stabbed down to illuminate the crest of the hill. There was enough light reflected upward to show what the tropical night had hidden.

"A goddamn flying saucer!" one of the troops shouted. There was a shot.

"Hold your fire!" Rick screamed.

Parsons looked at him curiously.

"That's nothing of Labon's. Why shoot at it? And—I'm not sure we *can* hurt it. . . ."

"It is landing," Parsons said.

"Of course." Rick felt an inane urge to giggle. Why not? he thought. We're defeated, surrounded, every one of us marked for a firing squad within the week, so why not flying saucers too? He felt lightheaded, and it was not just the wine. He was glad that he hadn't tried the local equivalent of pot.

Flying saucers weren't real. They weren't even science fiction. The girl he liked to think of as his mistress—he knew she'd have resented the label, and he'd never used it in her hearing, but he liked to think of himself as a man who'd once had a mistress—had been interested in science fiction, and had got Rick to read some of the classics; but neither she nor her friends "believed in" flying saucers.

The thing settled on the hilltop. It was very large, as big as a 707, and it wasn't precisely saucer-shaped, although seen edge on at a distance it might give that appearance. It was more like half a football sliced lengthwise, nearly flat at the bottom. It did nothing for a moment. Then a bright orange rectangle opened in the center of one side.

Sergeant Elliot caught up to him. Other troopers crawled into the CP trench. "What do we do, Captain?" Elliot demanded.

"Keep the men at their posts. There are still a thousand Cubans out there," Rick said. He studied the bright opening. Nothing happened. The only sounds were mutters from his own troops, and no one—or no *thing*—came out. "Take over," he told Parsons. "I'm going to have a look."

Parsons spread his hands in a wide gesture, a typical French shrug. "You are mad. But I will go with you—"

"No." Rick stared at the ship again. For a moment he felt rising hope. Could this be an experimental plane, something kept secret by the CIA and sent to get him out? The Agency had got them into this mess and would be embarrassed if they were captured. "Elliot, get headquarters."

"Can't, sir. Radio stopped working about the time we saw that thing."

"Flying saucer," someone muttered.

Rick had heard the stories. When people saw flying saucers, electrical gear stopped working. Ignition, radios, TV—anything electrical. But so what? He willed himself to believe that the Agency had sent this craft to rescue him. It made sense, even to risk a secret craft, in order to save the embarrassment of political trials and—

There was no point in just looking at it. He didn't want to go alone, but Parsons would have to remain in command, and Elliot would be needed to control the troops. He looked at the others who'd crawled into his CP. "Mason, come with me."

"Right." Mason was a corporal; a short, stocky man with a lot of self-confidence and a phlegmatic temperament. He'd do.

Rick slung his rifle and started forward. Mason carried his at the ready, walking just behind Rick. "I never believed in flying saucers," Mason said.

"Neither did I. Not sure I do now," Rick told him. "Could be the Agency coming for us."

"Yeah. Sure," Mason said.

Rick could guess how the man felt. Rick Galloway didn't believe it either. This was no illusion, no swamp gas. It wasn't the planet Venus or a weather balloon. This was a real ship which had silently landed on his hill, and it was too damned advanced to be anyone's secret weapon. Anyone with a fleet of ships like that could dictate terms to the whole world. The way it had come in, zipping along in silence and changing direction in random ways, it would be unstoppable by any missile or interceptor Rick had ever heard of.

He reached the lighted square. He could feel the troops behind staring at his back. The sounds of gunfire started up again off to the south, and probably half his troops had left their posts to come look at the ship. Others, though, were dug in, grimly waiting. They'd make the Cubans pay for the hill. But how long could they hold? Rick looked inside the ship.

The lighted square was a doorway into a small chamber about three meters on a side. There was no one inside, and there were few features to see except for what appeared to be sliding doors, closed, on three of the walls. The opening was less than two meters high, a bit low for Rick's six feet and a fraction. He stood outside looking in until he felt silly. Finally he shouted. "Anybody home?"

"Come in, Captain Galloway," a voice said. It was a perfectly ordinary male voice, nothing unearthly about it. "You have very little time, Captain. Come aboard."

"My God, maybe it is the Agency," Rick muttered. Whatever he'd expected, it hadn't been an ordinary human voice with an accent he couldn't place.

It spoke again. "You may leave your weapons outside. You will not need them, and they might tempt you to rash actions. If we wished you harm, Captain Galloway, you would be dead now."

That, Rick thought, was for sure. This thing—whatever it was—couldn't be worse than the Cubans. He unslung his rifle and laid it on the ground. Mason did the same, but threw him a significant look. Rick nodded. They both had knives, and Rick had his .45 automatic pistol under his jacket. He was certain that Mason had another.

The opening was inconveniently high off the ground, above waist level. "No gangplank for us," Rick told Mason. He put his hand on the sill. It felt like metal, but was slightly warm to the touch. "Here goes," he muttered, and vaulted in. Mason followed closely.

He had half-expected the opening to close once he was inside, but it did nothing. The doorway to his left slid open silently, revealing a short corridor. Rick gestured to Mason to follow and went down that. Another door slid open at the far end. The room beyond was very brightly lit.

He went in gingerly, feeling very much alone. Corporal Mason hadn't hesitated to lead an infantry attack on a Cuban tank two days before, and had himself crept up to it and blown off a tread with a satchel charge; he looked far more nervous now than when he went off to attack the tank. Rick wondered if he were as shaky as the corporal, tried to straighten up and get control of his face. It wouldn't do to let the troops see their officer shaken.

His eyes adjusted to the bright light. There were—beings—in the compartment. Three of them, and they were not human.

2

They were shaped like humans. They had two arms and two legs and two eyes, but the proportions were wrong. The shoulders were too high, almost as if they didn't have necks, and their heads rose from too-thick bodies. They wore clothing, coveralls of a shining metallic appearance, one dull grey, the other two in brighter colors that shimmered when they moved.

Their hands had only three fingers, but there were two thumbs—one on each side of a thick palm. They had no hair that Rick could see. Their lips were thin—far too thin to be human—and their mouths were too high on their strangely flat faces. Mouth too high, eyes too low, nose—not really a nose at all, Rick decided. Instead there was a fleshy snout-slit like a vertical second mouth. It rose until it almost reached the line joining the eyes.

It took an effort to look away from them and inspect the compartment. The room was nearly bare. All around the upper parts of the compartment there were screens, like TV sets but very thin. Some showed images: Rick's troops standing outside, Lieutenant Parsons and Sergeant Elliot talking and pointing, the machine-gun emplacements. The aliens seemed to have most of his defenses spotted, and their TV gave bright images although outside it was nearly pitch-dark.

The creatures sat at a long table placed crosswise to the door he had entered. It was too high—at least a foot higher than a table for humans would have been—and was transparent, but without the shimmer of glass, so that it was almost invisible. A small box with lights and colored squares rested on the table.

Rick had the impression of controls below some of the screens; at least there were flat plates about an inch square, some lit in bright colors, and others colored but dark. They might have been pushbuttons or touch-sensitive plates, but they might have been anything else. The room was as alien as the creatures.

Despite a strong desire to curl up in a corner and gibber, Rick studied the room carefully, trying to categorize and file the new information. He kept trying to convince himself this was a dream, but he knew better. Finally he was able to speak. "Hello."

When the aliens spoke, both the mouth and nose slits moved. "You have very little time, Captain Galloway," the grey-clad alien said. The voice was very matter-of-fact. It sounded masculine, but Rick reminded himself that he didn't know the creature's sex. Or, he thought, if they even *had* sexes. "Perhaps too little. We may have waited too long. We are here to rescue you and your men."

"Who the hell—"

"Later. There is no time."

Sure, Rick thought. Later. But the alien was right. The Cubans were approaching rapidly. He tried to organize his thoughts, but it was difficult to accept what he was doing, that he was talking with—things. The spokesman—man? No. Not a man. Not a spokesman, either, his mind gibbered. He had no concepts to use. Finally he found his voice. "What do you want with us?"

"For you to get your men aboard. Quickly, before you have none left." The alien spread its hands, palms down, in a gesture that meant nothing to Rick. The tone of its voice had not changed, but it was not difficult to guess that the alien was impatient. "As we have said before and doubtless must say many times again, if we wished you harm, you would be dead. What can we do to you that the Cubans will not accomplish within a few hours?"

The alien was obviously right, but that didn't make Rick feel much better. The "rescue" was not very appealing. "How do you know my name?" he demanded.

"From your radio. You have no more time for questions." This came from one of the creatures in bright coveralls. "You must act. Now."

"What about our weapons?"

"Bring them. Bring all of your equipment," Grey-coveralls said. "But quickly. When the Cubans are close enough to see us clearly, we must be gone. With or without you and your men."

"That's no choice at all, Cap'n," Corporal Mason said. "Better them than the Cubans." The trooper's voice was flat and without emotion.

"I'd thought of that," Rick said. He stood another moment in indecision, but he had made up his mind. "All right."

"Quickly," the alien urged.

"Sure. Come on, Mason—"

"You will leave him here," Grey-coveralls said. "As an earnest of your good intentions."

"Now, wait just a damned minute—"

"It's okay, Captain," Mason said. "I'm as safe here as out there."

"All right." Rick went back to the doorway. It opened for him. When he reached the entry chamber, another door opened on the side opposite the entrance to the chamber where the aliens sat. He saw a large empty compartment, more than fifty feet long and perhaps fifteen wide.

"Have the men go in there with their weapons," a voice said. It seemed to speak from the walls, but there was no sign of a speaker grille.

Rick jumped out of the ship and ran to his command post. Half the troops—perhaps more—had gathered there to stare at the ship. They stood clutching rifles and grenades for what comfort weapons could give.

"I did not entirely expect to see you again," Lieutenant Parsons said. "Welcome back."

"Thanks. We've got no time at all. Get the men aboard. Men, weapons, food, equipment, everything. Fast."

"But—" Sergeant Elliot was stammering. Rick had never seen the big sergeant confused before.

"That's a CIA ship," Rick said. He spoke loudly so that many of the troops could hear him. "Secret stuff. They've come to get us out, but they don't want the Cubans to see the ship, so we've got to load up quickly. Now move it."

"Sir!" Elliot ran over to the mortar emplacement, and some of the other troops gathered their gear and headed for the ship. Rick didn't know if he had fooled them or not, but the "CIA ship" explanation seemed the easiest and fastest way to handle the situation.

Parsons looked at him with raised eyebrows. His expression said clearly that he knew Rick was a liar. Then he shrugged and began urging the men onto the ship. Sergeant Elliot rounded up more.

Good troops, Rick thought. And each one had probably made the same decision: They *knew* what the Cubans could do. This was at least a chance.

The mortar team ran by with their tube, followed by others with the base and packs of mortar bombs. Men grabbed boxes and bandoliers of ammunition, stuffed their pockets with grenades. They were going aboard well armed.

Not, Rick thought, that it will do a hell of a lot of good. Weapons won't make us safer. But they do make us *feel* safer, and that's important.

"What is this nonsense?" Parsons demanded in a low voice. "You know that is not—"

"Can it. Hold onto the questions." Rick held up his hand and gestured toward the south. There was sporadic firing down there, some of it much closer than Hendrix could possibly be. The Cubans were mopping up the last pockets of resistance before coming up the hill. "Hendrix has had it," Rick said. "His last orders were to get as many men out as we could. Got a better way?"

"No. But—"

"But nothing. That ship won't wait, and we can't do anything for Hendrix and his people." Fear and a sense of guilt at abandoning their wounded made Rick speak more sharply than he had intended. "Shut up and get the men aboard. There's no time for talk."

André Parsons shrugged. "As you say. But there are questions you will answer."

"Don't I know it. Christ, André, don't argue. Just do it. Please."

"Very well." He went out to assist in dismounting the light machine-gun.

More troopers ran past. They carried packs, sleeping bags, helmets, ammo boxes, mess gear; the usual impedimentia of a marching army. They were not making much noise, and there was surprisingly little confusion.

Good troops, Rick thought. We did damned well, considering how little support we had. Not our fault we were beaten. For a collection of soldiers who had never served together before, we did damned well.

"That's the last," Elliot shouted.

Rick had been counting. "Only thirty-four went aboard."

Elliot looked ashamed. "I can't find any more, Captain."

They've run, Rick thought. Well, I can understand that. I thought of it myself. "Get aboard, then," he ordered. After Elliot climbed in, Rick followed. They were the last.

As soon as Rick cleared the entryway, the outer door slid closed. When he went through into the compartment with the troops, that entryway closed also. They were blocked off from the outside and from the control room—or whatever that room was, Rick thought. Mason was still in there with the aliens.

There was a loud musical tone, and a voice said, "Everyone will please sit on the floor. Quickly."

"Get down!" Rick shouted. "Hit the deck!" He sat heavily, just in time. There was a feeling of far too much weight, and some of the troops who hadn't obeyed quickly enough fell heavily. Loose equipment fell and rolled around the compartment.

There were sideways accelerations. The feeling of motion went on for a long time. Then it stopped and they had normal weight again.

"Medic!" someone shouted. One of the troopers was holding his wrist, broken in a fall to the deck. Sergeant McCleve went to the downed man. McCleve was an older trooper, a career soldier rumored to have graduated from a Mexican medical school and unable to obtain a license to practice in the United States due to heavy drinking. Rick didn't know, but McCleve had always seemed very competent.

The troops were all talking at once. Some swore, and one or two prayed. Others got up and roamed around the compartment. There was nothing to see.

They were in a large rectangular metal room, and very little more could be said about it. Rick couldn't even tell where the light came from; it was just there, and although there were multiple shadows, they were very faint.

"I think we got away," Rick shouted. "Let the Cubans figure that one out!"

There was a cheer that sounded artificial. Rick smiled grimly. He didn't feel much like cheering himself.

"Level with us, sir," Corporal Gengrich said. "How'd the CIA get a thing like this? And why the hell did they need us if they've got—" he waved expressively— "these?"

It was a good question, and Rick had no idea of how to answer.

"All in good time," Lieutenant Parsons said. "All in good time. Count your blessings."

"But—" Gengrich began.

"Shut up." Sergeant Elliot was nervous and fell back on military tradition as something familiar and understood. An officer had spoken, and that was that.

It won't last, Rick thought. Elliot had strong views about officers: he assumed they were competent, wanted them to be, *demanded* that they be. He knew that there were plenty of incompetents with bars and leaves, but he was proud enough of his Army that he'd kill himself trying to cover for them. But Rick suspected that Elliot would not hesitate to frag a bad officer for the honor of the corps.

There were more accelerations, this time not so violent. The ship was turning. Rick felt trapped, but he tried to keep his expression calm and unworried. He didn't know how successful he was at that, but he thought it was important that the troops think he was confident.

We are, he thought, thirty-six armed men and some heavy weapons, in a ship controlled by aliens—*aliens!* I don't have the faintest notion of where I am, where we're going, or what those creatures want with us.

He was certain they were in space. That decided one thing: they certainly didn't need any shooting. Not that there was anything to shoot at, but there were a lot of weapons available, and some might punch holes in the ship. The metal walls didn't seem too thick, and Rick had no idea of how strong they might be. Even supposing they could blow open a door and found air beyond it, and that they could go through the ship and kill or capture every alien in it— what then? They couldn't fly it; they couldn't land it; they couldn't even operate the food and water and air system.

And so far no one had threatened them.

⋄   ⋄   ⋄

Two hours later they were all certain they were in space. There was a brief warning tone, and a voice said, "There will be a period of no-weight. Please secure all equipment and secure yourselves."

The only thing they could secure themselves to was a low bar a bit above waist height that ran around two sides of the compartment like the rails ballet dancers use for exercise. Rick managed to get most of the troops over to those walls. They tied lines to as much of the gear as they could. They were just finishing when there was another musical tone.

They had no weight at all. Loose objects drifted slowly. Several men looked sick, and one was. The vomit floated around in large pools. Other men turned green.

"Jesus, we got to get *out* of here!" one soldier yelled.

"Shut up!" Elliot didn't look too good himself. "Captain—"

He didn't finish the question. The ship went through more gyrations, none very severe. Then, slowly, everything drifting in the air began to settle toward the deck. They felt increasing weight, building up to what seemed almost—but not quite—normal again.

This time it was much harder to calm the troops. They hung onto their weapons and stared around the compartment looking for someone to fight, something they could do. Rick thought he could literally smell the fear in the compartment, and it was contagious. He felt like a caged animal.

"For God's sake, where are we going?" Gengrich demanded.

"The journey will last two more hours," the voice said. It spoke from nowhere at all.

"So they can listen to us," Parsons said. He lowered his voice to an undertone. "Are you certain there is nothing else you wish to tell me?"

"Not just now."

Parsons shrugged. "As you will. But I hope this does not last much more than a few hours. It will be difficult to control the men if it goes on much longer." He made a wry face. "It will be difficult to control me."

"Yeah," Rick said. He knew exactly how André Parsons felt.

❖   ❖   ❖

The voice's time estimate was accurate. Rick's watch said they had been aboard for four hours and five minutes when the warning tones sounded again and they were told to secure themselves.

This time they never had a period of no-weight, but the accelerations were short and sharp, in little spurts. There were periods of varying gravity between spurts. Finally they felt a slight impact, no more than they might have felt jumping from a chair to the floor. The accelerations ceased.

They didn't weigh enough. Nowhere near enough, and this was steady. Rick looked around in surprise, a wild suspicion coming to his mind. Some of the troops were muttering. Corporal Gengrich thoughtfully took a cartridge from his pocket and dropped it, watched it fall slowly.

About one-sixth gravity, Rick thought. There was no hiding that, and no hiding what it meant.

Gengrich shouted it first. "God Almighty, we're on the friggin' Moon!"

3

The troopers had little time to react to Gengrich. The compartment door opened, and Corporal Mason came in. His face looked like grey ashes, and he held his right arm against his chest. The compartment door remained open to the entry chamber, but all the other doors were closed.

"Mason—"

"Where the hell you been?"

"What's wrong, Art? What in hell did they do to you?"

The men were all shouting at once. Sergeant McCleve went over with his medical kit.

"At ease!" Rick shouted. Sergeant Elliot repeated the order more loudly. There were mutters, but the shouting stopped.

Rick joined Mason and McCleve. "What happened?"

"Jesus, Captain, we're on the Moon," Mason said. "The bastards brought us to the moon!"

"Yes," Rick said.

"I saw it all," Mason said. The troops crowded around to listen.

Rick nodded to himself. It was time the men found out what had happened. He thought he should have told them before.

"Those screen things," Mason was saying. "It was like TV. We lifted off, straight up, it seemed like, and the world kept getting further and further away until I could see all of it, just like on TV during a space mission."

"What happened to your arm?" McCleve asked. He slit Mason's field-jacket sleeve and examined the wound. It looked like a neat round hole, thinner than a pencil, and it went through the jacket, the arm, and out the sleeve on the other side. There was no blood.

"They wouldn't talk to me," Mason said.

"Who?" "Who wouldn't talk?" the troops demanded. Elliot glared at them, but he didn't try to keep them quiet. He wanted to know too.

"Those critters," Mason said. "The—Captain, you saw 'em. I don't know what they are. Not men. Look something like men, but they're not."

Now there was a lot of excited babble. "Shut up," Rick said. "Let Mason tell his story."

"They wouldn't talk to me. We kept getting further and further away from the Earth, until I could see it—all of it—up to where I could see daylight and clouds over the ocean, just like on TV from Skylab. And they wouldn't talk. So I took out my pistol and pointed it at one—the one in the grey suit—and told him if he didn't tell me where we were going, I'd shoot him."

"Stupid," Lieutenant Parsons muttered.

"Yes, sir, it was stupid," Mason said. "The critter didn't do anything. Just waved his hand, kind of, and some kind of beam, like a laser beam, came out of the wall. Right out of the wall. I never saw any opening. Just this green light and it burned a hole right through. I dropped the gun and the critter came around and picked it up, and he said I should sit there and I should tell him if I needed medical attention—he talked that way, like a professor. Then he gave me a pill. I thought about it and then I took it, and after that it stopped hurting. And then we came on straight to the Moon. I saw us land. We're on the back side, Captain. The back side of the Moon. There's a big cave, and two other ships like this one."

When Mason stopped talking, the men began again. "You

didn't tell us it was a goddamn flying saucer!" Gengrich shouted. His voice was hostile and accusing. "You said it was a CIA ship!"

"They were in a hurry," Rick said. "Would you rather be back on the hill waiting for the Cubans? Would any of you?"

They didn't know what to make of that. Nobody spoke of going back.

"We can always die," Rick said. "At least we can find out what these—people—want with us."

"Good advice." The voice came from everywhere and nowhere. "You will know very soon. The exit port will open and you will please carry all your equipment and weapons out of the ship. You will be told what to do after that. Please be careful. You are, as you have been told, on your planet's Moon. The air pressure will be lower than you are accustomed to, but there is more than enough air and oxygen for your species if you do nothing violent. Now please gather your equipment."

Rick felt totally drained of emotion. "Let's get with it," he said.

Elliot stood a moment in indecision, then evidently made up his mind. "Get that gear together. Move!" he shouted.

There was a cave beyond the door. Heavy material that looked like thick rubber sealed the door to the cave. The seal, which reminded Rick of the materials wet suits are made of, stretched for twenty meters or so into the cave. Beyond that the tunnel walls were made of rock, but shiny, as if it had been varnished. Rick felt it; the stuff was very hard, and he thought it had been sprayed on—probably to keep the air from leaking out through the rock walls.

When they had unloaded the ship, the entryway door closed, and they had no choice but to go down the tunnel. It went inward and down. They had no difficulty with equipment; everything weighed only a sixth of what it would on Earth, and one man could carry ten mortar bombs without great effort.

The tunnel was lighted, not with glowing walls as the ship had been, but with ordinary fluorescent lights. Rick examined one of the fixtures; it was stamped "Westinghouse." Common house wire ran from light to light.

As they went deeper into the cave, doors closed behind them. They seemed to be made from the same wet-suit material as the passage from the ship to the cave, and they appeared from the walls in a circle that closed together so tightly that it was difficult to see they weren't solid.

They reached the bottom of the ramp. Rick estimated that they had come nearly a kilometer. At the ramp's end was a big cavern, as large as a basketball gymnasium, and furniture. Rick saw tables, chairs, bookcases with books and magazines. Beds and army cots were clustered at one end of the area. A table held a coffee urn and bags of styrofoam cups, and a can of Yuban coffee stood next to the urn. On another table he saw loaves of bread of various American brands; jars of Jiffy peanut butter; cans of Campbell's soup. Paper plates and cheap plastic forks. Canned milk. Bricks of cheese; Vienna sausage; tins of sardines. There were no signs of fresh foods, meats or vegetables, but Rick was certain they wouldn't starve.

At the far end of the cavern was a TV set. It looked strange. Rick saw no maker's marks, unless some curious squiggles on a plate at the bottom meant something. It had no controls at all. A man's face looked out at them, and from the way his eyes and head moved, Rick thought the man was watching him.

Man. Rick stood staring at the TV. The face on the screen was human. He was certain of it.

"You are in charge?" The figure on the screen spoke without warning. The phrase wasn't precisely a question, but it did not sound positive either. The voice held a slight accent, but Rick was certain he had never heard anything like it before.

"As much as anyone is," Rick said.

"Then you are Captain Galloway. I must have information. First, is it true that you voluntarily boarded the ship that brought you here? There was no coercion from the *Shalnuksis*?"

"Shalnuksis?"

"The beings who brought you here. Were you forced to board their ship?"

"Not by them. There were some Cubans who didn't leave us many choices—"

"That is my second question." The man's expression did not change at all. Rick got closer to the set and examined the image carefully.

He saw a man who appeared to be in his forties. He wore a rust-colored upper garment that resembled a tunic, no buttons, a V-neck lined with blue and studded with decorations: a stylized comet and sunburst. The man's hair was short, and his complexion was darker than Rick's; about the same hue as an American Indian, but not quite so dark.

"Is it true that you would now be dead if the *Shalnuksi* ship had not taken you aboard?" the man asked.

"It's likely," Rick answered.

"One of your men was injured by the *Shalnuksis*. They have said they were merely defending themselves and did the least damage possible to the man. Is this true?"

"Yes—"

"Thank you. We regret that we do not have better accommodations. You are welcome to whatever you find there. You may eat now. We will have more to talk of later."

"Hey—damn it, what's going on?" Rick demanded. He was talking to a blank screen.

❖   ❖   ❖

They examined their prison. There was a hot plate and an electrical outlet on a long cord. The wire ran into the wall, and the hole it came out of was sealed with the wet-suit material. The hot plate had been made by General Electric. The coffeepot was Japanese, with Japanese labels. Everything in the compartment had come from Earth. Most had come from the United States, but there were articles from many other places. Some of the gear was new, much still in packing cases. Other equipment and stores had been used. There were radios and television sets, but they produced nothing beyond a few random hisses and howls.

After half an hour, they settled in to cook dinner. There was plenty to eat; soup and canned bacon and ham, canned vegetables, and pudding for dessert. André Parsons found a water tap—Kohler of Kohler—near the coffee urn. There was a drain beneath it. Other troops found cases of warm beer and several jugs of wine, enough so that everyone had a beer and a full cup of California red. There was plenty of coffee.

When they had eaten, they all felt better. The troops prowled about restlessly, but eventually began making themselves comfortable, using what was in their packs and whatever else they could find to bed down. Elliot pulled two of the single beds off to one side for Parsons and Rick Galloway. No one had eaten or slept for more than twenty-four hours, and soon most of the troops were sprawled onto beds and cots, or onto air mattresses on the floor.

The floor, Rick found, was uneven at the edges near the walls, but away from the walls it was artificially smooth and flat. It felt warm to the touch.

Rick sat with Parsons at a table near the TV set. They ate in silence. Finally Parsons said, "I see why you did not explain earlier."

"Yeah. Not that I could have," Rick said.

Parsons shrugged. "Five hours ago, I was prepared to be killed on that hilltop. Now I have eaten, I have a cup of wine and coffee to follow, and it is warm. No one is shooting me, and there is a comfortable bed. We have been lucky."

"Maybe."

"Have you thought of the implications of your television conversation?" André asked. "A human. A human who asks interesting questions. Are we volunteers? How was Corporal Mason injured? Would we be alive if we had not boarded the alien ship? All asked by a human in a voice of authority, as if he had every right to the answers."

Rick nodded. "I thought of that. It means somebody cares what happens to us. Maybe not a lot, but somebody cares. I keep hoping that's a good sign."

"It cannot be a bad one," André said.

"Dammit, you're calm enough—"

Parsons laughed. "I would have said the same of you. Rick, I am terrified, but it would do no good to let the men see that. Obviously you must feel the same way."

"Yeah. But I sure wish they'd let us know what they want with us."

"Perhaps nothing," Parsons said. He shrugged again in his expansive French manner. "Perhaps they rescued us for humanitarian reasons. Are we not worth it?" His smile was broad.

❖   ❖   ❖

"Captain! Cap'n, that TV's going again. They want you."

Rick struggled to wakefulness. His watch showed that he had slept five hours. It seemed longer, and he felt far better rested than he would have expected from five hours' sleep.

A dozen men were crowded around the TV. They were trying to talk to the man—as near as Rick could tell, it was the same one who had spoken to him before—but they had no success. It was only when Rick stood in front of the set that the man responded.

"It is time to discuss your situation," the screen figure said. "You will not require weapons. Leave them all, and any other large metal objects, and enter the doorway which will open in the wall behind this screen."

As he spoke a steel plate set in the wall swung away. A rubberlike airtight door stood behind it. "Alone, please," the screen said. "You will not be harmed."

"Maybe a couple of us ought to come anyway," Sergeant Elliot said.

"Thanks, Sarge, but I guess not," Rick said. "If they really want us dead, they'll let the air out of this compartment. And don't forget that. Elliot, for God's sake, don't let the troops do anything stupid while I'm gone."

"No, sir. But when will you be back?"

"I don't know."

"Cap'n, if you're not back in four hours, we can blow that door open—"

"No. Wake up Lieutenant Parsons and tell him he's in

charge. I'll be back." Rick sounded a lot more confident than he felt as he went through the doorway. It closed behind him before the airtight in front of him dilated.

There was another corridor, and no one in sight. Rick followed that for a hundred meters until it bent sharply left, then led through two more rubberized pressure doors. He emerged in another cavern, one much smaller than the one he had left. It was well lighted, and there were at least a dozen of the TV screens of the kind he had seen in the ship and in the cavern.

There were both people and aliens in the cavern, perhaps a dozen of each. Several were studying the TV-like screens. An alien in grey coveralls, possibly the one who had spoken to him in the ship, came over to him.

The alien was six inches taller than Rick, but the extra height seemed to be all in the legs. The torso was not much longer than Rick's. The arms were longer than a human's, but not so much longer as were the legs. "There," the alien said. He indicated a door. "You would—do well—to be— careful—of what you say."

Rick nodded. "I understand." If this were the same alien, and Rick thought it was, it no longer spoke as easily and confidently as it had aboard the ship. Why? he wondered.

The door opened into an office. A desk faced the door. There were papers on the desk, along with two keyboards that Rick thought must connect to a computer. The desk held two of the flat TV screens, and there were other screens higher up. All were blank. The office had metallic square walls and floor and ceiling; a room built into the cavern. There was a rug on the floor which Rick thought was Persian; it had that pattern and look to it. There were other art objects that appeared to be from Earth: seascape paintings, a color photograph of the Golden Gate bridge, a Kalliroscope with its swirling shock-wave patterns.

The man he had seen on the TV screen sat behind the desk. The desk itself looked Danish modern and was probably from Earth. The man stood as Rick entered, but he did not offer to shake hands.

He was perhaps five feet ten, two inches shorter than Rick, and looked thoroughly human. He was a bit darker than Rick, face rounder, but he would not have attracted attention on any street in the United States or Europe. His expression was not unfriendly, but he looked harried, very busy and preoccupied.

The man spoke. It sounded to Rick more like the twittering of a bird than any human speech. "A parrot in a cageful of cats," Rick told André Parsons later. The alien answered in the same language, and the human nodded.

"Excuse me, Captain," he said. "Please be seated." He indicated chairs, both of aluminum and plastic, one a normal-height chair, the other like a highchair for an adult. "Doubtless you have many questions."

Now there's an understatement, Rick thought. "Yes. Beginning with, who are you?"

The man nodded, tight-lipped, again his expression more of impatience and mild annoyance than anything else. "You would find my name hard to pronounce. Try 'Agzaral,' which is close enough not to offend me. I am—you do not have the occupation. Think of me as a police inspector. It is close enough for our purposes. And do be seated."

Rick took the normal chair. The alien went to the highchair. It fitted perfectly. "And my—rescuer?" Rick asked. It was difficult to know how to speak. There were no referents, and Rick had no idea of what would offend either the human or the alien. Obviously he should avoid terms like "this critter" or "stretchy here," but what could he call the creature?

"His name translates as 'Goldsmith,'" Agzaral said. "Many *Shalnuksi* names derive from ancient occupations. That seems a nearly universal cultural trait among industrializing peoples. If you prefer his own language, it is 'Karreeel.'" The last was said with a twitter that Rick couldn't possibly pronounce.

"Pleased to meet you," Rick said. "An expression that we don't always mean, but given the way we met, I certainly do. Only—"

"Only you would like to know why he made the effort,"

Agzaral said. "I listened to part of your conversation with the other officer." He switched to the twitter-and-snarl language again and spoke briefly.

"We have need of you," Karreeel said. His facial slits flared briefly. "We have need of human soldiers, and we went to great expense and difficulty to locate you."

"But why us?" Rick demanded.

"Because you would not be missed," Agzaral said. "And you could be taken aboard his ship without anyone seeing it. There are severe regulations against allowing the ships to be seen."

"Flying saucers," Rick said. "But you *have* been seen—"

"*Some* have," Agzaral corrected. "Not Karreeel. The ships that have been seen were employed by students. Fortunately, none of those sightings can be proved." He sighed. It seemed to Rick a very human sigh. "It is my unpleasant task to investigate every instance in which a ship had been seen and reported."

"I see," Rick said. "And then what?"

"We have agents on Earth," Agzaral said. "They discredit the sighting reports."

"They've done a good job," Rick said. He remembered what he had thought of UFO stories, and the people who 'believed in flying saucers.' Brass-plated nuts. "The" —he hesitated at the unfamiliar word— "*Shalnuksis*—are studying us?"

Agzaral's lips curled in what Rick thought might be a thin smile. "No. Others study Earth. Including other humans. But the—" He paused. "I will not in future stop myself when I require a term that you will not quite understand. I will simply use the nearest equivalent. There is a High Commission which regulates trade with primitive worlds, particularly with Earth, and protects primitive peoples from crude exploitation. The Commission forbids trade or other intercourse with your planet."

"But why?" Rick demanded. He was surprised at how calm he felt. One part of his mind wanted him to scream and run in circles, flapping his arms, but instead he found it easy enough to sit calmly and politely conversing with a human who was not from Earth and an alien who resembled a stretched-out chimpanzee with a single nostril and no neck. It was all so completely ordinary; the conversational tones, the gestures—

"Your planet is in an interesting stage of development," Agzaral said. "Trade will not be allowed until it is decided what—until the studies are completed."

"What the hell do you want with *me*, then?" Rick demanded.

"I want nothing," Agzaral said. "You are, for me, a great annoyance. Karreeel has an offer which I believe you should consider."

"Shoot—uh, go ahead. What's the offer?"

"My—colleagues—and I are merchants. More correct would be 'merchant-adventurers,'" Karreeel said. When he spoke, he paused frequently, and Rick wondered if he had some kind of translating machine, so that he could think of what he wanted to say and get the English. There was no sign of wires or a hearing aid, but that wasn't decisive.

"'Merchant-adventurers,'" Rick repeated. He couldn't help remembering that the Gentleman Adventurers of the Honourable East India Company had gone out and conquered India for England, and he wondered if the aliens had a similar fate in mind for Earth.

"Yes," said Karreeel. "We now have a need for human soldiers. The price of mercenaries has become—excessively high. We gambled that we could find soldiers here and yet not violate—Inspector—Agzaral's regulations. If you will agree, we will have succeeded."

"If we agree," Rick said.

Agzaral wagged his head in a manner that Rick thought strange; when he saw Rick's reaction, he checked himself and nodded. "You are under no compulsion to accept," he said. "When he has made his offer, I will tell you what alternatives are permitted for you."

"There is a planet, far from here," Karreeel said. "It has a primitive society, much more primitive than yours. The planet can support a highly valuable crop, one that cannot be grown easily anywhere else. We need assistance in getting those crops planted and harvested."

Rick shook his head. This didn't make sense. "Why don't you grow your own?"

The alien made a gesture with his left hand, and both his facial slits flared wide. "Why should one of us be condemned to live on a primitive world?"

"But we're not farmers—"

"We do not expect you to do any farming. There is a local population. Unfortunately, the planet is very primitive, in a state of—feudalism. Our need is not farmers, but soldiers to impose a government which will wish to plant our required crops, harvest them, and deliver the harvest to us."

"And what makes you think we'll be interested in living on a primitive world?" Rick demanded.

"Your reward should be obvious. You will rule as you will, without interference. You will have wealth and power, and you will have only to see that our crops are grown. We will supply you with luxuries and comforts in trade."

"This sounds like a long-term project," Rick said.

"Of course," Karreeel said.

Before Agzaral spoke, Rick knew what he was going to say.

"The task will last your lifetime," Agzaral said. "Captain Galloway, surely it must be obvious to you that you and your men will never return to Earth."

4

"Just a damn minute!" Rick exploded. "You kidnap us, and then—"

"Rescued," Agzaral said. "I asked you about it. I have taken the trouble to check the story. It is obvious to me that you would be dead if Karreeel had not taken you aboard his ship. Do you dispute that?"

Rick felt the anger drain out to be replaced by fear. "No. I can't dispute that. But why can't we go home?"

"Because you would be believed," Agzaral said. "Too many witnesses. Karreeel planned on that, of course. By deliberately taking aboard such a large number, he made it certain that someone would take you seriously if you returned to Earth."

"You mentioned alternatives," Rick said.

Agzaral nodded. "You have few enough. None include going back to your own world. You would have to stay here, in that chamber where you are now, until transport could be arranged to another planet. Some of you could probably find positions as experimental subjects for the university. Others might—find different work. I do not know what would happen to the majority. The High Commission would have to decide. I would have to report that you have been offered employment and refused it. Humans unwilling to work do not always have a pleasant life on most of our worlds. And it may be several years before transport could be found—at least for all of you."

33

"That's not much choice at all."

"Or you may commit suicide," Agzaral said.

"That's even less." Rick touched the grenade through his pocket. It was a new variety; a small grenade not much larger than a golf ball, made mostly of plastic. It would explode into thousands of tiny fragments, surely enough to kill everyone in the room—including himself. It didn't seem a very useful weapon at the moment. "May I smoke?" he asked.

"I would prefer that you do not," Agzaral said.

"Okay. Look, how the hell do you expect thirty men to take over an entire planet?"

"Not an entire planet." Karreeel's tone didn't change; it remained matter-of-fact, calm, unworried. "Most of" — he twittered something incomprehensible— "is of no interest or value. Only one region will be worth controlling. Surely your men with firearms and other military equipment will have no difficulty dominating primitives with lances, bows, and swords?"

That seemed possible. Rick didn't care much for the idea. If the planet were that primitive in weapons, it would also be primitive in hygiene and medical science. Living there would not be much fun.

He wondered what it would be like to be on welfare in one of Agzaral's cultures. It hadn't sounded pleasant, but Agzaral was undoubtedly used to more luxuries than Rick was. But then there was that phrase "experimental subjects," and that didn't sound good at all.

There was another problem that would be even worse. "We're all men," Rick said. "And you'll be sending us to another planet for the rest of our lives—"

"Ah," Karreeel said. "I understand. Permit me to explain that there will be human females."

"You've kidnapped women?" Rick demanded.

"No. Providing a sufficient number might be difficult without—violating—the regulations. The planet—let us call it Paradise. That is a good name for a planet. Paradise is inhabited by humans."

"Bull puckey," said Rick.

There was silence for a moment. Rick wondered if he had offended the alien.

"It is quite true," Agzaral said. "There are humans in many parts of the galaxy."

"How?" Rick demanded.

Agzaral smiled thinly. "Don't your own scientists suggest that humans are not native to Earth?"

"I never heard of that theory being taken seriously. If people—humans—are spread all over the galaxy, how'd they get that way?"

"I doubt that you will ever find that out," Agzaral said. His voice had become very serious, with no trace of warmth at all. Then he shrugged. "There are no English translations of galactic history, and I have no time to give you lessons. For the moment, believe it."

Rick frowned. He wondered if it could be true. There were legends of early astronauts: Ezekiel and the wheel, cherubim, the biblical four-faced flying creatures; even the so-called evidence of commercial writers. Genesis could be interpreted as the transplantation of a very small number of people—the story said only two—onto a world where they hadn't evolved.

It was beyond Rick. He had never been a brilliant student. One reason he had worked in ROTC classes was that he had thought he might need the army for a job. The only subject he had consistently done well in was military history, and that hadn't promised a very good living.

Paradise. He smiled lopsidedly as he remembered a lump of uninhabitable ice had been named "Greenland" in the hopes of attracting suckers who might go there to settle. "Real people," he said. "*Homo sapiens.*"

"How sapient is debatable. Not merely for those on Paradise, but everywhere," Agzaral said. "But depend upon it; union with females there will be fertile."

Something else nagged at Rick. "You're a policeman," he said. "I get the idea that you're here to protect the people of Earth. All those regulations. Can't kidnap people who aren't going to die anyway. Yet you're sending us off to conquer this primitive place you call Paradise. Why aren't you concerned about the people there?"

Agzaral frowned. Rick wondered if he'd hit a sore spot. "Paradise—you may as well know the place's real name," Agzaral said. "In the dominant language it is called 'Tran.' Tran is not covered by the same regulations as Earth." He stopped and pressed his lips grimly together. "Besides, you can't do anything to the people there that they haven't been doing to themselves. You may save them much misery."

There was some mystery here, Rick thought. Agzaral's expression did not match his words. But what? "If it's that easy, why don't you do it yourselves?"

"We can't." Agzaral pointed to Karreeel. "Discoverers, colonizers, and developers have their rights, too. But when you arrive on Tran with your weapons, you might recall that the people there are as human as you or I. Captain Galloway, you must make a decision."

"How much time do I have?"

Agzaral looked to Karreeel.

"There is no vital hurry," the alien said. "Shall we say twenty-four hours?"

⋄   ⋄   ⋄

Rick put the proposition to the troops. He wasn't surprised when there was a long silence, then babble. He knew how they felt; he'd wanted to babble himself when he left the interview with Karreeel and Agzaral.

Then a loud voice cut through the chatter. "Another planet? That's not possible."

Private Larry Warner, called "Professor" by the other troops, had a voice that could be heard in the middle of a battle. He was a college graduate, and Rick had no idea why the man had volunteered for the army, still less why he had volunteered a second time for a CIA operation. He argued with everyone: officers, noncoms, anyone who would listen. Only threats of severe punishment could shut him up. For all that, he was an educated man, and Rick had found his knowledge valuable in the past.

"Faster-than-light travel is impossible," Warner said. "We

can't get to another star system—and there sure aren't any inhabited planets in the solar system. They must be lying to you."

"It seems a pointless deception," André Parsons said.

Sergeant Elliot had a simpler way. "Shut up, Warner."

"Where did the aliens come from?" Jack Campbell shouted. "Not this solar system. You said so yourself, Professor." Campbell was a college dropout who'd joined the army for lack of something better to do. He enjoyed teasing Warner. "Hey, I like it! Captain, I take it there'll be some changes in our status. Most of us can hope for something more than twenty years in the army and retirement—"

Rick shrugged. "I hadn't much thought about it, but I guess so. They talked like we could do pretty well what we wanted to."

"I have always fancied myself as a king," André Parsons said. "I see no reason why we cannot all become kings— or at least dukes and barons. Presuming we succeed, of course."

"We have to get out of here," someone shouted.

Babble broke out.

"Where to?"

"I've got a wife and two kids—I got to get back home!"

"Ten—hut!" Elliot's command quieted them for a moment. Before they could speak again, Rick said, "We aren't going home. They made that clear, and I don't see any way to get there. They can let the pressure out of here anytime they want to. Anybody know how to breathe vacuum?"

"So what do we do, Captain?" Campbell asked.

"Stick together. Do what they want," Rick said. "Lieutenant Parsons is right. We can all get rich out of this. We can't go home, but we can be rich. If we stick together."

"Fight a whole planet?" Campbell asked.

"Not quite," Rick said. "But we could. We have the edge in weapons and tactics. There'll be a lot of people down there, though. A lot. If we don't stay together—well, when does anyone sleep?"

"First we need a new contract," Warner said. His voice

had a smug quality that instantly irritated Rick. "A new contract. We can begin by electing a chairman—"

Sergeant Elliot looked as if he were having a stroke. "Elect! We got officers—"

"Who have no authority over us under the circumstances," Warner said. "Their commissions are from the United States, and we don't live there any longer. Why should we have to take orders from them?"

"Warner, one more goddamn word out of you and I'll break your neck." Elliot moved to stand near Private Warner.

"He has a point," André Parsons said. "Those who volunteer to go are also volunteering to accept Captain Galloway and myself as leaders." He turned to Rick and said, very formally, "Sir, I accept you as leader and captain of this expedition." Then he saluted.

Parsons had turned away from the troops, so that only Rick could see his face. His eyes showed sly amusement, and as Rick returned the salute, Parsons gave an exaggerated wink.

❖   ❖   ❖

Rick had told Parsons that the aliens—and the human "police," who in some ways seemed as alien as the *Shalnuksis*—were probably listening to all their conversations; after that they were guarded, saying nothing they did not want their employers to hear. It made Rick lonelier than ever. He was losing Earth and everyone he knew, and he couldn't talk about it without risk of being overheard.

And yet, he thought, it might be fun. As Parsons had said, everyone at one time or another dreams of getting a chance to become a knight or baron or duke. Even a king. That didn't happen on Earth anymore, but it might happen to Rick Galloway on Paradise.

He had other fantasies. He knew enough of Earth's history to know of the mistakes made in going from the Middle Ages to an industrial society. He had seen pictures of Bombay and Calcutta. Perhaps, he told himself, he could help this new world avoid some of the mistakes. For Karreeel and his merchant-adventurers, this was a routine operation to make some money—or whatever passed for money in their culture—but for Rick it was a chance at adventure.

It was also inevitable, and he was uncomfortably aware that many of the arguments he used with himself and the men were born of necessity. They had no other choices.

✧   ✧   ✧

The first task was preparation. They would need supplies and equipment. Agzaral had told him that a reasonable amount of equipment could be obtained from Earth. He hadn't said what would be reasonable.

Rick set the troops to making lists. Weapons, ammunition, special equipment, communications, survival gear, medical supplies, soap; luxuries and conveniences that couldn't be manufactured on Tran even with all the help Rick and his people could supply. The lists became endless, and they began to cut them back.

They had very little information about Tran. Karreeel was certain there was no petroleum industry there, but neither knew nor cared whether there was petroleum at all: thus no internal-combustion gear. The other decision information was just as sketchy.

Rick asked the television set for an interview. Eventually Karreeel came on the screen.

"We need more data," Rick said. "How big is this planet? How much water? Are there hurricanes? How can I prepare when I don't know what to prepare *for*?"

"Your questions are reasonable. Unfortunately, we have not translated the data you require. That will be done later."

"Can you get the equipment I've asked for?"

"Some. Most."

"How?" Rick asked.

"It can be bought. Or stolen," Karreeel said. "I have little time for you. You will later meet someone who does. Until then, please do not annoy me further."

"Who is this—"

"A human. If you give me your list, I will see what can be obtained."

The screen went blank. Rick and André looked at each

other. "They must have agents on Earth," Parsons said. "They spoke of purchases—"

"Yeah." Rick thought about that for a moment, then laughed. "Aliens among us. Agents of the Galactic Confederacy move about studying us. We read about it for years, and it's all true."

André Parsons laughed also, but neither of them thought it was really very funny.

PART TWO:

THE SHIP

1

Gwen Tremaine was in love. Given that she was twenty
years old and not at all unattractive, this shouldn't have been
astonishing; but in point of fact she was more than astonished.
She couldn't really believe it.

She had resigned herself to a lonely life. Not lonely in
the sense of having no friends, although she had few enough;
but she was convinced that she would never be in love,
and even doubted whether anyone else ever had been. She
had strongly suspected that all the poetic passages, all the
lyric descriptions of how one felt when one was in love,
had been invented by poets and writers who felt there ought
to be such feelings but who had never experienced them.

Physical attraction she understood. She'd had several affairs
and enjoyed them all. But what she couldn't seem to arouse,
in herself or others, was whatever the poets felt when they
spoke of love.

She had tried, and a few times she thought it was
happening to her, but it never developed into anything more.
The strong affection, the need for someone else's company
that she saw in the few girls she got along with, sometimes
she felt stirrings of it, but it never lasted. Generally what
few stirrings she did experience happened after physical
encounters, and usually hadn't lasted past the cold light of
morning. For a while she had blamed her inability to fall

in love on the men in her life, and indeed there was some
justice in that. She'd been attracted to as thoroughgoing a
collection of cynics, bounders, and just plain cads as it was
possible for her to imagine. Even her friends said so. Not
that it was so obvious when she met them. She didn't seek
out the most popular boy in her high-school class, or lust
after the jocks who could and did have every girl in the
school. She was more likely to date the quiet ones with
glasses who read a lot. Some had never had a date before
her. Yet they invariably left her for her friends as soon as
she'd built up their confidence to a level where they dared
ask someone else for a date.

In truth, she scared hell out of everyone who tried to
take her seriously. She was intelligent, she talked a lot, and
she was interested in everything. She wrote for the school
paper. She did so much extra classwork that she could get
an A in any subject even if she turned in a blank final exam.
She earned real money at such unfeminine activities as buying
stale bread and reselling it to chicken farmers. In short,
she was real competition for any boy she met, and the ones
she liked were never secure enough to survive that threat.

When she was sixteen and a senior at John Marshall High,
she met Fred Linker in the school library. Fred had never
had a date in his life and was terrified of girls. Gwen was a
bit cynical about men by that time, but she was enough of
a product of her culture to wish she had someone to take
her on dates. Fred seemed perfect. He wasn't at all bad
looking, just shy. He liked to read and knew of works like
Silverlock that she adored as soon as he told her about them.
He was a good listener, and they shared many opinions. So
she worked on him until he asked her out, and three dates
later, he got the nerve to kiss her goodnight. He didn't know
how to do that very well, but Gwen was a good teacher.
She'd found books that told how.

Fred wanted to be a writer. He wrote constantly. Someday
he'd sell a story. He was certain of it. He'd even sent a few
off to magazines and got rejections slips.

Gwen read the magazines Fred liked, and three weeks

later got a short story accepted in one of his favorites. She thought he'd be proud of her, and she knew she could show him how he could sell, too—it was only a matter of studying the editor's prejudices—but a week after that Fred took another girl to the sock hop. Later he sold three stories himself, but he never asked Gwen out again.

College hadn't been much different. Gwen's physical urges got stronger, and sometimes she was so lonely she'd read in an all-night restaurant rather than sit in her room; so lonely that she made resolutions about not competing with the next man she liked. She even tried to carry them out. It did no good. Even when she didn't actually do whatever her current boyfriend thought he was good at, eventually it would come out that she could if she wanted to.

Or maybe, she told herself as she dressed in her compulsively neat one-room apartment, maybe that's all wrong. Maybe they just didn't like me in the first place. God knows there must be *something* wrong with me.

I'm not ugly. She studied herself in the mirror. Too short, yes. Five foot two and eyes of blue sounds very good in songs, but in fact that's pretty short, and besides my eyes are more greenish-brown. Nose too pointed, face too angular, but there are plenty of girls with longer and pointier noses and they aren't ugly. And I've got all the right equipment. Not a *lot* of it, but in good proportion. I bounce all right if I go without a bra, and my hips aren't bony. I don't wear clothes well because I'm too thin, but I don't look too bad. Men don't turn away.

And everyone tells me I talk well. I'm bright and witty. They say it just after we meet, and just as they're walking out.

But this time it's different.

She dressed carefully. This time for sure, she thought. Things will happen tonight. She felt a delicious sensation of anticipation. Maybe this will last, she thought. Please. Let it last.

She grinned at her image in the mirror. To whom was

she praying? Her image of the universe had room in it for
a god, but not one who paid much attention to that kind of
prayer. If prayer worked, there were a lot of people worse
off than Gwen Tremaine praying their arses off. They didn't
get what they wanted. Why should she?

But there was a chance. Les was different.

She'd met him in an all-night coffee shop near the
university library. It had been quite late, and she was ready
to go home. She was carrying a half dozen books, and he'd
seen the anthropology book. "That looks like a new one,"
he'd said. "I think I have not seen that one before. May I
look?"

And then they'd got to talking. He was brilliant. She could
tell that from the few things he said. But mostly he wanted
her to talk. He liked listening to her—about everything,
about *anything* she wanted to say.

He got her to tell him about growing up in Iowa, about
moving to California when she was fourteen, about high
school and college and her unsuccessful love affairs, about
her theories of history and physics and mathematics and
especially anthropology and—

He liked her. He listened, and he liked her, and to Gwen
that was devastating.

And she couldn't compete with him. Partly she couldn't
because she didn't know what he did. He never said directly,
but she had the impression that he was in advanced physics.
Once he'd got her talking about the origin of the universe.
She'd told him what she thought, and he scribbled some
equations on a napkin. They meant nothing to her. He'd
thrown the napkin away. She went back the next morning
and retrieved it from the garbage behind the restaurant
and went to the library. After spending all day working on
them the equations still meant nothing to her. She couldn't
even find many of the symbols.

Which meant he was a liar—only it didn't. Les didn't
have to lie. He talked about himself only when she urged
him to, and never to impress her. He'd already done that
on the first night, when she found he'd read nearly every

anthropology book ever written and understood all the major theories. When she could get him to talk, she learned more in an hour with Les than she did in a month of classes.

For three weeks she had never seen him except in the coffee shop. He came in late, always after midnight, sometimes not until dawn. He drove a truck for spending money and had no fixed schedule; but he always came, and she was always waiting. They'd never discussed it, but she knew he came just to see her.

For three weeks they talked in the shop. He waved good-bye to her when it got so late she had to go home (or to morning classes).

Until yesterday. Yesterday he got up when she did, paid his check, and walked home with her. It seemed perfectly natural that he come in with her and that they go to bed together, and that he aroused her to flights of passion she had never supposed possible.

He stayed until noon.

And now he was coming back and wanted to take her somewhere. She dressed carefully. A skirt that didn't wrinkle. They didn't have to wrestle in a car—he was welcome in her bed—but who knows? she thought. She grinned at her image in the mirror. "Painted hussy," she told it.

The image grinned back. "We like it, don't we, ducks?"

"Damn straight," Gwen said. "Damn straight. Never thought I would—"

She laughed at herself, but she studied her small collection of jewelry and perfume just the same. What would he like?

"Independent. Liberated. And working my arse off to make him want me," she told the mirror.

"Hang on to this one," the image said.

"Right." If we can. Please. Let this be all right. Let this last.

❖   ❖   ❖

When the doorbell rang an hour after midnight, she ran to it, then caught herself. He knew she liked him, but she didn't want him to think she was *that* nuts over him. Still, she was a little breathless when she opened the door. Would

he leap at her? Carry her to bed? She damned well wasn't
going to resist—

He kissed her, but broke away quickly before that could
lead to anything else. Then he grinned. "Later. We'll have
a lot of time."

"Good."

"Go for a drive?" he asked.

"Sure. Where? Do I need a coat?"

"Actually, I had in mind a weekend trip. Can you pack a
bag?"

She frowned. Was he *that* confident? But then he had
reason to be. And why not? "I can get away," she said. "For
a couple of days. but I ought to call my landlady and tell
her—"

"Leave a note. It's late."

"What should I pack? Swimsuit? Ski clothes?"

"Do you like boats? Sailing?"

"I never went on one before. I don't get motion sick—I
guess I've told you that."

"You have."

There it was. The tiny accent. "Just where did you grow
up?" she asked.

"I thought you were the professional who'd guess from
my speech patterns." He grinned.

It's a nice grin, she thought. A nice grin, on a nice face.
She moved closer to him. "Wheedle, wheedle."

He pulled her against him and held her for a moment.

"You're just the right size," she said.

"How's that?"

She shrugged. "Big enough that I think of you as a big
man, but not so big you tower over me. And not so big in
other ways, if you know what I mean—"

He laughed. "We do seem compatible."

"Yes, I like that. I'll pack my sailing clothes," she said. "I
won't be long."

❖   ❖   ❖

"I didn't know they kept boats in the mountains," Gwen
said. "Just where are you taking me?"

It seemed a reasonable question. The road climbed steadily higher into the Angeles Mountains, directly away from the sea. At first she'd thought they were driving up the coast toward Santa Barbara, but he'd turned east.

The truck hummed along the road. It was a heavy Ford pickup, and the bed was crammed with odd shapes covered with a tarpaulin. That seemed strange too. Why a loaded truck for a weekend date? "Where are we going, Les?"

"Don't you trust me?"

"I—I don't know. I don't—Les please. Don't play head games with me."

"I don't want to, Gwen." His voice was very serious. "But I don't have much choice." He hesitated a moment. "You told me you want to learn. You like anthropology because you want to learn. To travel, see strange people and learn how they live—"

"Yes—"

"I can give you a chance to do that. Right now. But it's a long trip. Will you come with me?"

"Right now? Just like that? Not tell anyone—"

"Yes."

"Les, I can't—"

"Sure you can. You told me yourself, nobody cares what happens to you. Your mother's dead, and you haven't heard from your father in years. Sure you can. Who'll care? The people at the university? Landlady? Not really."

"But—right now? Just like that? Where do we go?"

"That's the part I can't tell you. A long voyage to exotic and distant lands. I can promise you that."

"With you."

"Yes. With me." He drove with both hands on the wheel, both eyes on the road; almost as if he were afraid of the truck. Now he let go to take her hand for a moment and squeeze it. "With me. I promise you that."

She thought about it. But it was all so strange. "What's in the truck? Your travel equipment? What—who are you? CIA?"

"What if I were?"

"I—wouldn't like that."

"Then I'm not," he said. "Let's see. Other question. The gear in the truck is for travel, but it is not mine. I get equipment for others. Get it and deliver it."

"But always at night—"

"Generally," he agreed.

"Les, where *are* we going? I thought Mexico for a moment, but we're going northeast. Where—"

"Can't tell you. But will you come with me?"

"If I don't?"

He let the truck slow. "I turn around and take you home."

"And then?"

"And then I leave. I have to go, Gwen. I'm sorry I haven't been able to tell you much, but I can't. I do want you to go with me, but you don't have much time to make up your mind."

"How long—how long will we be gone?"

"A long time. Years. But you'll see exotic places, faraway places, places you'll never see unless you come with me."

"I didn't pack very much," she said. "Not for being away that long. Will you buy me a grass skirt?"

The truck ran on for a second more. Then he stopped, turned, and kissed her. "I'm glad," he said. Then he started up. "We don't have a lot of time. They won't wait all night."

"Who won't?" she asked.

An hour later she knew.

2

Gwen was on the Moon. She had to keep telling herself that. She was on the Moon and talking to a TV set.

The face on the TV was human. Strange, but human, and after what Gwen had seen on the ship, any human face was a relief.

The man looked bored. "You have come voluntarily?" he asked.

An embarrassing question. Gwen was naked, except for a sheet that she wrapped around herself when she realized that the TV screen worked *both* ways. She sat on the edge of the bed to talk to the man in the rust-colored tunic who'd appeared on the screen. Les lay partly covered on the bed, and his expression was—worried? Why worried, she wondered.

"Yes, I came voluntarily," she said. "Les asked me to come. He said I would visit strange and exotic lands and—"

"You boarded voluntarily," the man said. "Will you be missed? Will your disappearance cause difficulties? Widespread search by the authorities?"

"I don't think so. I left a note for my landlady that said I was going for a weekend trip. She'll worry when I don't come back after that. She may call the police."

"They will probably assume you were murdered. That is no problem of mine." The screen went blank.

51

"That's over," Les said. He looked relieved.

Why relieved? And why had he been worried? There was a lot that Gwen didn't understand. But certainly she was glad she had come. There were marvels enough, even here in the compartment. It was lavishly furnished, mostly with goods from- Earth; but some of the furnishings were new and strange. There was the TV with its strange control box that could call up books and maps and all kinds of interesting material—the only problem was that she couldn't read a word of it. And there had been the aliens, and the experience of seeing Earth from space. Now she felt the low gravity of the Moon and could see the lunar surface on the TV screen. It was all frightening, but exciting, too.

"Who was that man?" she asked.

"A policeman," Les said.

"What would have happened if I had said you kidnapped me?"

"He probably would not have believed you. But if you had said the *Shalnuksis* had kidnapped you, there would have been trouble."

Gwen shuddered, but not in fear. It was all so marvelous. Aliens. Spaceships. And they were so nice to her. Les had given her clothes and jewelry—not that the gifts meant anything, but he had got them for her. He cared. She knew that. He cared.

"And you don't come from anywhere on Earth?" she asked. "I still can't believe that."

"It's true, though," he said. "My home is twenty light-years from here."

"How long have you been on Earth?"

"Four years. A bit more than that."

"But you speak English so well! No wonder I couldn't tell where you came from. How did you learn to speak English so well in four years?"

"It's a gift," he said. "I speak a number of human languages. Four from your planet."

"A number of human languages—Les, what do you do for these—for the aliens?"

"You can think of me as a civil servant," he said. "I pilot ships, make studies of primitives, buy equipment and see that it gets aboard ship—any number of activities that the traders or the confederacy need done."

"A civil servant."

"Sort of," Les told her. "That is, most humans work for the confederacy, but they sometimes rent us out to traders when the work involves other humans. Just now I'm doing some errands for the *Shalnuksis*."

"But why don't you go to Washington and tell them? Or someone? Why such secrecy?"

"Time enough for questions later," he said. "We will have a lot of time. For the moment, we are together, and we have a few hours before we go to the other ship."

"Another ship?"

"Yes. I'm supposed to take some people—human volunteers, soldiers—to another planet. I'll have to brief them on the way."

"Soldiers. Volunteers. You mean mercenaries." She made no attempt to disguise the contempt in her voice.

He laughed. "You don't like warriors? You ought to feel a bit sorry for these. They've got their work cut out. More than they know."

"Who will they fight? What are they going to be doing?"

"All in good time. You'll know more about them than you want to by the time we get to Tran. For now—" He reached for her.

For a moment she resisted, but she could feel his urgency.

Why resist? she thought. Why resent his need? A need for me. He cares. I can lose myself in him. And he keeps his promises.

He'd already showed her marvels beyond her imagination. What more would there be? She shuddered in anticipation.

❖   ❖   ❖

The screen came to life while the troops were cooking lunch. Rick Galloway went over carrying his new lists of equipment. There was a lot they needed, and they hadn't received much of what they'd asked for.

"No time," Agzaral said. "No time at all. Gather your equipment. You must leave this cavern immediately. There is a ship outside, and you must be aboard it with everything you propose to take with you. You have two hours." He seemed very excited. "You must hurry."

"Why? We can't go now. We don't have anything like the gear we asked for—"

"Some is aboard the ship. The rest may be supplied later. But hurry. Those who remain behind will not be happy with the consequences."

"Why?"

"You will learn," Agzaral said. "But you will not go at all if you do not board the ship now. Recall the alternatives I gave you. They have not changed."

"This is ridiculous," Rick said. "It makes no sense at all."

There was no reply. Agzaral continued to stare out from the screen.

At least, Rick thought, at least he doesn't look bored. Is that a good sign? It seems pretty frightening, actually.

"I cannot say I care for this," André Parsons said. "But I think of few alternatives." He turned to the screen. "Why should we trust you?"

"You would be surprised at how little that matters to me," Agzaral said. "But you will regret not having boarded the ship."

Parsons shrugged, then looked to Rick. "I think we should do it."

"Agreed," Rick said. "Load it up. Elliot, get them moving. We board ship."

"Move your equipment to the upper corridor," Agzaral said. "The ship will be ready to board shortly, and you should have all your possessions at the airlock."

They sweated the weapons and other equipment up the corridor. "Now get that other stuff," Rick ordered. "Clean out the cavern."

"Why?" Warner demanded. "What do we do with a gasoline lawnmower?"

"I don't know," Rick said. "But we'll never get another one. Now carry it up, Professor."

"Yes, *sir*," Warner said. "And the toaster, too?"

"Everything," Rick said. He picked up a coffee urn.

When they had all left the cavern, the entrance to it closed off.

❖   ❖   ❖

The ship stank. Although they couldn't see very much of the ship, it was obvious that it wasn't the same one they had come up in. The paint was stained and chipped in places. There were stains on the deck.

When they got the last of the equipment aboard, the entryway closed. There was no warning at all. Their weight increased. It was obvious that the ship was in motion. Rick estimated the acceleration at about twice the Moon's gravity.

After two hours, he began shouting. "What the hell's going on," he demanded. There was no one to talk to. The only TV screen was blank. It seemed silly to be shouting at empty air, but it was sillier not to do *something*.

Nothing happened. Some of the troops prowled the areas they could reach. They found doorways that would open, and beyond them were latrines, storage compartments, another empty area. They found food in two other compartments.

The rest of the system was closed. There was no way into the rest of the ship.

"What the hell's going on?" Rick muttered.

André Parsons shrugged. "There is wine and whiskey in the storerooms. I suggest we have a drink."

"Is that all you think of?"

"No, but I think of nothing better to do at the moment."

More than fifty hours went by. They still had no word from anyone. They had been under acceleration the entire time. Rick worked out the distance, assuming two Lunar gravities. The answer seemed so unreasonable that he worked it again. Thirty-two million miles. A third of the distance from Earth to the Sun.

There was nothing on the TV. Warner began to complain that their employers had violated their contract. Rick privately agreed, but he saw no point in talking about it. If the

Shalnuksis were listening, he didn't want them thinking in those terms. Finally Elliot shut Warner up.

A couple of troopers got roaring drunk, and Rick had to post guards at the door to the liquor compartment. The problem was—whom did he trust? Discipline was going to hell, and there wasn't much he could do about it.

Another forty hours went by.

"TEN MINUTES." The voice sounded through their compartment. "You have ten minutes to prepare for no gravity. Ten minutes."

There was netting in the storerooms, and they put the loose equipment under that, but they kept their weapons. No one wanted ship's doors between them and their rifles.

The acceleration stopped, and they were in free fall, but not for long. The ship moved in short jerks. Then there was a deep tone—nothing like the warning tones they had heard from the speakers. This was a deep thrum that sounded through the whole ship, as if the ship itself were vibrating to the noise.

Rick's vision blurred. He could see, but not well, as if he were looking through heavy astigmatic lenses. The thrumming note got louder and increased in pitch. Then, gradually, the note died away and his vision returned. They began to feel weight again, more than before—almost a full Earth gravity.

The TV set came on. It showed Karreeel seated in his highchair. He looked almost comical, and some of the troops laughed nervously.

Then they crowded around shouting obscenities. There was no response. Instead, Karreeel began to speak in a flat monotone.

"I regret that this is a recorded message," the alien said. "Please listen carefully."

"Shut up," Rick ordered. The babble died, but he missed the first words.

". . . . was unavoidable. You are now on your way to Tran, and you cannot regret your lack of proper equipment more

than we do. Your success is important to us, and only great
need forces us to send you with so little preparation." The
alien spoke in a calm and detached manner, but Rick noticed
that the mouth and nose slits flared more than they had
during the interview in Agzaral's office.

"We will provide you with as much information as possible.
The pilot of this vessel is of your species, and he has tapes
of what we know of local conditions. He will translate the
information and provide you with copies of the planetary
surveys.

"You will be aboard the transport ship for approximately
forty of your days. During that time the acceleration will
be increased to that of Paradise to accustom you to the
gravity you will find there.

"I regret that most of the information on local languages
is very old, but doubtless you will learn those currently in
use. You may need only one. We are interested in only a
small area of the planet. You will also be given all the
information required to plant and harvest the crops. The
cultivation of the *surinomaz* is complex, and it is important
that you follow instructions exactly. The harvest will be
valuable to us, and thus to you. When next we visit Paradise,
we will bring luxuries and necessities. You need have no
concern, provided that you have grown what we require
and are prepared to furnish it to us.

"Of course you must understand that if you have nothing
to sell us, we will have nothing to sell to you.

"We wish you great success."

The screen went blank. Then a human face appeared.

The man was not as dark as Agzaral, and his eyes were
lighter in color, but there was a faint resemblance to Agzaral
even so. His voice had no accent at all. "You can call me
'Les,' " he said. "I'm the pilot. I'll try to answer questions."

"Take us back!" Warner shouted. "You have no right to
change our contract! We enlisted under specified conditions
and you have changed them. We quit!"

The pilot laughed. "You'll do it on Tran, then. I don't
think anybody every jumped ship in phase drive before,

but you're welcome to try. Unfortunately, there's no known way you can report to us on what happens. Telepathy? Are you telepathic?"

"That's enough, Warner," Rick said. "Elliot, sit on him if that's what it takes."

"Sir." Sergeant Elliot grinned. This was the first thing he'd completely understood since they left the Moon, and he was eager to be useful.

"Equipment," Rick said. "We don't have what we need— we don't even know what we need."

"Yeah, that's too bad," Les said. "Karreeel is very sorry about that. You see, we got word that a ship-load of government people had just come out of phase drive and was about to make a visit. That would have delayed your trip for months, maybe longer. Might have canceled it entirely. This ship is under charter to Karreeel's trading company, and you wouldn't believe what it would have cost to have it sit idle all that time."

"But—we don't know what to do when we get there," Rick protested.

"You'll get all the information you need," Les said. "Well, all we have, anyway. Look, this has all been done before. You'll manage."

"This is absurd," André Parsons said. "How do you expect us to establish control of an area and raise crops with almost no equipment and very little ammunition?"

"Don't know," the pilot said. "But you'd better try. Karreeel will keep his part of the bargain, but he won't trade with you if you've got nothing to trade."

"But it makes so little sense," Parsons said. "If they wish this crop, why send us with inadequate gear?"

"Well, it's too bad," Les said. "But his outfit can afford the loss. What they couldn't afford was the time they'd lose if you were still around when the Commission people arrived. You wouldn't have liked that much either. Hearings, committee meetings, more hearings, and all the time they'd insist they were interested only in what was best for you."

"Can't you explain some of this?" Rick asked. "Somehow

you people don't act the way we always thought an interstellar civilization would—"

The pilot laughed. "I've read some of your speculations. Why did you think we'd be so different from you? Or that we'd treat Earth any different from the way the English treated India? Excuse me, I've got work to do. Among other things, I have to translate all this stuff."

"Can't a computer do that?" Rick asked.

"Yeah, but it's not as easy as you think. Have to set up the right programs for it. I'll be back." The screen went blank again.

André Parsons looked thoughtful. "What was it that the East India Company called native soldiers?"

"Sepoys," Rick said.

Parsons nodded. "Sepoys. Well, now we know our status."

3

The computer control system was complex, but eventually Gwen was able to use it for simple tasks, such as calling up pictures and documents. A good thing, too, she told herself. Otherwise she'd be bored to distraction.

Not with Les, of course. He was attentive and kind. He spent hours preparing dinners to be served in a romantic setting, with exotic music from a dozen worlds, wines and liqueurs from as many more, so that their evenings—and nights!—were more exciting than anything she could imagine.

But that was a few hours a day. You can spend only so much of your time being charmed. Or in bed, she told herself. Les had his work; he was translating documents for the mercenaries. That left her with mornings and afternoons (ship time, of course; since they had left the solar system there was nothing to be seen outside the ship—no star or sun to mark days or seasons) with nothing to do. Les wouldn't let her talk to the mercenaries; they weren't to know she was aboard. He insisted on that.

Which left her curious. Who were they? Why were they going to a primitive world called Tran?

When she first learned to use the computer's information-retrieval system, she could only look at pictures. The languages were a total mystery. The pictures were amazing enough; stars and nebulae, time-lapse photographs of multiple star systems with the stars so close they touched and sent streams of star-stuff spiraling off into the universe; another time-lapse of a black hole devouring its companion, taken from close enough and with long enough time delay that she could actually see the real star diminish in size, torn into gases which spiraled down and down to vanish into a central nothing; and more. There were intriguing pictures of life on a hundred planets. She counted a dozen races. *Shalnuksis*, of course, and others; Centauroids. Octopoids. A race like humans, but obviously reptilian in ancestry. A world where humans—real humans—kept as seeming pets small winged reptiles looking for all the world like tiny dragons.

And it was frustrating because Les didn't want to answer questions. Not that he flatly refused, but he would put her off, ask what she thought of what she had seen, ask what it reminded her of, until the evening was over and once again she had done all the talking. His desire for knowledge about Earth was insatiable. He wanted to know everything, trivial or profound. No detail seemed unimportant.

An anthropologist studying her. But few anthropologists were so charming about it.

Eventually she found the file on Tran, the place where the mercenaries were going. She could read none of it, of course; but she had learned how to make the computer pronounce the words it displayed on the screen, and from that she learned the phonetic alphabet used by the Confederacy. She made very little progress learning that language. There were too many words referring to places and people and things and ideas that were thoroughly unfamiliar. This didn't surprise her. The real shock came when the computer showed her the languages of Tran.

She spent a day being certain. Then, in the evening, when they were together with a glass of amontillado ("One of Earth's finest products," Les had said. "Nothing to match it anywhere. Too bad regular trade with Earth isn't allowed."), she could stand it no longer.

"I was listening to Tran languages," she said.

He raised an eyebrow. "Nothing there to interest you."

"But there is! Les, I recognized some of the words! A lot of them. That language is based on an ancient Indo-European tongue! Some of the words are unchanged from Mycenaean Greek!"

"Astute of you to notice," he said. "I expect you're right."

"Les, you're teasing me. You know what this means. It means that there was an exchange of people—a lot of people, enough to bring languages with them—between Tran and Earth as far back as four thousand years."

"Other way," he said. "From Earth to Tran."

"I meant that. It's obvious that humans didn't evolve on Tran. It's only a colony. But why is it so primitive? Even relative to Earth. And Earth is primitive by your standards—Les, is *Earth* a colony?"

"No." He looked thoughtful. "Perhaps that's not the right answer. Perhaps you're right. Earth is a colony—"

"Les, you're not making sense. Did humanity evolve on Earth?"

"What do you think? You've read Darwin and Ardrey and Leakey. More sherry?"

"I don't want sherry, I want answers!"

He came over and filled her glass. "Don't be so serious," he said. "Now. You obviously think humanity is native to Earth. Tell me why."

An hour later, it was time for dinner. He still hadn't answered her questions.

Dinner was exotic, as usual, but she wasn't interested in food.

"Hey. You're crying," he said. "What's the matter? You don't like *nastari*?"

"You treat me like a child."

"No. I treat you like an adult," he said. He was very serious.

"I—what do you mean?"

"You are an intelligent woman. You raise fascinating questions. Don't you want to find answers for yourself?"

"But you know, and I don't—"

"Do I?"

"You mean you don't know? You don't know where humanity evolved?"

"I don't even *know* that it did."

"But—" The enormity of what he'd said struck her. "But you—your culture—you've had space travel for four thousand years," she insisted. "If you don't know the answers, at least you have a lot more data! Give me some."

"I'm doing that. How much can you absorb in a few weeks?"

"Oh." She was silent for a long time.

"Gwen." His voice was very gentle, his expression very serious. "Gwen, accept it. All of it. Believe me, I care for you. And believe me when I say I'm trying to do what's best for both of us." He laughed. "My, aren't we serious. And the dessert will melt."

✧   ✧   ✧

Gradually she realized it: he was interested in what she thought. He wanted to know her ideas, and more than that, her reactions to what she was learning. But he was getting her talking to herself.

"What am I?" she asked her mirror. "Lover or laboratory animal? Anthropologist's informant, mistress, or—" She broke off. She'd been about to say "wife" and she didn't have any right even to *think* that.

And he did want to know. When she pointed out that some of the intelligent races she'd seen in pictures were identical to descriptions found in ancient mythology: centaurs, an aquatic race that might be mistaken for mermaids, a saurian race that might or might not have inspired the Minotaur legend—he not only listened, he insisted on having her describe and sketch the legendary creatures.

He also encouraged her to study Tran. She might think of something useful, something that would aid the mercenaries. "It would help a lot if you could," he said.

"Why?"

"If they succeed, they'll make a lot of money for the traders.

Traders have influence with the Council. Won't hurt my career."

She stared in disbelief. "I—I thought I knew you better than that," she said. "Don't you care about the people on Tran? They're *human*. Don't you care?"

"Oddly enough, I do care," Les said. "Enough, in fact, to see if I can think of any way to help the mercenaries succeed with a minimum of slaughter. Because, you see, they really have to succeed—"

"Why?"

He ignored her question. "Can you think of anything that would help?"

"I don't know," Gwen said. "All the information I've seen is very old—"

"About six hundred years old," Les said. "No one's been there since, except for one fairly recent fly-by. We know they're still pretty primitive down there. No railroads, industries, paved roads. No technological civilization."

"But no one has landed for six hundred years?"

Les nodded.

"But I thought this crop was valuable—"

"It is. But there are some powerful reasons for the *Shalnuksis* to stay far away from Tran." He looked thoughtful for a moment. "It's best you know. Tran's not in the Council's data banks. Except for the *Shalnuksis* and a few humans who work for them, no one knows the planet exists."

He seemed very serious, and she knew he already regretted trusting her with even that much information. She wanted to tell him that he could trust her with anything, that she'd always be loyal to him no matter what he was doing. That thought shocked her because she'd never thought such a thing before. And was it even true? "What would happen if the—the Council found out?"

Les shook his head. "I don't know." He was silent for a moment.

She waited, hoping he'd trust her again, but instead he said, "But it wouldn't be good for me. The *Shalnuksis* would lose control. They'd never get their crop harvested."

"But without information, how can they expect a small group of mercenaries to get them anything?"

"Maybe they can't." There was definite worry in the pilot's voice. "But it is important. Have you any suggestions?"

"This doesn't make sense," Gwen said. "You say the crop is valuable, but they don't visit the source for hundreds of years—"

"Oh. Yes," Les said. "But you see, the real *surinomaz* won't grow under normal conditions on Tran. Just for a few years out of every six hundred. But for about five years, starting a couple years from now, it grows very well. The mercenaries could demand a pretty stiff price if they knew it." He sighed. "I guess the best thing will be to set them down near a small village in the right geographical region and hope they're intelligent enough to manage."

"They won't even know the languages—"

"They'll have to learn them."

"Why six hundred years?"

"Orbits," the pilot said. "Tran has two main suns. Both a little bigger and a little hotter than Sol. Planet's farther away from either of them, so it's not as warm. Reasonable climate, actually. But even with both suns, *surinomaz* won't grow properly. It's only a weed until the third sun comes close, but then for a short time it's the best stuff in the galaxy."

"But what is *surinomaz*?"

"Ever hear of Acapulco Gold?" the pilot asked.

"Marijuana—you mean drugs?"

"In a way. Look, back on Earth, you've just discovered endogenous morphiates. Know what I'm talking about? No? Well, it turns out that the brain manufactures its own painkillers and euphoric drugs. Chemicals similar to morphines. Enough of them in your system, and you have a natural high. *Surinomaz* makes the stuff, only by the barrelful. It has about the same effect on *Shalnuksis* as on humans, and they use it about the same way Americans use alcohol. And Tran Natural gets a premium price, like Talisker scotch, or the rarer wines."

Gwen stared at him.

"I see you don't approve," Les said. "Look, what is it to me if the *Shalnuksis* use drugs? Or to you?"

But there has to be more, she thought. There has to be. Or is it that I can't accept being in love with a drug dealer? "Isn't all this illegal?" Gwen asked.

Les shrugged. "The drug traffic isn't precisely legal, but no one really cares. Keeping Tran a secret—now, that's highly illegal."

"But the crop is important to you," Gwen said.

The pilot was very serious now. "More important than you can guess that the mercenaries succeed."

"Then you should stay and help them," she said.

"Can't. The ship's too valuable. And this trip has to be kept secret, which means the ship must return as quickly as possible—"

And then, as he always did, he changed the subject.

✧   ✧   ✧

The computer's files on Tran were sketchy. As nearly as Gwen could tell, the planet had never been visited except to obtain a harvest, and there had never been any systematic studies made. No one had been sufficiently curious. There were only groups of traders who had brought mercenary soldiers from Earth with instructions to seize a particular area and cultivate *surinomaz*, harvest it, and sell the product to ships that would come later.

That had begun in Indo-European times, as Gwen had deduced from the language. She was pleased to find confirmation in the computer's records. The first humans had been sent to Tran because a dominant life-form, centauroid (vaguely similar to the Greek centaur of legend, but the intelligent and unrelated centauroids she'd seen in other pictures far more so) and about as intelligent as a chimpanzee, could not be trained to do cultivation. She could not find out why humans had been chosen, or why, once they had decided on humans, they had brought a band of Achaean warriors and their slaves instead of planting a high-technology colony.

The original expedition had been expensive. In addition

to the Achaeans, the *Shalnuksi* traders had brought a variety of Earth plants and animals, scattering seeds broadside on the planet and returning years later with more animals and insects. There had been no scientific rationale to what they had brought, no attempt at a balanced ecology. It was instant natural selection; adapt or die.

The records didn't say so, but Gwen wondered if one of the reasons that *surinomaz* had become increasingly difficult to cultivate might be the competition from Earth plants, animals, and insects. Tran's native life forms used levoamino acids and dextro sugars, like Earth's, and thus competed for many of the same nutrients.

Tran's history and evolution was dominated by its suns. The two major suns together gave it at best only a bit more than 90 percent of what Earth receives from Sol; Tran was normally a cold world, with only the regions near the equator comfortable for humans. But then came the cyclic approach of the third star; for 20 years out of each 600, Tran received nearly 20 percent more sunlight, a combined total of 10 percent more illumination than Earth ever got.

In those times of burning, ice caps melted. Weather became enormously variable, cycles of drought and rainstorms alternating nearly everywhere. The higher latitudes, in normal times too cold for humans and resembling the Alaska tundra, were warmed and became temperate, experiencing a brief but glorious bloom of life.

The effects of the invader's passage were devastating to the human cultures. They never rose higher than an Iron Age feudalism. Gwen thought that curious and wanted to talk to Les about it, but she didn't feel very good and went to bed early.

The next morning she vomited her breakfast.

❖   ❖   ❖

In a week she was certain. She went to find Les. He was seated at the control console dictating notes for the mercenaries. When she came in he looked up with a slight frown, annoyed that she'd disturbed him at work. "Yes?"

"I'm pregnant."

His face ran a gamut of emotions. Surprise, but then something else. It looked almost like horror. He said nothing for what seemed like an eternity. Then, his voice calm, he said, "We have reasonably complete medical robots aboard. I can ask the computer if they're up to an abortion."

"Damn you!" she shouted. "Damn you!"

"But—"

"What makes you think I want an abortion? I suppose this is an inconvenience to you. It—"

"Hush. There's more involved than you know."

He's serious, she thought. Deadly serious. Deadly. Now there's an appropriate word. "Les, I thought you might be pleased." Tears welled despite her effort to control them. Couldn't he understand?

"There's so much you don't know. Can't know," he said. "Gwen, we can't have a family life. Not as you think of family life—"

"You're already married. I should have known." She was alone again. Alone, and she couldn't go home.

His reaction startled her. He laughed. Then he said, "No. I'm not married." He stood and came toward her. She moved away. His face changed, the expression softening. "Gwen, it's going to be all right. You startled me, that's all. It will be all right. You'll see."

She wanted desperately to believe him. "Les, I love you—"

He moved closer. She was afraid, of him and of everything, but she didn't know what to do; and when he came to her, she clung to him in despair.

Two weeks passed. Les did not mention their future again. They entered Tran's star system, and Les busied himself finding a suitable place to land the mercenaries.

PART THREE:

TYLARA

1

Tylara do Tamaerthon sat at the head of the great wooden council table beneath banners and armor taken in a hundred battles. Her blouse was fine silk, dyed a cornflower blue to match her eyes, but under it she wore mail. The dagger at her belt had jewels and a pommel carved to the likeness of a gull's head; a work of art, but the blade was made in Rustengo and was honed to a fine point. Her braided raven-black hair was crowned with a cap of hammered iron.

She was young and beautiful, and every man in the room felt her presence; despite her armor and the dagger at her waist, she seemed small and vulnerable, in need of protection.

Everyone seemed dwarfed in the great hall of Castle Dravan. Like all of the ancient castles of Tran, Dravan stood above caves of ice; there was a faint smell of ammonia in the council room as an acolyte opened a massive door far below them. Above ground, stone arches and great wooden beams stretched massively. Other rooms in the fortress sported rich tapestries and wood paneling, but here the bones and sinews of the castle showed nakedly. The only decorations were mementos of battles won.

There were many of those. Banners from places a hundred leagues and more distant gave mute testimony to the strength of Dravan and the skill of the Eqetas who had ruled here.

Tylara looked up at them as if to draw strength down from the rafters.

It was her first meeting of the full council, and she had no real confidence in these westerners. They seemed so little like her husband! And there were only two bheromen in attendance. The others were knights and merchants, a local priest of Hestia—this was a grain-producing region—and the inevitable priests of Yatar, two representatives of the yeomanry, a scattering of guildmasters. They called her Great Lady, and for the moment they respected her as Eqetassa of Chelm; but she was still a stranger who had never lived among them.

Her only real friends were the retinue she had brought from Tamaerthon, and they had no place in the council of this western land.

A messenger stood at the end of the table. What he read was full of flowery phrases and elaborate compliments, but his meaning was clear enough. She heard him out with impatience, then waved to have him led from the room. When he was gone, she looked down the length of the heavy wooden table. "Well, my lords? Wanax Sarakos makes us an offer. Have you advice?"

There was profound silence. Tylara smiled thinly. The silence was more eloquent than any speech could have been. Her bheromen wanted to accept the offer—or at least bargain with Sarakos while they still had something to bargain with. The yeomen and guildmasters—could they want Sarakos here also? Tylara looked at the impassive faces and read nothing. She knew too little of these people, and they were accustomed to hiding their thoughts from the great ones.

But if one of the bheromen spoke for accepting Sarakos, others would join. Or would they? These were her husband's people. Could they be so little like him? The memory of him stabbed at her, and she saw him as he had been: tanned, laughing, coming to her. She thrust the image from her mind before the tears came, for she had had this dream before, and it ended with reality—with Lamil cold and stiff in his bier.

She keenly felt her youth and inexperience. She was only twelve as they reckoned years here (in Tamaerthon they counted a child a year old at birth and added four more at age nine, so that she would be called seventeen there). She had lived far from these iron hills, and she did not know these people. It said much for her husband—and for the strength of his family—that they obeyed her at all.

"Captain Camithon," she said. "It seems no one wishes to speak. Perhaps you will advise me."

Camithon had served three generations of Eqetas of Chelm; his beard had greyed in that service, and his body was scarred with wounds. A long scar from a lance that had narrowly missed taking his eye ran diagonally across his cheek, giving him a somewhat ferocious appearance that he sometimes took advantage of in councils of war. He stood hunched over as if his very bones were tired, and as he stood he muttered about his estates which he had not visited in a year. But his voice was steady enough when he spoke. "The usurper marches with two thousand lances and a great train of foot," he said. "We have but a hundred lances, and we stand in Wanax Sarakos's way."

Tylara nodded gravely as she had seen her father do in clan meetings. Inwardly she wished to shout. Camithon was broadly proclaimed a splendid soldier and perhaps he was, but he could never come to the point until he had reviewed everything a dozen times and more.

She hid her impatience with good grace and thought no one noticed. She had learned endurance if not patience, and that would have to do.

"Dravan is strong," mused Camithon. He brushed his fingers against the scar on his cheek, as if to remind everyone that he had held Dravan in the battle that earned him his distinctive mark. "Our lady has seen to the granaries and magazines, and well done that was, too. This old castle has killed five armies—but it has never before been held with only a hundred lances, and it has never before been so thoroughly cut off from aid."

"As if there were any aid to send," one of the guildmasters muttered.

Camithon's sword rested on a map unrolled on the table. He lifted the weapon and used it as a pointer. "The Protector is here, ten days and more to the northwest with our Wanax Ganton. He has no more than a thousand lances, and the Protector cannot allow the young king to be penned up in any castle, no matter how strong. Thus he cannot come to our rescue himself, and I doubt he can spare any great strength."

Tylara wanted to shout. *I know all that*, her mind screamed. Outwardly she smiled and said, "You give us a hundred lances, but you have forgotten my Tamaerthon archers. I hope this usurper Sarakos makes that mistake. He won't make it twice."

There were murmurs of approval from behind her. Tylara's people could not sit at the council table, but she was attended by them; and the Tamaerthon yeomanry wasn't afraid to be heard in any council room. In their mountainous plateau by the sea, the clans did not live as peasants lived among the great lords and bheromen of the west.

She had a momentary twinge of homesickness. She longed for her high ridges, with the blue sea to the east, stark mountains rising from it to stand deep blue in dusklight and dawn. It would be so easy to go home. She had only to give up this castle to Sarakos and she could return as the wealthiest lady in Tamaerthon—or she could stay, with all her husband's lands restored. Sarakos would give her that, and the council would approve. She had only to say the words—

"A hundred lances and two hundred archers are still but five hundred fighting men," Camithon said. He spoke as if proud of his arithmetic. "Fewer, for not all our knights have squire and man-at-arms. And these walls, though strong, enclose a great area. We have no reserve. Every man is needed at his post. What happens when they tire?"

Now, she thought. Say it now. But she couldn't. She had sworn. And how could she host her husband's murderer in his own home? Receive Chelm as a telast of Sarakos? It was unthinkable.

Yet—how do else? If the chief captain had no stomach for a fight, there was no chance at all. She fingered her braids restlessly.

"Yet honor demands that we fight," Camithon said. He looked down the length of the council table. "Do any dare dispute that?"

Some may have wanted to, but none spoke.

"I have never been one to fight merely for honor," Camithon said. "I prefer to win. But we can do no good elsewhere, so if we fight, we must hold Dravan. We sit astride the only good road south. Until we are taken, Sarakos can take no great force in search of our young Wanax. We buy time for the Protector."

"Yatar knows what he'll do with it," Bheroman Trakon said. His voice was overly loud, nervous, yet Trakon was a good man who had stood by the old Wanax in his troubles, and had lost much for doing it.

"Unfair, my lord," Camithon protested. "The Protector is the greatest soldier of Drantos, and he has won before when all seemed darkest."

"And the Dayfather may produce a miracle," Trakon said. He did not turn to see the red face of Yanulf, Archpriest of Yatar. "Yet what else can we do? I trust Sarakos not at all. Of the bheromen who have gone over to him, more than half have lost all to his favorites."

"Which hasn't stopped dozens more from joining him anyway," the weavers' guildmaster muttered. "Half the bheromen—no, three parts of four—have welcomed Sarakos. We fight to no purpose."

"Do you counsel surrender?" Camithon demanded.

The portly guildmaster shrugged. "It would do no good. Sarakos has his own weavers, and they like not our competition. But it's a forlorn fight all the same."

"It is more than forlorn." Yanulf had stood silent and impassive thus far; now the priest drew himself to full height and spoke with contempt. "Fools. The Time approaches, and you babble of petty dynastic wars."

"Legends," Trakon said.

Yanulf smiled thinly. "Legends. Is it legend that the Demon grows in the night sky? Is it legend that the waters rise along the shore? That the lamils breed, and the madweed flourishes in your very fields? Is it legend that we sit in council hall with no fire burning, yet we are not cold?"

"A warm summer," Trakon said. "No more than that. The Firestealer has been banished from the vault of the sky and stands at zenith each midnight. Of course it is warm."

There were murmurs from the yeomanry and guildmasters. Yanulf's voice rose. "And in the Time of Burning," he intoned, "then shall the seas smoke and the lands melt as wax. The waters of ocean shall lap the mountains. Woe to them who have not prepared. Woe to the unbeliever." He laughed. "Woe to you, Bheroman. But Yatar will forgive you. My lady, this is not a time for war. It is a time to gather food, to fill the holy caves. Do you not smell the breath of the Preserver? When the Stormbringer approaches, Yatar takes care of his own; and his first sign is the breath of the Preserver."

"Aye," one of the yeomen muttered. "My nephew's an acolyte, and he says the ice has grown half a foot in the past forty-day. Grown, when the Firestealer stands overhead at midnight!"

"How long?" Tylara demanded. "How long until the Time?"

"The writings are not clear," Yanulf admitted. "The worst may not come for a dozen years. There will be other signs first. The Demon Gods will visit and offer magic in exchange for *soma*. Strangers will come, with strange weapons and a strange language."

Trakon laughed.

Yanulf gave him a look of contempt. "It is written," he said. "Thus came the Christians, and thus came the Legions; and thus came *your* forefathers. It matters not whether you believe. Before the Firestealer plunges through the True Sun five times, these things will have come to pass."

"Plenty of time, then," Trakon said.

"Nay," Yanulf said. "When the signs are seen, all will seek

refuge in the great castles. The petty wars you fight now will be forgotten as those who have built castles upon bare rock know their folly and bring their armies to strike. Soon, soon all will know that there is no safety beyond the caves of the Protectors."

Tylara let them talk, half-listening in case one said something new. There was little chance of that. The situation was simple enough, if you left out religion.

But dared she? The priesthood of Yatar was universal. Whatever local gods might hold this land or that, Yatar was everywhere that humans lived. In her own land were ice caves, deep beneath the rocks, and sacrifices of grain and meat were taken there to be preserved against the days of Burning, even though few believed in the tales carried by the priesthood. If the Time approached—a time of storms when no ship sailed, and the seas rose to lap at the foothills; when Tamaerthon itself became an island; when fire fell from the sky; a time when rains would not fall, and then deadly rains fell in torrents—

She had heard the tales. No one she knew believed them except for the priesthood. Yet everyone knew of them.

But there was time. Religion could wait. And for the rest the situation was simple enough. Wanax Loron had not been a good ruler, and three years before his death civil war had broken out. The bheromen who fought him had justice on their side. Even Chelm had wavered, closing the gates of Dravan against Wanax Loron when he sought refuge from the bheromen, yet never quite joining the revolt either. That had been under Lamil's father, before plague took him.

(Plague. The legends said that as the Demon Star approached, the plague ran through the land; and certainly the plague struck every year now, with more killed each time. . . .)

But Loron had hired mercenaries and had driven the bheromen back and back, until the great ones of the land had done the unpardonable thing and invited outside help. They had offered the crown of Drantos to Sarakos son of

Toris, Sarakos in his own right one of the Five Wanaxxae, and son of Toris High Rexja of the Five.

Before the invasion began, Loron died; but Drantos was left with a boy king and depleted treasury. When the bheromen rallied to their new Wanax with one of their number as Protector, they were too late. Sarakos continued to press his claims. Twenty years before, the council of Drantos had arranged a royal marriage between Lana of Drantos, sister to Wanax Loron's father, and Toris Wanax High Rexja of the Five. It had been a brilliant diplomatic stroke, but now Sarakos could claim the throne of Drantos by blood, as the most legitimate adult claimant. A few minutes with a pillow would make him the only possible claimant.

And who could blame some of the bheromen for preferring Sarakos and peace to a boy king and war? Especially now, with the Demon growing visibly brighter in the night sky, and the priests of Yatar reading from their musty books and telling of the Time which would come. These were no times for a boy king. If only Lamil had joined Sarakos! He would be alive, and he—

"I say we fight." The accent was uncultured—the blacksmith at the foot of the table. "I have heard how they live in the Five. Better be dead for one such as me. Is my forge to be used to hammer slave collars for my friends?"

"Well said," Bheroman Trakon said. "Aye. Well said. For our honor, then. Yet—honor does not demand that we hold after all is lost. I say fight, and I will be on the walls; but when Sarakos brings up towers and siege engines, I say make the best bargain we can. For all of us."

"You may bargain, my lord," the blacksmith said. "But when the Demon stands high in the day sky, what do we folk do? Sarakos would like well enough to hold Castle Dravan for his people, but will he take my family into the cool of the donjon?"

"If he will not swear to that, then I make no bargain with him," Trakon said. "We of Chelm protect our own, even against the gods. But I think you fear too much the tales of the priesthood."

"When the Demon grows large and sky fire falls, you will regret those words," Yanulf said.

"We fight," Tylara said. "For the rest we must wait, but we fight. See to the defenses. And bring all who wish to come within the walls. Have the herds we cannot bring inside driven into the mountains. Leave nothing to sustain Sarakos. Nothing to eat. Hide all wealth. Cover and hide the very wells. Let Sarakos find our land unpleasant for his stay."

"It is evil to destroy food," Yanulf said. "Evil."

There was muttering from the low end of the table, but the peasantry could see it was necessary. One of the guildmasters spoke for all the townsmen and crofters. "Do we make it hard enough, he may depart, leaving our own as our masters." He fingered his neck. "It will take a heavy collar to circle this. I cannot wish to carry such."

"See to it," Tylara repeated.

"Aye, Lady," Captain Camithon said. He paused until the bheromen were leaving, but had not gone so far that they could not hear him. "The young lord made no mistake in his choice. You're more of a man than half the bheromen of Drantos."

✧ ✧ ✧

The great hall was empty except for Tylara and her archer commander. Cadaric was almost as old as Captain Camithon. His skin was tanned by wind and sun until his cheeks were cracked like worn leather. He wore the jerkin and kilts of his own people; they had never cared for trousers. "You've made no mistake, Lady," he said. He seemed pleased. "We'll show these westerners what Tamaerthon shafts can do."

"Until we have shot them all," Tylara said. Now that the others were gone, she could slump in her chair. She seemed smaller and more vulnerable. She was afraid, and there was no need to hide that from Cadaric. He had known her from the day she was born, and had served her brother and her father before him. There was no one else within five hundred leagues whom she could trust completely. "I've brought you here to be killed in a strange land, old friend."

He shrugged. "And will that be worse than to be killed

at home? I doubt not the Chooser can find me here as easily as in our mountains. When it is time to guest in his lodge, then guest you will. And yet," he mused, "and yet the Dayfather holds higher sway here. Do you think old One-eye has lost sight of this land? It would be pleasant to know."

"They say he sees the wide world," Tylara said. "Cadaric, I think they trust me not."

"They know you not. You are a young girl to them, and all they know is that their lad chose you. And because he did, they love you. Och, Lady, I know you mourn him."

And that was more than true. Tylara touched her cheeks, determined not to let the tears start again. A widow before she was properly a bride. It was the stuff the minstrels sang of.

Certainly Lamil had loved her. Eqeta of Chelm, one of the great counts of Drantos, he could have had his choice of a hundred ladies; but his ship had been wrecked on the rocky Tamaerthon coast, and after a summer (overly warm— could the priests be right?) he chose the daughter of a Tamaerthon chief. Tylara had no dowry, nothing to bring to the marriage—only two hundred archers, and a hundred of them free to leave after five years' service—but Lamil had chosen her above the great ones of his homeland.

She had loved to watch him; young and strong, calf muscles as hard as granite and standing out like thick cords from his slim legs. He browned to a deep copper in the sun. At night they ran on high ridges lit by the Firestealer. By day he laughed in the surf, climbed high on the ledges above the sea in search of young eagles. And he had laughed. Those were her favorite memories, of his laughter; laughing and swearing that he would have no other but her when she knew it could not be, laughing again at the furor he caused in rejecting the great ladies of Drantos and the Five.

And yet—it had been no silly match. Tylara brought nothing—and did not give anyone cause to fear an expanded county of Chelm. If no great lady caught the most eligible man in Drantos, then there were no jealousies. Yet she knew he had loved her.

She was married to him before he left Tamaerthon, but she was too young to go with him. The law required that the marriage be "consummated," and so it had been, but with a thick quilt between them in the wedding bed, and her father's dour henchmen standing by through the night.

' And for a winter, while the Firestealer plunged through the True Sun, she had made ready to go to her new home, to join this strong and handsome young husband. She sang the winter through until her father pretended disgust that she could be so happy to leave. In spring, when shadows stood doubled at noon and the ice was thin, she sailed north with the yearly merchant fleet, too strong for pirates to molest. They sailed north, then west through the chain of islands and swamps, and then upriver. When they landed, she was so eager that she set out the same day. She drove so hard that her maidservants were exhausted and the archers muttered ribaldries.

They reached Castle Dravan only hours ahead of the news. Lamil had chosen to stand with the boy Wanax Ganton. There had been a great battle, and Lamil was dead. Most of his troops had died covering the retreat of the boy king and the Protector. Captain Camithon told her that the Eqeta had charged Sarakos and struck him on the helmet before the guards beat him from his saddle. A dozen men had held him while Sarakos personally delivered the death stroke.

"I mourn him," Tylara said, and there was ice in her voice. "Have your fletchers make true shafts, Cadaric. We will teach this Sarakos what plumage the Tamaerthon gull wears."

2

There were none but fighting men in the great hall of Castle Dravan. The council was not needed; and now Cadaric and three subcaptains of archers sat at the table among the knights and bheromen.

They all stood respectfully when Tylara entered. If the bheromen resented her archers sitting as equals to armored knights, they kept that to themselves. Their lady had shown how sharp her tongue could be during the few weeks that she'd been with them—and they had seen what those shafts could do. They waited until she was seated at the head of the table. Then all began to speak at once.

"Hold! Silence!" Bheroman Trakon pounded the table with a dagger hilt. "That's better." He smiled at her. "My lady."

She nodded her thanks. Trakon had been most attentive lately. His wife had died of the plague ten months ago. He was twice her age—but only that, and handsome enough. Certainly she could not remain a virgin ruler of this county forever. She would never find another like Lamil, and Trakon would do as well as another when her mourning period ended. But so soon, so soon—

"They come, lady," Captain Camithon said. "Two days' march to the north."

"Two days if they're lucky," Trakon said. "They're so swollen

82

with plunder, they're lucky to march two thousand paces an hour."

"But all of them?" Tylara asked.

"Aye, Lady," Cadaric said. He glared at the others, ready to resent any objection that a mere Tamaerthon archer would speak. But there was only silence. Trakon, Cadaric, and Camithon had seen the advancing enemy, and the others had not. "I counted five hundred banners in their vanguard alone."

"You scouted the land well?" Tylara asked.

"Aye, Lady," Cadaric said. "It's more than suitable. We could blunt them, aye and blood them as well, and not lose a handful were it done well."

More babble. Trakon pounded for order again. One of the knights shouted. "Blunt them? What madness is this?"

Tylara noted Trakon's grim smile. He had not been too proud to listen to Cadaric as they rode back from scouting. A good man, she thought.

"The passes are narrow," Tylara said. "The maps remind me of my home. In narrow passes one man is the worth of ten—"

"Narrow they are, but not that narrow," Captain Camithon said. He sounded hurt. Strategy was a matter for professionals, not for girls hardly old enough to bed lawfully. "Do we stand in the passes with our hundred lances, we would blood Sarakos, aye, but then his strength would ride over us. Then who would there be to defend Dravan?"

Trakon's grin widened. "Our lady does not propose a stand," he said.

"Then what in the twelfth name of Yatar are we talking about?" Camithon demanded.

Cadaric grinned. "It is plain that you in the west have not heard the tales of how Tamaerthon won freedom from Ta-Hakos and the other greedy ones about us," he said. "I propose to have a ballad sung for you. With my lady's permission?"

Tylara nodded, and before there could be any protest one of the younger archers began to sing.

There were mutterings at first, but the boy's voice was good. They listened in silence, not trying to hide their astonishment at this intrusion in a council of war. As the song went on, Camithon leaned forward eagerly and Bheroman Trakon began to grin broadly. Before the ballad ended, the knights and captains were huddled over the map. For the first time in weeks, there were shouts of laughter in the great hall.

✧   ✧   ✧

Tylara sat astride her horse. This in itself was shocking enough; but worse, she rode no gentle mare but a great stallion—a war-horse any knight would be proud to own. She sat atop a small knoll, surrounded by a dozen men-at-arms and as many archers.

This was the price she paid for coming herself to the battle. She had never got her people to agree to that—but she'd come anyway, and no one dared lay hands on her. One soldier, ordered by Trakon to seize her bridle and lead her back inside Castle Dravan, would bear the welt from her riding crop for weeks. She must see at least one blow struck against the man who had killed her husband.

Below were not only all her fighting men, but hundreds of peasants with brush hooks and axes. They were using these to cut the low scraggly wax-stalks from the hillside and carry them into the pass. For five hundred paces from the top of the pass to where it widened below, the narrow road was carpeted with the newly cut brush. More was piled high to either side.

Bheromen and knights and men-at-arms waited where the pass widened a hundred paces beyond the last brushpile. The armored knights sat on the ground, giving their mounts ease until they would be needed. A few polished mail and plate. Others threw dice.

About half the knights were mounted on horses. The others rode centaurs; not as reliable as horses, harder to tame, and more likely to bolt when threatened. Horses were far superior, but they were more costly. They had to be fed cultivated grains and hay; they could not live by grazing.

Priestly legend said that horses, like men, were brought to this place by evil gods. This did not seem reasonable, but like the other tales of ships in the sky, the story was universal. "Why else," the priests said, "must we labor so hard to eat, if the Dayfather intended us to live here?" They said that the stars were suns, and the wanderers other worlds, one of which was the true home of men. Whether or not the stories were true, men were more comfortable with horses than with centaurs, and she wished that more of her knights rode them.

Between the top of the pass and the broader area where her knights waited, the pass was quite narrow—no more than a hundred paces wide at one point. The hills rose steeply on either side. One of the peasants went up into that area with his brush hook. Before he could cut any of the upthrust stalks, a dozen voices halted him.

"Not here, you Dayfather-damned fool!" A guild journeyman ran up to show the brushcutter the proper place. It was important that there be no signs of activity on the hill above the narrow pass—

A horseman clattered over the top of the ridge. He drew his sword and waved it vigorously. "Enemy in sight," an officer muttered. Tylara nodded.

The knights and men-at-arms climbed to their feet, clumsy in their armor, and helped each other mount. This took time. The armor was heavy, and centaurs resented heavy burdens; although a few were so well trained that they assisted their riders. Before all were mounted, Tylara, from her vantage point, saw the leading elements of Sarakos's army.

The Wanax had deployed well. There were only fighting men in the van, and when the pass began to narrow, they fell into column in good order, not pushing each other or crowding together. Horsemen led; then a group mounted on centaurs; then more horsemen. They climbed the twisting road into the pass twenty abreast—a long column—lances high with banners fluttering in the chill morning wind.

The group behind was not so orderly. Carts drawn by

mules and arrocks, crossbowmen mingled with spearmen, camp followers, cooks, prostitutes, and priests all mixed together.

A trumpet sounded, and Camithon's heavy cavalrymen trotted forward over the piled brush toward the top of the pass. They raised their banners. The brushcutters scrambled away behind them, down and onto the road, running back to Dravan, raising a thin cloud of dust as they ran.

Another trumpet sounded from the leaders of Sarakos's army, and the column halted. The group behind became even more disorganized as the marching horde piled onto one another. Trailing elements caught up and mingled with the leaders. Pity, Tylara thought. If the knights could get among that press for ten minutes, Wanax Sarakos would feel the losses. But the lead group was not disorganized, and it outnumbered her entire army.

Once again she felt doubts and fear, and she looked up into the vault of reddish-blue sky above, searching for a sign. But there was none. A cloudless cold day in the mountains; rare enough, the Dayfather showing himself in all his glory—but he showed no signs of favor. Would he care? Or would the ancient One-eye govern the day, choosing the most valiant to be slain, sending victory by whim?

There were more trumpets from Sarakos's column, and the vanguard knights spread across forty abreast. They moved forward at a walk, then at a trot. The lines rippled as lances fell into place, and the trumpet sounded once more. The trot became a canter as the charge swept forward.

"Now," Tylara prayed. "Now. In Yatar's name, NOW!"

Her own trumpets sounded. Her knights wheeled, and spurred their mounts ahead, trotting down the road toward Dravan, riding after the dust cloud raised by the retreating woodcutters.

Tylara muttered thanks to the Dayfather. That had been the first of the many things that could go wrong. If the knights would not run, if the sight of the enemy had brought them to a hopeless charge because it would be dishonorable to run—more than one battle had been lost through blind obedience to the dictates of a cavalier's honor. As this one might yet be.

"They flee! The cowards run!" The shouts rose from Sarakos's charging knights.

As her own knights rode away, there were tiny movements in the brush at the roadsides. Men hidden in holes beneath the brush thrust torches upward, then fled toward the sides of the pass. Thin wisps of smoke rose, here and there a flame. The waxy stalks caught fire quickly.

Her knights reached the wide place where they had waited earlier. They wheeled as one, facing the enemy. Their lances came down.

"The cowards hide behind fire!" someone shouted. "We will teach them!" The charging enemy came on harder, a hundred paces into the brush. Two hundred, and still they rode. Tylara held her breath.

When the leading elements were three hundred paces into the brush-strewn pass, a hundred paces beyond the top of the pass, her own trumpets sounded. There was a flash of movement on the hillsides above the pass. Bright kilts, dull leather, the dull shine of steel caps painted with earth colors. A moment before there wasn't a man to be seen. Now almost two hundred archers were standing behind shrubs, behind rocks, seemingly having risen from the very ground. They raised their bows, nocked arrows, and drew back to cheek and eye.

There were shouts from Sarakos's troops, but it was obvious to even the most stupid that there was no halting the charge. Safety lay ahead, through the screen of knights, out of the growing fire and away from the archers. The leading horsemen spurred harder.

Another pause. Then a shout from the hillside. "Let the grey gulls fly!"

The arrows flew with a deadly sound. In a moment the air was thick with them. Even as the first flight struck, another was on its way. Shafts the length of a tall man's arm and tipped with steel sped from bows drawn by men who'd used them since childhood. The second flight struck, and another arched out.

The slaughter was terrifying. The arrows pierced horses, saddles, even armor itself. Horses reared and bolted, crashed into each other, tripped and fell and stumbled over fallen horses. The centaurs screamed in rage and pain, their stubby arms flailing wildly, their half-hands frantically plucking at the arrows, their heads twisted to lick wounds. They seized their riders and tried to throw them off, or fell into the brush and rolled on their backs. Some plunged uphill off the road, to be shot down before they could climb far.

Still the arrows flew. The charge was broken into scattered groups, driblets of twos and threes and fours; not a solid wave of armored men with lances, but a disorganized horde fleeing past the archers, away from the growing fires, out into the broad area beyond—

To be struck by the countercharge of Tylara's knights. With a hundred paces to build momentum they struck the leading elements of Sarakos's forces, driving their enemy back toward the flames and the falling arrows, then wheeling away as yet another wave charged through to strike and turn. They too wheeled and joined their fellows; halted and dismounted.

Dismounted. One-eyed Vothan had smiled on her, had not maddened her knights as he so easily might have done. They had obeyed orders. Most western knights wouldn't fight dismounted; the Eqetas of Chelm had trained these well.

They stood with leveled lances, poised just beyond the burning brushwood, an impenetrable wall on which Sarakos's men could break themselves again and again, but never get through. They could not have withstood a mounted charge by an organized group, but there was no danger of that. Sarakos's force milled about in the smoke and flame, galled by the ceaseless shower of arrows, held by the fire and the bodies of their own comrades. The dismounted line was more than able to kill the few who rode out of the smoke.

A brisk wind came up to whip the flames. They grew and flamed higher, until for five hundred paces the pass looked like the very Pit—a tangle of smoke and fire, shouting men, men unhorsed, dying horses, riderless centaurs maddened by fire and plunging into everyone. And through it all the Tamaerthon gulls flew with their deadly bite, flight after flight of the grey shafts.

The Sarakos trumpets sounded a frantic retreat, but for far too many there was no retreat possible.

The arrows did not come in flights now. The archers picked single targets, concentrating on men still mounted, bringing down their mounts to leave the armored men helpless in the burning brushwood. The pass filled with sounds of pain and terror.

Tylara sat her horse grimly, her mouth set in a hard line. I thought I would enjoy it, she thought. These are the men who killed my husband. I should enjoy their agony.

But she felt no joy at all, only sickness and horror which she must hide from her shouting escort, and the numbing realization that this was only the beginning. There would be far more, weeks more.

I hadn't known the horses would scream so, she thought. I expected to see men die, but I had not thought of the horses.

She continued to watch in sick fascination until she suddenly realized what she was doing. She had almost made a fatal mistake.

Sarakos was bringing up his own archers. Most were crossbowmen, or mounted archers with short bows they drew only to the chest; none were a match for her Tamaerthon clansmen, but two hundred cannot fight a thousand. It was time to go. She raised her hand and waved vigorously.

Her trumpets sounded in the pass. Cadaric waved acknowledgement and began sending his archers out; the forward ones first, then others, leapfrogging so that they kept a continuous fire onto the Sarakos troops piled up at the edge of the brushfire.

Another trumpet call. Nothing happened. Her knights stood at the pass. A few left the line, but they went only for their mounts, and when they were mounted they came back.

"Fools!" Tylara shouted. She spurred her horse down the knoll to where the knights and bheromen of Chelm stood. More mounted as she came, but they showed no signs of leaving.

"Ride!" she shouted. "Before the fires burn down and their whole army comes through! Ride, my lords. You've done well. One-eyed Vothan smiles on you. Sarakos will not soon forget this day. Now, in the name of the Dayfather, ride!"

Bheroman Trakon sat motionless. "The fire protects them no less than us. There was nothing behind their vanguard but foot. We have more work to do this day."

"Not true," Tylara shouted. "They were bringing up their horse archers even as I watched, and they have their crossbowmen. You will ride into their volleys, and the remnant will be charged by their cavalry."

Trakon didn't move.

"My lord," Tylara said. She tried to control the panic in her voice. "If you mean to die here today, I will stand with you. It will be no victory no matter how many we destroy, for we will have given Dravan to Sarakos. If we are caught here, anywhere but within the walls, we are finished.

"I would rather be killed with my husband's knights than ride to Dravan and live to see it fall to Sarakos. Is that your will?"

Trakon sat motionless for a moment, then shook his head as if to clear it of the morning fog. "You speak well, Lady. We have won no victory if we stay to be killed." He rose in his stirrups to shout orders. "Carry the dead and wounded away. Leave nothing for Sarakos. Let him believe that he has lost the quarter of his vanguard to ghosts, to achieve nothing." He turned and rode down the pass. After a moment, Tylara followed.

I follow, she thought. It was my victory, but I follow. She sighed, knowing what would be thought by everyone who saw.

❖   ❖   ❖

A week later, Sarakos reached Castle Dravan. The first attempt to storm the castle was repulsed; attack and defense might have been the opening steps in a ritual dance. The next move was also set; Sarakos dug in and erected pavilions and defenses around the castle.

There was no entry or exit from Dravan. Sarakos and his army waited for their siege train.

3

The siege towers rolled forward slowly. The armored heads of picks thrust out of them as if eager to attack the walls and gates of Dravan. Hundreds of men strained to push the monsters forward. Overseers shouted cadence. Boys poured melted fat on the axles. They would reach the walls by afternoon.

"It is time, Tylara," Trakon said. "Time and past time."

She looked helplessly at him, then at the others: Cadaric, his son Caradoc, and Yanulf. "Have I no other advice?" she asked.

"You know mine, Lady," Cadaric said. He clutched his bow. "There are no more shafts. As for me, as well to die; but it would be waste to no purpose."

Cadaric's son Caradoc opened his mouth to speak, but was silenced by his father's look. The young man looked down at the towers in hatred.

Yanulf nodded sagely. "What choice is there? In a day they will be inside, and it always fares ill with the populace when a place is taken by storm." He paused. "You need not stay, Lady. My place is with the acolytes in the caves of the Preserver, and we could find you a place there as well."

"No," Trakon said. "I will have a better bargain for her than that."

Yanulf bowed. "I will not wait, then." He turned to leave the battlements.

"I will send my son with you," Cadaric said. "Perhaps Yatar will aid him to return to Tamaerthon."

"And perhaps not," Yanulf said. "But it is well to have young men as apprentices." The old priest waved toward the armies below the walls. "Fools all. The Time approaches, and still men fight."

"But not for long," Tylara said. She turned to Trakon, but for a moment she could not find words. Finally she said, "Make a good bargain for our people."

"I will. It will be for the best."

Tylara stood at the battlements as Trakon went to the gate and hoisted the green branch of truce.

❖   ❖   ❖

Her ladies dressed her, and one of Sarakos's officers led her to the council chamber. She felt strangely light without mail and steel cap, and stranger still to be unarmed. Strangest of all was to see Sarakos in her place at the head of the table.

He looked young to be so powerful. He was a big man, but not fat; even his eyes showed strength. He was handsome, but she did not forget for a moment that this was the man who had killed her husband while others held him helpless.

His smile was not pleasant. "Welcome, Lady." He stared at her and she shuddered.

Sarakos was not alone in the room. Guards held Bheroman Trakon. His shirt was open; there was blood on his bare chest. "What is the meaning of this?" she demanded.

"You are all traitors," Sarakos said. "Traitors do not die easily, as you will learn." He motioned to the guards. "Take that carrion out and kill him with the rest."

Trakon shook off the guards and stood straight, although he winced to do it. "Is this how a Wanax keeps his promises?" he demanded. "You gave your word that the lady Tylara and I—"

"Would marry," Sarakos said. "After the traitors were killed. And so shall you be. Joined forever." He turned and looked appreciatively at Tylara. "I can see why you wanted her. You may have to wait for her, but you will have her for all time when I am through." He waved dismissal to the guards.

For an hour, Castle Dravan sounded with the screams of the dying. Tylara was forced to stand at the window and watch as her soldiers were killed; some beheaded, the archers used as targets for Sarakos's crossbowmen, the officers flung from the castle battlements.

Then she was taken to Sarakos's bedchamber, and another kind of horror began.

❖   ❖   ❖

She heard the massive door opening and whimpered, trying to draw her knees tighter to her chest. She kept her eyes closed. Which would it be; the crone with the whip or Sarakos himself? She remembered his parting words; "You have not pleased me. I would as soon have a corpse. But before you die, you will please me. You will beg for the chance."

"My Lady."

The voice seemed different. Familiar, and youthful. It was not Sarakos—

"My Lady. There is little time. You must come now."

She was afraid. Was it a trick? But the voice was urgent. She found the courage to open her eyes and turn her head, although she dared not hope.

She saw kilts—her own plaid—and looked higher. "Caradoc!" she cried. He reached for her and she let him help her stand. He gasped when he saw her back, and she leaned on him as he led her urgently out of the bedchamber. There were two dead men lying at her door.

❖   ❖   ❖

The hour was early. They saw no one as they went down the back stairs to the large cistern below ground; then to the massive doorways that led still farther below; to the caves of the Protectors. The ammonia smell was strong. She hesitated, but Caradoc hustled her through and closed the doors behind. Two acolytes with torches came to help her now. Their faces showed disapproval of this invasion of their realm.

They went through darkened tunnels, turning until she was lost. Finally they came to a larger room lit with another torch. Yanulf was there.

"The guards were drunk," Caradoc said. "I killed four. No one else was awake."

"We must be gone before they are found," Yanulf said. The priest turned to the acolytes. "Fetch bladders."

They stared at him in horror.

"Do you think Yatar prefers his secrets to the torture of his friends?" Yanulf snapped. "This lady treated us well. She will not reveal what she sees, nor will Caradoc."

The acolytes hesitated a moment more, then left. When they came back, they carried inflated sheep's bladders.

Yanulf pointed to a door in the chamber. "We will go through there. You must breathe only from the bladders, and you must hold your breath as long as possible. The journey is steep, and we cannot pause to rest until we are through the tunnels and outside the door on the far side. It will be dark. Is this understood?"

Tylara stared at him in confusion. She wanted to lie down, to rest, to sleep, to forget the pain in her back and the terrible pain between her thighs. Pain filtered the memories, but not entirely. "There is no need," she said. "Give me your dagger, and—"

"Don't be a fool," Yanulf told her. "Do you think I have invited Sarakos to violate Yatar's house just let you die?"

"I may carry Sarakos's child," she said. "I'd rather be dead."

"Time enough when you know. But it's unlikely," Yanulf said. He was thoughtful for a moment. "Very unlikely, even leaving out your virginity."

The priests of Yanulf were said to know when women could conceive.

"Alive there is hope of vengeance," Caradoc said. "For you and for my father. Until I see Sarakos gull-feathered, I will stay alive."

"Come." Yanulf handed her the bladder. "Before you use

the bladder, breathe deeply. Many times." He demonstrated. "More." When he was satisfied, he motioned to the acolytes to open the heavy doors.

There were more doors beyond. These next were sealed with leather. Tylara felt the ammonia stinging her eyes, and even through the bladder she could smell the pungent odor when the last doors were opened.

Cold welled out of the caves. She took an acolyte's hand and let herself be led into darkness.

❖   ❖   ❖

There was no light at all. She felt the walls as they went through. There were shelves with baskets, and slabs of meat hanging below those. Between the shelves were slimy bulbous things, cold to the touch. Then there was ice.

They seemed to go on forever. The air in the bladder was stale, and her lungs ached so much that she nearly forgot her other pains. She was certain that she would faint from lack of breath, but at that moment they stopped. Light burst in from a door opened in front of them. They hurried through, past another door, and stood outside in the dying light of the night sun. To the east was the red of dawn.

There were horses. She felt herself lifted up behind Caradoc. She clung to him and they rode away. After a while, she fell asleep clinging to the archer. In her dreams, she had Sarakos flayed alive, and she smiled.

❖   ❖   ❖

The true sun was high overhead when at last they stopped at a crossroads.

"We must hurry on," Yanulf was saying.

"This horse must rest," Caradoc answered. "Carrying double has nearly foundered him." He reached up to help Tylara down, then led the horse to the watering trough that stood next to the stone heap. He bowed to the heap before allowing the horse to drink.

Tylara bowed as well. Crossroads were sacred to the Guide of the Dead. Then she turned to Yanulf. "Thank you."

"Thank him." He pointed at Caradoc.

"I have. But we would not have escaped if you had not—" she stopped herself.

"Broken my oath of secrecy?" Yanulf said. "Yes. Doubtless I will answer for that. But I spoke truly to the acolytes. Yatar cannot wish his secrets held at such a cost."

"Where are we going?" Tylara asked.

Caradoc answered from behind her. "This is the east road," he said. "Perhaps we will find the boy Wanax and the Protector. And if not—it leads home."

Home. She looked to the east, but Tamaerthon was more than a hundred leagues, across salt flats and pirate lands. "There's someone coming," she said. She pointed eastward. Two men and a woman were walking up the road. The woman wore strange-trousered clothing like the men.

PART FOUR:

THE CROSSROADS

1

The planet below did not look like Earth. The polar ice-caps were too large, and there was much more water, too little land. Despite the vast empty seas—because of them? Rick knew too little to guess—there were great deserts ringed by mountain ranges.

From high orbit there was no trace of man at all.

The pilot seemed to be afraid of them. He made them store all the ammunition for the rocket launchers and mortars in one locker and the guns in another. He made it clear that the two would be offloaded a considerable distance apart.

The last few hours had been continuous briefings with the pilot insisting that both Rick and André Parsons attend them all. They were told how to raise *surinomaz*, which had a complex ecology and even more complex harvest procedure; how to use the transceivers to communicate with the traders when they came for the harvest; endless details, and always an underlying note of warning that the people of Tran were human and deserved to be well treated.

The landing area had been chosen: far enough from the equator to have an endurable climate even after the rogue sun came close; far enough from the poles to be inhabited even during the centuries when the invader was far away; at high enough altitude to remain dry when the polar caps melted and raised the sea level a hundred meters. There were several areas that would do, and Rick had no way to know which was best. He had pleaded with the pilot to let them spend several days observing the planet before landing, but that request was refused. The pilot seemed to be in a frantic hurry. Rick wondered why, but there was no explanation.

They moved to a lower orbit, and the TV screen showed images of the country below: a few large cities, but mostly a land of villages and fields. Many of the villages and all the cities were dominated by massive castles. There were few roads.

Parsons wanted to land near a city, but Rick chose a village near a major road, fifteen kilometers from a castle. The orbital photographs showed an army encamped outside the castle and massive siege towers nearing completion.

"If there's a battle we may decide to join it," Rick said. "After we get some political intelligence."

"Nearer a city would be better," Parsons said. "And if you intend to take that castle, why land a day's march away?"

Rick again protested that they didn't know enough and should land a safe distance from conflict. Eventually Parsons stopped arguing.

They landed at dusk, just after the major sun had set but before the distant secondary was up. When the secondary sun fully rose, it would light the planet with a blaze like a thousand full moons, making the night as light as a heavily clouded day on Earth. When they landed, the tricky light—dusk from the sun, rays of dawn from the secondary—made weird images and shadows.

They offloaded the guns first, then the ammunition nearly a kilometer from their first touchdown spot. Rick was the last to leave. Before he could jump out, the hatch closed and the ship lifted.

"Stop! I'm still aboard!" he shouted.

"I know." The pilot's voice was impassive. The ship moved half a kilometer and settled to the ground. Rick heard the whine of machinery, but the hatch didn't open for several minutes. Then the voice said, "Now you can get out."

When he jumped to the ground, the ship lifted. Rick watched it rise into the clouds until it was gone. He hadn't really believed it would leave until then. He felt completely alone.

"It's really gone."

He fought a moment of terror as he realized the voice had been a woman's. He turned.

She was a tiny girl, not very pretty in the half-light. She was dressed in coveralls much like his own. "You're human," he said.

"You don't sound very sure of that."

"I'm not very sure of that."

"I'm human. My name is Gwen Tremaine, and I come from Santa Barbara."

"Santa Barbara. As in California? On Earth?"

"Yes." She tried to laugh, but she didn't succeed. "Oh, yes, I'm from Earth."

"We'd better get over to the others," Rick said. He moved closer to her and saw tears in her eyes. "Are you all right?"

"I'm scared as hell," she said.

"So am I. Uh—"

"I was the pilot's mistress," she said. "That's what you wanted to ask, wasn't it? I got pregnant and didn't want an abortion, so he put me out here." This time she managed a laugh. Rick thought it sounded horrible. "Pretty convenient. I asked him if this was the traditional way for flying-saucer pilots to get rid of excess baggage, but he didn't answer."

"Jesus!" Rick muttered. He led her through the scrub brush—it seemed a lot like the chaparral of the western United States, but there was a strange pungent odor to it— toward the distant lights where Parsons and the guns had been unloaded. He wanted to say something to comfort her, but he couldn't think of anything. God Almighty, he thought. She must be as alone as anyone has ever been. "Do you know anything about—about why we're here?"

"Probably more than you," she said. She walked beside him, but several steps away, as if repelled by him.

"If you know more than I do, I'd appreciate the information," he said.

"We've got plenty of time. Let me get used to the situation, will you? When he had me read up on Tran, he didn't tell me it was because he was leaving me here."

"When did he tell you—"

"That he was ditching me? About five minutes ago."

"That was—" He tried to think of something to say, but couldn't.

"A rotten thing to do?" she asked. "Sure was. You see, I thought I was in love with him." She walked on for a few steps. "Do I sound like you?" she asked.

"How?"

"Scared and trying to be calm about it when what you really want to do is run in circles flapping your arms."

"Do I sound that way?" Rick asked.

"Yes."

"I guess I do," he said.

❖   ❖   ❖

Parsons had assembled the troops on the hilltop. He seemed as surprised to see Rick as he was to see Gwen. "I thought they'd taken you on to wherever the saucer was going," Parsons said.

Rick didn't like the edge to Parsons' voice. He didn't much care for the way Parsons held the M-16 rifle, either. "They didn't," he said. "I guess he wanted an escort for Miss Tremaine." Rick explained who she was.

"I see. And now what do we do?"

"There are about a thousand things to do," Rick said. "When there's more light, we can go down to that village. The first thing is to start learning the local language. And figure out which side to take in that war we saw. Then—"

"There's one thing a bit more urgent," Parsons said.

"What's that?"

"I think it time we restructure the command," he said. The rifle swung around until it almost pointed at Rick.

"What the hell do you mean?"

"You are not an experienced officer," Parsons said. "An

ROTC boy, with almost no combat experience. Under the circumstances, do you really feel qualified to lead?"

"As qualified as you—"

"No. This is my career. For you it was an accident," Parsons said.

"So you're taking over."

"Yes." Parsons shrugged. "If you like, I'll fight you for it."

"Isn't that a little barbaric?" Rick demanded.

Parsons smiled broadly. "Of course. We are on a barbarous planet. In fact, that is one major objection to you, Rick. You are unlikely to have the proper instincts for survival here. I have long noticed a regrettable tendency toward softheartedness in you. That was bad enough in Africa. Here it is likely to be fatal."

A circle of men had gathered around them. Rick looked at them. "Elliot—"

"Cap'n, I'm truly sorry. I thought about this a lot when Mr. Parsons first brought it up, back aboard ship. He's right. You just don't have the experience."

And he sounds really sorry about it, Rick thought. And probably is. One thing was certain. If Elliot and the NCOs accepted Parsons' takeover, there was nothing Rick could do about it. At best he'd cripple the command. They were all staring at him.

He had to say something, and quickly, before Parsons decided to shoot and be done with it. "Maybe you're right. André, you do have more experience than me. All right, you command." As he said it, he felt a wave of relief. Someone else could do the worrying.

"Glad you understand," Parsons said. "Sergeant Elliot, get our perimeter defense set up."

"Sir."

"And the rest of you clear out," Parsons said. He waited until the other troops were gone. "Rick, there is another problem. Surely you can understand that you can't stay with us."

"Why not?"

"You were in command. Some of the men would look to

you every time I gave an order. It wouldn't work," Parsons said. His voice was low and urgent, almost pleading. "I ought to shoot you out of hand," he said. "That would be the intelligent thing to do."

"Bull crap. The troops wouldn't stand for it," Rick said.

"You see?" Parsons said. "Some of them do admire you. And there can be only one commander."

"So you're sending me off alone."

Parsons shrugged. "What else can I do? Look, I don't want to kill you. You can take your personal weapons—"

"Damn generous of you," Rick said.

"It *is* generous, and you know it. Also dangerous for me. Fair warning, Rick. I offered to fight you for the command. You refused, which was intelligent. But the next time I see you, I'll assume you've changed your mind. And I'll kill you, Rick. Make no mistake about that."

"You mean that, don't you, André?"

"Yes." He used his foot to indicate a backpack lying near them. "I've made you up a kit. A rifle. Two hundred rounds, which is more than your share of the ammunition. First-aid packet. A week's rations. You may keep your binoculars. You have your pistol, and I've included a box of cartridges for it. I haven't been ungenerous—"

"Damn you—"

"Please," Parsons protested. "Do not make me regret my generosity." He pointed. "The road is that way. Do not go toward the castle. Go east."

"I'm going with him." Gwen's voice was tightly controlled.

Parsons looked startled. Like Rick, he had forgotten that she was listening to them. "Surely you do not mean that," Parsons said.

"Surely I do," she said. She shook her head. "You're crazy. I've listened to both of you for weeks. Between the two of you, I'll take Galloway."

"Why?" Parsons asked.

"I just will. Or do you intend to keep me here?"

Parsons frowned deeply. "No, I suppose not. Very well. But get moving. I have a lot to do."

"You certainly do," Gwen said. Her voice was sugary sweet. "And you're less likely to manage it than you think. Let's go, Captain Galloway."

❖   ❖   ❖

Lower down, near the road, there were trees. They looked like gnarled evergreens, but the leaves were too broad, and like the chaparral they had a strange odor. Rick moved into the trees before he spoke.

"Are you out of your mind?" he asked.

"No." The girl's voice was strong, almost too loud.

"You didn't even act surprised . . ."

"I wasn't. I told you, I've been listening to both of you for weeks. Before we went up the hill I knew what was going to happen."

"You might have warned me—"

"To what purpose?" she asked. "There wasn't anything you could have done about it. He'd have beaten you in a fair fight, and you wouldn't shoot him without warning. Would you?"

"No. I guess not. So you knew they were going to mutiny. Did the pilot?"

"Yes. He predicted that you'd go your way and they'd go theirs."

"And you decided to come with me. Why?—careful, it's slippery here—" He put out his hand.

She moved away from him. "Let's get something straight," she said. "I've had one lover boy, and I don't need another."

"I wasn't—"

"No, I guess you weren't," she said. "But I did want to make it clear. And maybe that will give you some idea of why you. I get the impression that you're a little more human than some of those animals back there."

"They're not animals, they're soldiers. Pretty good ones. Gwen, this is silly, if you're scared of getting raped, you'd batter stay with Parsons. Not that I'm going to leap at you, but I'm not likely to live very long."

"Neither are they."

"What the hell do you mean by that?" Rick demanded.

"Nothing." She scrambled down the slope. "The road's down here," she said. "Which way?"

"Left."

"Away from the castle," she said. "See? At least you've got sense enough to walk away from a fight." She stopped to look intently at his face. "And don't get your macho image bent out of shape—I'm not calling you a coward."

"No, but you hit pretty close to home," Rick said.

"How's that?"

He told her how he had chosen track instead of football. "And don't tell me how sensible it was," he said. "I know it was sensible, but it bothers me."

2

The road was excellent. It reminded Rick of the old Roman roads he'd seen in Europe; cobblestones placed over enough rock fill to prevent settling. From the wear on the stones, the road had been there a long time, centuries at least. Unlike Roman roads, though, this one wound through the low hills and trees. Roman military roads had been unfailingly straight no matter what obstacles were in the way.

The trees and underbrush were strange, but they didn't seem particularly alien; no stranger than Africa had been when he first went there. There were no birds—at least he'd seen none—but twice he saw flying squirrels. At least, he thought, they look like the pictures of flying foxes in my old school books. I never saw a real one on Earth.

Gwen walked beside him, still keeping her distance.

"You decided to come with me. Do you have any—" Rick cut himself off and lowered his voice. "There's someone behind us," he said. They looked back to the last bend but saw nothing. Rick motioned Gwen off the road and into the trees. They took shelter in the underbrush. Rick held the rifle in readiness. Whoever was coming was making no attempt to be silent; footsteps clattered on the cobblestones.

Corporal Mason came around the bend. He stopped and looked ahead, then very carefully slung his rifle and held out his empty hands. "Cap'n," he called.

"In here," Rick said.

"Yes, sir. Figured you'd hear me comin'. Just didn't want to get shot."

Rick led Gwen back to the road. He slung his rifle, but made certain the strap on the shoulder-holstered pistol was released. "What brings you here?"

"About a dozen of us volunteered to come off with you, but Parsons and Elliot wouldn't let 'em. Elliot said it was all right for one of us, so we cut cards for it, and here I am."

"Flattering," Rick said. And, he thought, just possibly believable. It was also believable that Parsons had sent someone to finish him off. Parsons was a careful man.

Parsons might do that, but Mason wouldn't take that job. There were some who might, but not Mason. Rick suddenly realized that he was glad to see the plucky little corporal. At least he had one friend to watch his back in this strange place. "Welcome aboard," Rick said. "But you might want to explain—"

Mason spat in the dirt. "Parsons is a Foreign Legion type," he said. "The Legion uses up men. I've known some mercs who put in five with the Legion, and no thanks."

"Is Parsons likely to be looking for you as a deserter?" Rick asked.

"It's possible," Mason admitted. "It was Elliot said it was all right to take off, but maybe he didn't ask Parsons first."

"And probably didn't tell him later," Rick added. Another complication. "We'd better watch our backs."

"More reasons than one," Mason said. "There might be some others want out of Parsons' chickenshit outfit."

"Maybe we should wait and see," Gwen said. "But—" she looked thoughtful. "You wouldn't want too many."

"Why?"

She shook her head. "Woman's intuition—"

"Bat puckey. You've hinted a couple of times that you know things I don't. Isn't it time to let me in on the secret?"

"No. It's not time." Gwen was very serious.

"When will it be?"

"I don't know. But I do point out that as long as the men might run away to join you, you'll be a threat to Parsons."

"So I hide from him—"

"It's not that," she said. "Look, you won't kill him from ambush. But if he decides to kill you, you won't even know until he's done it. The only way you'll be safe from him is if he doesn't know where you are."

It made sense. It didn't sound very manly, but it made sense. Rick said so.

"There's another thing," she said.

"Yeah?"

"If the *Shalnuksi* traders learn where you are, they'll tell Parsons—"

"That's what really concerns you, isn't it?" Rick asked. "You don't want the Galactics to find you. Why?"

"Does it matter? You won't be trading with them. You can't possibly manage to grow those drugs alone—"

"Drugs?"

"I'll explain later. Rick, you won't be trading with them. It's certainly better for us if Parsons can't find us. All I'm suggesting is that we don't call attention to ourselves. Get out of this part of the country, and don't leave traces of where we've gone. Doesn't that make sense?"

"I suppose—"

"That's all I'm asking."

"It's enough. We don't even know where we're going. For that matter, we'll be out of rations soon enough. I saw what might have been a deer—"

"It probably was. There were a lot of Earth animals released here."

"Damn it, you're doing it again! What else do you know that might save our lives?"

She didn't answer.

✧　✧　✧

They rounded another bend. There was a crossroads marked by a small thatch-roofed shelter whose roof drained into a stone cistern and watering trough. The side road was dirt, heavily rutted with cart tracks and the prints of shod horses, but deserted at the moment.

Mason inspected the cistern. Leaves floated on top of the water. "We trust this stuff?" he asked.

"We'll have to eventually, and we'll want to start drinking local water while we're still pumped up with gamma globulins and the other shots we got—but I think we can wait a day or so until we've got a permanent base. Got purification tablets?"

"Yeah. I'll use them. Hand me your canteen."

They filled the canteens while Rick thought about their situation. The main road would have more traffic, but it would also be easier going. Not far down the side road he could see patches of water and mud.

"Horses comin'," Mason said. He pointed back the way they came.

"Off the road," Rick ordered. He led them into the trees beyond the crossroads.

There was a click as Mason released the safety on his H&K battle rifle. "They're slowin' down," he said softly.

"If they don't want trouble, we don't," Rick said. Two horses came into view. One carried an elderly man in yellow robes. There was a blue circle with a stylized thunderbolt across it sewn to the breast of the robe. The other horse was ridden double. The rider in front wore kilts and an iron cap, and carried a short sword slung at his left side. The other was cloaked and hooded. They stopped at the crossroads, and the other robed man swung down easily and led his mount to the watering trough, first pausing to bow to the stone heap.

The other two dismounted.

Gwen stared interestedly. "Notice the reverent gesture," she whispered. "Hermes. Guide of the Dead. He was originally a god of crossroads. Evidently he hasn't lost that function here."

The second rider threw back the hood and removed the cloak. Mason gave a nearly inaudible whistle. "That's a looker!" he whispered.

Rick gestured for silence. Mason was right. The girl was young—about twenty, Rick would guess, with long raven-black hair. Even at this distance her eyes were startlingly blue. She had a classic Scandinavian shape to her face, and the woolen frock she wore would have brought a high price at Magnin's.

Only the kilted rider seemed armed, and Rick examined his weapons carefully. A leather case was fastened to the saddle; from its shape, it probably held a longbow. Otherwise there were no missile weapons. The man's sword was quite short. He also carried a dagger about the size of Rick's Gerber Mark II combat knife.

"This may be a good chance to talk to the locals," Rick said.

"They'll probably think we're horse thieves," Gwen warned.

"So we stay away from their horses. Mason, don't start anything unless there's no other choice. And keep an eye out back the way we came. Just in case."

"Sure."

"Not just for Parsons," Rick said. "The girl looks nervous, and they all keep looking back. And notice how lathered those horses are. They didn't stop because they wanted to. Okay, let's go make contact with the locals."

❖   ❖   ❖

The girl saw them first. She pointed and the younger man went toward his horse.

"Sling arms, Mason," Rick ordered. He spread his empty hands. "Gwen, can you tell them we're friends?"

"The last languages I was able to study from Tran were six hundred years old," she said. She raised her voice. "*Amici. Filos. Zevos.* No, dammit, that doesn't get through. Rick, bow to the stone heap. At least that will show we're religious."

"Right. You too, Mason. And keep your hands clear."

"Yes, sir."

Reverence to a stone heap. It did seem to have a beneficial effect. The others watched them warily, but they did nothing as Rick came closer.

The kilted warrior stared at Rick in frank curiosity. He eyed the slung rifle as if aware that it was a weapon. He seemed very interested in the scabbarded Mark II which hung hilt-down from Rick's suspender webbing.

The older robed man dipped water with a gourd and held it out to them.

Rick hesitated, thinking of the various amoebic life-forms that probably inhabited the unpurified water.

"He's a priest," Gwen said. "Blue sky and thunderbolt. Zeus? Jupiter?"

The priest nodded in comprehension. "Yatar."

"It really is," Gwen said. She seemed delighted. "Zeus Pater, the Sky-father. See, blue for the vault of the sky, and the thunderbolt—"

Rick let the priest hand him the gourd, gulped hard, and drank, hoping that when the inevitable happened it wouldn't be at an inconvenient time.

"You carrying wine, Mason?" he asked.

"Yes, sir."

"Hand it here."

Mason took the plastic liter flask from his belt. "Wine," Rick said. "Uh—vino."

The priest looked interested, and said something to his companions. They looked interested, too.

Rick tilted up the bottle and drank a swallow. It wasn't wine at all, but Scotch. Now what have I done? he thought. The others were gesturing toward the girl, and she held out her hand expectantly.

Rick handed her the bottle. "Strong. *Fuerte*. Not much. Uh—take it easy—"

The girl drank, looked startled, then drank again, slowly. She didn't seem shocked, which meant they must have some kind of distillation here. She said something which Rick took to be thanks.

"Cap'n, no wonder they wanted her to have a drink," Mason said. "The back of her dress is all bloody."

"Yeah? Have a look, Gwen—"

"If she'll let me," Gwen said. "Keep an eye on her

boyfriend." She went over to the girl. *"Permiso?* Uh, medico."
She tapped herself on the breast. "Magister?"

"Magistro?" the girl said. She looked at Gwen with what
seemed to be respect and stood still while Gwen tried to
peel back the blouse. "Good Lord!" she muttered. "Rick,
someone's abused this child badly."

Child, hell, Rick thought. "How?"

The girl reached up and unbuttoned the front of her dress
and slipped it off her shoulders, leaving her back and breasts
bare. Apparently they didn't believe in modesty here—at
least not for the upper body. It was hard not to stare at the
nearly perfect figure. She evidently didn't usually go without
clothing, though; she had no tan at all.

She also had no objection to Rick looking at her, and he
went over to examine her back. Someone had beaten her
badly. Her back was a mass of bruises, and twice whatever
had beaten her had flayed open the skin. It was going to
scar. He took out his first-aid kit. "Know much about this?"
he asked Gwen.

"No." She looked mildly ill.

"Better let me, then." He took out a swab. "Got to clean
this and it's going to sting. Gwen, watch her boyfriend."
He tapped himself on the chest. "Magistro," he said.
"Medico." She winced when the swab touched the wound,
but she didn't cry out. Rick painted it with Merthiolate and
put a loose gauze bandage over the broken skin areas. "No
tetanus inoculations," he warned. "Make sure you don't cut
air off from the wounds. Better to risk aerobic infection.
With all the horse crap on the roads, there's a high tetanus
risk." He stepped away. "All right, you can cover yourself
again." He gestured to show what he meant. "And have
another drink. You earned it."

The girl smiled tentatively, then downed another slug of
Scotch. She tapped herself on the chest. "Tylara do
Tamaerthon, Eqetassa do Chelm."

"You get that, Gwen?" Rick asked.

"I think so. Eqetassa. That's right out of old Mycenae. If
I'm not mistaken, she's a countess. If that's right, her name

would be Tylara and she's from that place with the guttural sound."

"Tylara," Rick said. The girl nodded happily. He pointed to himself. "Rick Galloway, Captain of mercenaries." If long names indicated high rank, he didn't want to claim to be a peasant.

"Riok," Tylara said tentatively. She pointed to the robed priest. "Yanulf, sacerdos pu Yatar." The priest bowed. She pointed again. "Caradoc."

"Latin and Greek all mixed up with Mycenaean," Gwen said.

"Mykenae?" the priest asked. He pointed to them.

"No." Gwen shook her head. The priest frowned.

The kilted man took out a curry comb and began working on the horses. He glanced warily back at Rick and Mason from time to time, but didn't seem excessively suspicious.

An auspicious beginning, Rick thought. And that girl! Were all the women on this planet as lovely?

3

"Company comin', Cap'n," Mason called. "Lots of horses riding hard."

The others heard, too. Rick gestured toward the thickets by the road. There would be no room to hide the horses, though, and from the sounds, not enough time either. Tylara shouted something and Caradoc ran to his horse. He took down the lather case and withdrew a longbow, stringing it with an easy gesture that made Rick's muscles ache to watch.

A dozen horsemen rounded the bend two hundred meters away. The sight was like a blow. They were not all riding horses. Three of the beasts were centaurs. The riders wore mail armor, and white plumes streamed out from their helmets. The lead men carried lances, and they lowered them. Others drew sabers. They didn't act friendly at all.

Tylara shouted. Rick understood none of it, but he heard the word 'Sarakos' several times. She ran to Caradoc and drew his dagger, holding it as if she knew how to use it. Caradoc nocked an arrow. He thrust another into the dirt in front of him. There were only the two.

Two arrows, a short sword, and a dagger; but his new friends were obviously prepared to fight a dozen horsemen. Yanulf stood impassively by the cistern, his arms spread to the sky.

"What do we do?" Mason shouted.

117

Rick didn't answer for a moment. There would still be time to get into the trees. This wasn't his fight. From the uniforms, the approaching riders might be the local police. For that matter, he had no evidence that Yanulf wasn't a con man and Tylara his accomplice in the local equivalent of the badger game. He could be setting himself up as an outlaw. Probably was. And they could still run . . .

But dammit, he thought, I'm tired of running. You've got to choose sides sometimes. Why not now? "We fight," he said.

"Would you if she were a crone?" Gwen asked.

"Shut up. Mason, fire a couple of warning shots."

The H&K blasted at full automatic; a burst of fire that must have zinged over the heads of the approaching riders. They didn't slow.

Caradoc drew the arrow to his cheek and released it in a smooth motion. The lead rider took it full in the chest and fell from his horse.

And that's torn it, Rick thought. He raised the H&K and began to squeeze off rounds at semiautomatic fire.

◇   ◇   ◇

When Tylara saw the strangers approaching, she first thought they might be from a local village despite their strange clothing; but moments later she knew better. They couldn't be locals, and she felt a twinge of fear. Who were they?

They were obviously wealthy. She didn't know what all the objects they carried or wore on their belts might be used for, but so much metal would be valuable. And all three spoke to each other as equals. She didn't know the words, but the tones made that clear.

"Evil gods," Yanulf muttered. "The Time approaches."

Caradoc glanced hastily at the stone heap, hoping for protection.

"Do your tales say how they will steal our souls?" Tylara asked. "They do not look like gods to me." Although, she thought but didn't say, the taller man was handsome enough to be, if not a god, at least from the tales of the heroes. "What have we to lose by their friendship?"

"Little," Yanulf admitted, and went to draw water to make the traditional gesture.

Their response had been surprising enough. Tylara was familiar with strong drink made by freezing wine and throwing away the ice, but she had never experienced anything like what she tasted when the man handed her his bottle.

The bottle itself was interesting, too. It was neither metal nor ceramic, and she had no experience with anything else. Then they had come closer, and examined her back, and the handsome one had done something that hurt at first but soon took the ache away. While he treated her she studied him close up. He was a warrior. The sheathed blade on his chest—what a strange place to carry it, but it looked handy enough, easily drawn, perhaps he had to fight often—was obvious. Less obvious was the weapon he wore slung over his shoulder. It resembled a crossbow, but there was no bow; and it was all metal.

He wore no armor that she could see. Only the one-piece garment that was jacket and trousers combined, mottled by dye to resemble the forest. His hat was a felt beret, and she had seen those before. The boots were green with black leather at the bottom, more like a peasant's boots than a warrior's. Then there were the bewildering things—all carefully crafted, all useful-appearing but totally mysterious—hanging from the straps over his shoulders and from his belt.

Rick. She caught that, but not the titles he named himself. And his companion—obviously a warrior and wealthy as well, certainly a knight, perhaps a bheroman—was named Mason. The girl called herself Gwen. Unreasonably, Tylara did not like her. She must belong to Rick, and Tylara knew there was no reason to resent that, but she did. One thing was clear enough. "These are no gods," she told Yanulf.

"Perhaps," the priest growled.

Old fool, she thought, but regretted that instantly; he had given up everything to save her. She had never heard of a priest of Yatar allowing anyone not a sworn acolyte in the lower caverns. Not even her husband's father had ever visited those caves below Dravan. Would Sarakos dare search there now?

The drink made her feel better. Much better, and she talked volubly with the strangers, almost forgetting the horror of the night before, until the one called Mason shouted warning and a dozen of Sarakos's hussars came toward them at the gallop.

She ran to take Caradoc's dagger, wondering what would have happened if she had asked—Rick—to lend her his own. Would he? With the dagger in hand, she felt little fear. They might kill her, but they could never take her back. And the strangers had taken their weapons from off their backs and held them like crossbows—

She was startled for the moment when Mason's weapon gave a crash like thunder, and even more startled when there was no effect. Caradoc's shaft killed its man, but no one fell to Mason's thunder. But then Rick raised his own weapon.

The result was unbelievable. Each time Rick's weapon spoke, a rider fell. Then Mason did the same. Caradoc stood with an arrow nocked but did not loose it. He watched in amazement, as Tylara did.

The fight was over before it had well begun. Men lay in the road, some dead, some groaning, while riderless horses and centaurs dashed past. Tylara had sense enough to grasp the reins of one of the horses, and Caradoc seized another. She saw that Rick did not seem to think of that, although Mason tried and failed. Why?

Caradoc handed her the reins of the horse he had caught and went out to give the fallen soldiers a final mercy. When he slit the throat of the first, though, Rick shouted, as if in horror. His companion said something, and the girl said more. Finally Rick turned his back. Did he hate Sarakos's troops, then? That much? And why? She would cheerfully let Sarakos die of green stinking fester, but his soldiers had not deserved such. Evidently Rick's companions convinced him, because he said nothing else; but it would be well to

remember that he was a cold-hearted man, ruthless toward
his enemies.

But he was a man. Of that she was certain.

✧   ✧   ✧

"Leave him to his work, Cap'n," Mason was saying. "When
in Rome and all that. Besides, if they're all dead, they won't
be tellin' anyone who did 'em in."

Rick swallowed hard. In classical times it was normal to
kill the wounded, even your own. It wasn't until Philip of
Macedon that armies had hospital corpsmen. Philip gave a
substantial reward to the corpsmen for each trooper they
saved.

It bothered him that he hadn't captured any of the horses.
They'd need them. Centaurs he could live without—they
looked mean. He didn't know much about horses, either,
but he'd rather ride than walk.

That problem was solved a few minutes later. After
Caradoc (that name—wasn't there a Welsh king by that
name? There was something wrong with Gwen's theory of
language development here) had finished his grisly work
among the wounded, he mounted his own horse and rode
down the road, returning a few minutes later with four more
he'd caught. He offered all of them to Rick.

Rick inspected the saddles. Wood, with leather trim, and
rigid wooden stirrups. The horses were large and sturdy,
and he suspected that they'd bring a high price on Earth.
"Can you ride?" he asked Gwen.

"On Griffith Park bridle trails," she said. She eyed the
horses nervously.

"We'll try to keep the pace down. Will our new friend
get upset if we strip the dead? There's a lot of valuable
equipment out there."

"I don't know."

"Me neither," Rick said. Homeric heroes always despoiled
their dead enemies. Sometimes they even mutilated them.
And they often made trophies out of any arms and armor
they couldn't use. "Mason, go see what you can find," he
said. "Swords. And if there's any armor that will fit either

of us, get it, but strip the plumes off the helmets." He thought for a moment. "And don't touch the one the archer knocked down."

That seemed to be the right action. After Mason went through the dead, Caradoc did the same. He retrieved his arrow and stripped the man he'd killed, then went over Mason's leavings. He brought the loot over to the cistern and said something to Yanulf. The old priest indicated a sword, a breastplate, and a leather bag which Caradoc took over and piled reverently against the stone heap.

Aha. "Mason, take our stuff over to Yanulf."

The priest's selection from Mason's pile was considerably larger. "Wonder what the PC is," Rick said. "And who gets the loot."

"Redistribution system," Gwen said. "It's fairly common in some societies. The first people down the road will help themselves with Old Stone-heapy's blessings. Uh—don't like to say it, but it would be better if you carried the dead away from the road. That way they just vanished, and maybe no one will look too closely at what killed them."

"Covering our tracks?" Rick asked.

"Yes."

It made sense. Rick thought he was using that line a lot since he'd met Gwen. "Let's get at it, Mason. Maybe Caradoc will get the idea and help."

Caradoc did, but he obviously didn't understand. When they got the bodies stacked in the woods a hundred meters from the road, Rick made symbolic gestures and threw a few dirt clods over them. When Mason frowned a question, Rick said, "I'd rather he thought we have a screwy religion than leave him wondering why we're carrying bodies around."

They loaded their spare horse with loot, while Caradoc piled his own excess gear on the horse the priest had ridden. Then he rode off on a fresh horse and returned with two more. After a questioning glance at Rick, he gave the new mounts to Yanulf and Tylara. They mounted.

"Cap'n, they're waiting for us," Mason said.

"Yeah. Mount up." He swung into his own saddle and gave an experimental cluck. The horse moved slightly. It seemed very well trained and responded to the reins about as he had expected. "I'll lead yours at first," he told Gwen. "If you want me to."

"Please."

Rick edged his mount over until he was next to Tylara. "Where?" he said. "*Quo vadis? Donde?*" He pointed helplessly in all directions.

She frowned, then seemed to understand. She pointed down the road. "Tamaerthon."

"Your home?" Rick asked. He pointed to her, then the road. Tylara do Tamaerthon, she'd said. It must be. "You. Tamaerthon?"

She nodded vigorously, then swung her hands in a broad sweep to include the whole party. "Tamaerthon," she said, and she sounded quite determined about it.

PART FIVE:

TAMAERTHON

1

Tylara had been away less than a year, but she had forgotten just how small her homeland was. The whole of Tamaerthon was no more than twice the extent her own lands of Chelm had been, and her father's holdings in The Garioch would have been thought suitable for a wealthy knight—almost too mean to support a bheroman. As for her father's great hall, it wasn't much larger than her council chamber in Castle Dravan, and indeed her father used it for council meetings, which usually—as now—were no more than a gathering of several of his henchmen.

That wasn't her only disappointment. Her reception was something less than enthusiastic. Her father had seen her leave as a great lady. He had sent more archers and more wealth than he could afford as her dowry.

Outside the council hall, the women of the village were keening the deaths of sons and lovers who had gone with their lady to die in a far land.

"I had thought ye might send me horses and knights," her father said. "And gold. But ye hae returned wi' no more than three men-at-arms and this priest."

"What choice had I? But I have come with more than men-at-arms." Tylara described the battle at the crossroads. "And twice more they fought when bandits and refugees would not leave us alone. Each time they left none alive."

127

She described the weapons; the large ones like crossbows carried over the shoulder, and the smaller one-handed weapons they carried concealed beneath their jackets.

"But where do they come from?" her father demanded.

"From the stars," Yanulf said.

Drumold stared at the priest and back to his daughter. "Weapons of fire and thunder . . . then the old tales are true?"

"They are," Yanulf said. "You can see for yourself, the Demon Star grows larger each ten-day."

"Aye, I hae seen it at dawn when the night sun is low," Drumold agreed. "But the tales speak of evil gods." He glanced nervously toward the stone house where the newcomers were lodged. "Are these—"

"Not gods," Tylara said. "They are men. Men with great weapons, but men. For days they were sick nearly to death. The lady with them is ill yet."

"She carries a child," Yanulf said. "I do not know whose."

"Not gods," Drumold mused. "Men. And they befriended you. With such power as they have—" He grew thoughtful.

"That had occurred to me," Yanulf said. "When I saw the power of their weapons, I had thought to find the Lord Protector and the boy Wanax of Drantos. With the aid of these star men, we might have driven Sarakos from Drantos and returned the lady Tylara to her home."

"But they would no' aid you?" Drumold demanded.

"They could not," Yanulf said. "In the ten-day we sought the Protector's army, the Protector sought Sarakos. We heard the story from refugees three days after their armies met. The battle was thought to be equal at first, even though Sarakos had many more lances. But as the battle was fought, Sarakos smote his enemies with weapons of fire and thunder." The priest spread his hands. "Our friends are not the only men from the stars. More than a score, with weapons more terrible than any Rick carries, now are allied with Sarakos and hold Drantos for him."

"Rick was once of their company," Tylara said.

"Then why is he not with them?"

"She shrugged helplessly. "I do not know. I heard from the lady Gwen that Rick was once the commander of the star men. I know that he does not care to have them find him again."

"Then dare we keep him here?" Drumold demanded. "Is he a danger to our land?"

"He is our guest. He saved me from Sarakos once and twice from bandits," Tylara said.

Her father studied her face carefully. "Aye, and he has done more than that," he said. "When your mourning is done, will we see another stranger wed the daughter of the Mac Clallan Muir?"

Tylara had no answer to that. I wish, she thought, I wish I knew. Whose child does Gwen carry? She does not act toward Rick as a woman does to her man, but the ways of the star men are strange. I do not understand them. Especially I do not understand Rick, who likes well enough to be near me, but who has never touched me except to heal wounds. . . .

And another memory. Rick's shouting rage when finally he understood what Sarakos had done to her. Almost, almost he had gone back to seek out Sarakos, but then Gwen spoke to him for a long time, and they rode on again.

But he did rage. He hates the man who harmed me.

"We hae our troubles here," Drumold was saying. "There was untimely rain, and the harvests will be poor. Wi'out the archers sent with you, we hae lost many of our pastures. Mac Clallan Muir does not stand so high as at the time you left, and when it is learned that my daughter can no longer send a thousand lances to my aid, it will go worse. Now you hae brought us guests who may draw the strength of Sarakos against us. Daughter, 'tis no' your fault, but this is not good."

He looked to his silent henchmen. They had no advice for him. Then he stared moodily into the fire. "But they are guests and they have my welcome, for what good it will be to them."

❖   ❖   ❖

"What's taking them so damned long?" Corporal Mason asked. "My stomach's growling. They could at least feed us."

"I expect that's what the debate is about," Gwen said. "Hospitality is taken very seriously in some cultures. If they feed us, they have to take us in and protect us from our enemies."

"Well, I wish they'd get on with it."

"Count your blessings," Rick told him. "At least there's a warm fire and we'll get a safe night's sleep." Which, he thought, was more than they'd had for weeks while they fled across Drantos, staying ahead of the occupation forces that Sarakos and his new allies sent out in waves. It had been a nightmare journey, with all three of them sick with classic cases of Montezuma's Revenge, knowing nothing of the language and customs . . .

"But we made it," he said aloud. "And without leaving tacks. So now what do we do?"

"Blend in," Gwen said. "Get established in the community."

"Sure." Rick pointed out the window. The scenery was lovely. The village stood on a flat alpine meadow high above the sea, ringed on three sides by snowcapped mountains. Except for the seacoast to the southeast, it might have been a scene from a picture postcard of Switzerland. "Beautiful," he said. "But I don't see a hell of a lot of cultivated land, and some of the fields I did see were gullied. No industry, and not much pasture land. Gwen, you've noticed more than I have, but it's obvious even to me that this is a warrior society. They probably get more of their food by raiding their flatland neighbors than they do by growing their own. There's only one way Mason and I can make a living here. Fortunately, it's a trade we know."

"Until we run out of cartridges," Mason said. "Which may not take long."

"So we get busy manufacturing muzzle-loaders," Rick said. "I've been trying to remember the formula for gunpowder. I think I've got it."

"Rick, you can't!" Gwen protested.

"Why not? You want them unspoiled? Think arrows are a cleaner way to go than gunshots?"

"It's not that," Gwen said. "God, I wish my head would stop aching. Rick, if you start using gunpowder weapons, you'll advertise our location as surely as if you sent Parsons a letter."

Mason growled low in his throat. "Cap'n, I don't know about you, but I'm sick of worrying about Lieutenant—ha, he's a general by now—about Parsons. You saw the country we came through gettin' here. With five hundred good men, we could hold those passes forever. To hell with bein' scared of Parsons and his crew. I just wish I could be sure he'd come."

"He's right," Rick said. "And he's not the only one tired of running scared."

"Have you stopped to think that the *Shalnuksis* may help Parsons?" Gwen said. "Probably will. Can you fight *them*? Not to mention that you're involving Tylara's father in a needless war with the most powerful force on this planet." She sniffed. "I'd thought better of you than that."

"What the hell do you want us to do?" Rick demanded.

"What we agreed. Leave as few traces of our presence as possible—at least until the *Shalnuksis* have done with their trading. Once they're gone, you'll only have Parsons to fight."

Once again, Rick thought. Once again she makes sense. But why do I think she isn't telling me everything?

2

The cave was cold and smelled of ammonia. Rick shivered as the old priest led him down winding corridors. "This is all secret," Yanulf said. "Although a secret better kept in the west than here. Still, secret enough."

"What is secret?" Rick asked. "Everyone knows there are caverns—"

"But not the size, or the location of the entrances, or how to enter them."

"Why show me?" Rick asked. He coughed from the ammonia fumes and the chill.

"They may believe you—they pay little heed to me," Yanulf said. "And I have learned this; that you star men put your own meaning to what you see."

"This is all strange to me," Rick said. "What makes it so cold?"

Yanulf held the torch close to a bulbous slimy mass that covered one wall of the cavern. "The roots of the Protector. A plant. It is why I know the stories of the Demon Sun are true. In all my life I have never seen the Protector larger than a man's body. Recently it began to grow, and now grows daily. The growth began when the Demon Star was seen in the night sky, as the legends said it would."

"How does a plant make ice?" Rick wondered aloud. "There must be parts above ground—"

"Aye. It is very large. Thick leaves. In the west the castles are built above caverns, and the Protector climbs the walls and battlements. In this impoverished land they build few castles, and the plant grows on the rocks. You have seen it."

"Ah." He remembered a broad-leafed vine with thick stems and ugly white berries. "Scientists—uh, those whose task it is to study nature—in my home would pay much to see a plant like this." Sunlight to ammonia, and somehow the ammonia produced cold; the evolutionary advantage for such a plant on a planet in a triple-star system was obvious. "What is it you want me to see?"

"The size of the caverns and the barren storerooms. When the Time is upon us, the only safe refuge is in these caves. There will be no crops that year or the next, and poor ones for two more. So say the legends. Your drawings of the suns make me believe them."

"Which is surprising," Rick said. "You are a priest of Ius Pater, the Dayfather. Did you not think the stars are gods?"

"Can they not be?" Yanulf demanded. "You say yourself that they are older than worlds and burn forever."

And I'd best leave it at that, Rick thought. I wonder why all the secrecy. Who are they hiding from?

Yanulf opened a massive wooden door. The smell of ammonia was very strong, and Rick thought the torch dimmed. The priest held the torch high, and coughing, said, "You see. A few miserable offerings. There is meat and grain, aye, enough for a few ten-days, but not enough even for a single winter. How will these people live in the Time?"

The legends said that the approach of the third sun heralded evil times: fire, flood, famine, and typhoon. Those not prepared would die. They were mixed in with tales of the wars of gods, the appearance of fabulous monsters, and garbled stories whose point was the futility of dealing with the evil gods from the skies. It was hard to sort fact from fable, but Rick didn't doubt there would be hard times ahead. The whole climate would change.

They went deeper. The caverns were quite large, and

some went far below ground level, back into the granite itself. Water trickled through some of the chambers. Others were choked with ice.

"It is said that Yatar demands sacrifices," Yanulf said. "These are stored away, to be cared for by the priests and acolytes. In some lands the storerooms are kept filled. But not here."

Eventually Yanulf led the way back out of the caves. Rick was surprised to see how far they'd traveled underground. "So it is in the other caverns of Tamaerthon," Yanulf said. "The priests and acolytes tell me that their storerooms are as barren as these."

"I'll take their word for it," Rick gasped. He walked faster toward the open air and sunlight.

❖   ❖   ❖

Drumold was horrified. "No harvests for two years? Then aye are we doomed. One year of poor harvest and we are starving before spring." For luck he spat into the log fire burning on the hearth of his council room.

"There should be a time of good harvest first," Rick said. At least I hope so. I'm not much at climatology, but the legends say so, and it's not unreasonable.

"You know little of Tamaerthon," Drumold said. "In the best years we hae little enough land, and must take our chances in raids on the Empire. Nae, nae, the gods hate us, to let us be born in such times. I had hoped the legends false."

"But we have to do something," Tylara said. "You are Mac Clallan Muir. You have sworn to protect the clansmen."

"And I have!" Drumold thundered. "Are we not free of the Empire? Have the imperial slavemasters come to our mountains these ten years? Lass, I do what I can, but I am no magician, to grow crops in a stone quarry!"

"We can help," Gwen said. "We have ways of farming that may increase the yield—"

"Lassie, I tell you there is no land to farm," Drumold said moodily. "You hae seen that our best land is now split and cracked—"

"Yes." She spoke to Rick in English. "Heavy rains when they didn't expect them. Just showing them contour plowing will do a lot to stop the gullies—"

"In time to help?" Rick asked. "If we've got this figured right, they'll need to work their arses off starting next spring."

Drumold stared at them suspiciously. "I like it not when you speak so," he said.

"My apologies," Rick said. "Is there no land not plowed, then?"

Tylara laughed. "There's land enough in the Roman Empire. Fields left as parks for Caesar. Forests of game for Caesar. Herds for Caesar's gods. There's food and land there."

"A cruel joke," Drumold said. "There's food and land, aye. And legions to defend them, and the slavemarket for those who enter the Empire without Caesar's leave."

"Do you forget Rick's star weapons?" Tylara asked. She turned to Rick. "Your friends have taken all of Drantos with their weapons. Can we not do the same with the Empire?"

Dammit, I wish she wouldn't look at me that way, Rick thought. I am not a god. "I do not think so," he said. "Besides, there have to be better ways than fighting. Can't we parley with the current Caesar?"

Drumold and Tylara both laughed. "The only way Caesar wants to see any kin of mine is in chains," Drumold said. "We have little to sell to him save wool. What we get from Caesar we take with sword and bow."

If Caesar wouldn't parley, there might be another way to get his attention. "How strong is this Empire?" Rick asked.

"Bring the maps," Drumold shouted. He waited while a henchman unrolled parchments. "The Empire is no' so large as it was in my grandfather's day," he said. "But they hold the fertile lowlands, and the foothills, here and here. They keep a legion of four thousand mercenaries in this fortress." He indicated a point some twenty miles from where the foothills became steep mountains leading to Tamaerthon. "Within a ten-day they can have two more, and another ten-day an additional three."

And we've got about a hundred rounds for the rifles, Rick thought. "That's pretty heavy odds," he said carefully.

"The other star men have taken all of Drantos," Tylara said. "Can you not do as well?"

"They needed the armies of Sarakos to do it." And I suspect Sarakos has reason to regret his bargain. He's not likely to be much more than a puppet for André Parsons. Serves him right.

Lowlands. In about five years, maybe less, that new Roman Empire was going to be under water—all but the high plateau that held Rome itself. And by that time the people of Tamaerthon would be starving. Except Mac Clallan Muir and his family. They wouldn't starve. According to Yanulf, the clan leaders and their children would—in theory, willingly—offer themselves as a propitiation to the gods. It came with the job of leader. In Drumold's grandfather's time, it had happened after three years of bad harvests, which was how Drumold's grandfather had got the position of high chief of Tamaerthon.

Damnation, there had to be something he could do. And he wasn't too likely to talk Tylara out of jumping off that cliff into the sea, either. That was one girl who was likely to take her duties seriously.

"You have raided the Empire in the past?"

"Aye," Drumold said.

"Tell me more of the Empire. How are the legions armed?"

"With lances and swords. How else?"

"Lances and swords—they're horsemen, then?"

Drumold seemed surprised. "Aye. Horses and centaurs. Mostly horses."

"Not foot-soldiers." Rick described a classical Roman legionary: square shield, pilum, and *gladius hispanica*.

"There are no such anywhere I know of," Drumold said. "Ken ye any in your western lands, priest?"

"No." Yanulf studied Rick's face. "What makes you think there might be?"

As near as he could figure it, the *Shalnuksis* had brought an expeditionary force from Earth in about 200 A.D., about

the time of Septimius Severus. That had to be when the
ancestors of these new Romans arrived. Severus still employed
classical foot-marching legionaries, a bit degenerated from
those of Caesar's time, but still the most effective infantry
Earth would see until gunpowder. Evidently the same thing
had happened to legions here as happened on Earth: they
fell to heavy cavalry and lack of discipline. Now the heavy
cavalry ruled everywhere that the terrain was suitable. This
Rome was more like the Holy Roman Empire—aha! There
would have been another expedition in about 800, the time
of Charlemagne. This Rome must *be* the Holy Roman Empire.
But he couldn't explain all that.

"One of the greatest kingdoms in our history was armed
that way," he said. "Uh—what religion is the Empire?"

"They call themselves Christian," Yanulf said. "But the
Christians of the southern lands say they are not."

"Yatar does not prosper in Rome, then?"

"No."

"Have they ice caverns? How did Rome survive the Time?"
Rick asked.

Yanulf spread his hands. "They do not welcome visitors.
Or rather, their slavemasters welcome them all too well. It
is said that there are caverns in Rome, but who attends
them I do not know. It is also said that there is a great library
with many records of previous Times, but again this is not
of my own knowledge."

Gwen had been listening with a growing look of amazement. "Rick, what are you thinking of?" she demanded.

That earned her a sharp look from Drumold, who wasn't
used to having women speak up that way.

"North is barren," Rick said. "West is the salt marsh and
west of that Parsons and Sarakos. South of us is mostly ocean.
If we're going to get anything to store up for the Time,
we'll have to take it from Rome."

"Man, are ye daft?" Drumold asked. "We raid the Empire,
true, and done quickly, we often bring back cattle and horses.
But we seldom escape punishment from the legions."

"He is not daft," Tylara protested. "He can—I have heard

him speak of battles before. Of his victories over the
Cubans—"

Yeah, I brag a lot when you're around, Rick thought. "What
kind of punishment? What do the legions do?"

"Sometimes nothing," Drumold said. "But if we annoy
them enough, they bring their army into the hills."

"And you fight them—"

"We try," Drumold said. "Aye, and we can win battles.
But they come on, and we must take to the hills. They burn
the villages and the crops and slaughter the flocks. Ofttimes
we lose more than ever we gained. The Empire is a giant
best left unawakened."

"But you have won battles against them," Rick said. "You
must have, or they'd have simply occupied Tamaerthon and
had done with it."

"Aye, we've beaten them in the passes," Drumold said.
"In the passes, in the hills. But no one has ever beaten the
legions on the plains. I think no one remembers the last
time anyone tried."

So far it sounded a lot like the Scottish border country.
Scotland remained free, but just barely. But there had
been a time after Bannockburn when England feared
Scotland . . . The rifles would probably win a single battle.
The result wouldn't be anything more significant than
looting a border province, but that could be the difference
between life and death for Mac Clallan Muir. And for
Tylara.

An organized raid, with a wagon train to carry out grain
and a properly organized force to delay the legions while
the wagons got into the passes. It was possible.

"How many men could you put into the field against the
Empire?" Rick asked. "For the biggest raid ever. Something
to sing about for a hundred years."

Drumold frowned. "Not all the clans would respond to
the summons," he said. "Perhaps three hundred lances. Two
thousand archers. Another three thousand lads wi' swords.
Perhaps a thousand more freedmen armed wi' whatever
they can find. No more."

"And the nearest legion is four thousand strong," Rick mused.

"Four thousand legionaries," Drumold protested. "Wi' mail shirts, and good horses. Man, on level ground they'll ride us down."

Two thousand archers. Edward had four times that many at Crécy, but Edward faced the entire chivalry of France, at least thirty thousand men. Proportionally, Tamaerthon could field more troops against the Empire than Edward ever had.

But there was a vast difference. Archers alone could never face cavalry. Edward's main line at Crécy had been dismounted men-at-arms, fully armored knights. From what Rick had seen, Tamaerthon's three hundred lances would be at most five hundred men with no more than half of them armored. There was no way five hundred could form a shield for the archers. The legionary cavalry would sweep through. Once at close quarters, it would be all over for the archers.

Gunpowder? No. Even assuming Gwen was wrong about the possibility of the *Shalnuksis* helping Parsons, there just wasn't enough time. They'd need at least a thousand arquebuses and a ton of gunpowder. They'd need ring bayonets, too. It would take years. No. It wouldn't hurt to have some of the younger clan warriors start a systematic search for sulfur, just in case, but gunpowder wasn't the answer.

But there was another way. Heavy cavalry had been finished on Earth well before gunpowder put the final nails in their coffins. "Have any of your clansmen ever drilled with pikes?"

"Pikes?" Drumold asked.

"A long pole with a sharp metal point."

"Ye mean spears. We have spears."

"No, I mean pikes. How long are the spears you use? What formation do you fight in?"

That took a while. Eventually a henchman brought in a typical weapon. It was about six feet long, far too short to be any use against cavalry. The pikes used by the Swiss, and later by the *landsknects*, had been eighteen feet long. As for formation, men who could afford no better weapon than a spear were peasants and didn't fight in any formation at all. They just went off to battle in droves and died in droves.

"How long can you keep the clansmen together without fighting?" Rick asked. "To drill." He had to explain the concept of training and drill. By now even Tylara was wondering about his sanity.

"The fields and herds would go to waste," Drumold protested. "And there's nae enough to feed such a horde in one place."

"There's food in the caverns."

"For the Time," Yanulf protested. "And not enough for that."

"Not enough for the Time," Rick agreed. "But enough to feed an army in training. What good will it do to keep what little we have? A properly trained army can beat the legions. We can march in—" he thought rapidly. There'd not be enough time for real training, and keeping the men too long without a battle would be disastrous for morale. "—in six ten-days."

"Harvest time," Drumold shouted. "Now I know ye're daft. You'd strip the land of the men at harvest time."

"You've said yourself it will be a poor harvest," Rick said. "Leave it for the women and children to gather."

"What do we eat for the winter?"

"It will be harvest season in the Empire, too. We take their crops. And they have to have granaries or they couldn't support regular troops in garrison. We'll have that grain, too."

"And you truly believe you can defeat a legion wi' your star weapons?" Drumold said.

No, I can't possibly. But they're not invincible—or wouldn't be if everybody didn't think they were. There's one way to fix that. "Sure. We've got other weapons you haven't even seen. But Mason and I can't do it alone. We'll need your lads properly trained and properly armed." Now's the time to back out, he thought. To hell with that. "If we're going to do it, late harvest season is the time."

" 'Tis a bold plan," Drumold said.

Tylara's brother had listened in silence. Now he stood. "I have lost comrades to the imperials," he said. "And I for one would like the chance to repay."

Tylara smiled happily. "It would be better to lose and die on the field than to starve in the Time," she said. "But with Rick's aid, we will not lose."

"You are crazy," Gwen said in English. "Stupid, bloodthirsty crazy—"

"Is it better if we all starve. Tamaerthon and the Empire alike? Do you have a better suggestion?"

"We don't have to stay here—"

"No," Rick said. "We don't *have* to. But I'm not running this time. I've given up running."

3

Drumold was arrayed as Mac Clallan Muir, High Chief of the Clans of The Garioch. His kilts were splendid, his armor covered over with silver badges. Gwen recognized some of the symbols: the horned bull of Crete splayed across a caldron; the ancient linked spiral found in virtually every Bronze Age site in Europe and which Yanulf said represented order grown from primeval chaos; a dragon. There were others which she thought might be fabulous creatures—but after what she'd seen in the ship's data banks, she couldn't be sure.

Other clan chiefs were arrayed around Drumold, all dressed in their finery. Some of the bright-colored plaids might have come from the ancient Celtic tombs found in Dalmatia on Earth. The splendor of the chiefs contrasted strongly with the drab clothing of their warriors and the even drabber robes of the various priests.

Gwen could not keep track of all these. There were too many gods, and each had an order of priests. Some, like Yanulf, were full-time and consecrated; many of the minor gods, though, were served by men and women who had other tasks—artisans, landholders, ladies of households.

They all assisted at this ceremony. Reverently they opened a tomblike chamber cut into the granite cliff that towered above the alpine meadow; reverently they removed a stone box and opened it with great ceremony. Balquhain, Drumold's oldest son, took a battle-axe from the box.

The axe was double-headed and made of flint chipped to resemble bronze. Gwen felt tingles at her spine. This double-axe might have come from Earth four thousand years ago!

Drumold took the axe from his son and displayed it aloft. Then he went to a log altar erected in the center of the village green. A ram was tethered there. Drumold felled it with a single stroke of the axe.

He dipped the axe into the flowing blood. Two priests came forward with stone bowls of blazing pitch and bound them above the axe blade. Drumold brandished the fiery axe and chanted. Everyone present took up the cry.

Where had Gwen seen this before? Then she remembered. Scott's poem, when Roderick Dhu had summoned Clan Alpine. Roderick had sent a fiery cross through the hills, but that was in a nominally Christian land. Here they sent a stone axe with two fires. The ritual Scott described must have been more ancient than he knew.

A priest chanted curses to befall any clansman who failed to respond to the symbol, and a henchman took the axe and ran from the glen. The Garioch clans were summoned to war.

✧   ✧   ✧

The rogue star was visible for an hour after dawn, and there was dark for several hours each night. Tran's two suns drew closer together. Summer was gone.

"We ready, Cap'n?" Mason asked.

"No, but we're as ready as we'll ever be. These lads won't stay around much longer."

Mason nodded. "Yeah, they don't like drill much. But they're not that bad. Cap'n, did those battles you keep talking about really happen?"

"Most of them. I've mixed them up a little. Truthfully, I don't recall any time when there was a combined force of longbows and pikes, but pike and musket was a pretty standard mix for a hundred years." Rick grinned. "Besides, the stories cheer up the troops."

They could use cheering. Even with all of his tales of victory—by his account, he'd led half the successful armies of history—and the demonstrations of their magic weapons, most of his troops didn't really believe they could beat an imperial legion on fair ground. The priests, and the rogue star to confirm the priests' stories had scared enough of them into trying, but not many really believed they could win.

Rick wasn't sure himself.

The glen was curiously still. All summer it had rung with the sounds of hammers. A dozen smiths had been brought—some at swordpoint—to forge iron heads for pikes. The new saplings of an entire forest had gone into pikeshafts.

The hammers were still, and so were the shouts and curses of the drillmasters. Drill time was over. Now it was time to march.

✧   ✧   ✧

Gwen was miserable. Her belly had swollen and she knew she was ugly. The midwives and even Yanulf himself had assured her that everything was normal, but they couldn't convince her. She had too vivid an imagination, and knew too well all the things that could go wrong even in a modern hospital. She'd had friends back on Earth who'd been ecstatic about natural childbirth—but she doubted that any of them had meant to be quite *this* natural about it.

Outside she could hear the sounds of the army assembling. They were about to march into the Empire, and there was nothing she could do about it.

She couldn't even run. On Rick's advice, Drumold had sealed the passes with armed parties of his clansmen. No one would leave Tamaerthon. Rick had made it plain that this especially meant Gwen Tremaine. He was certain that she knew more than she'd told him, and he was going to make sure she stayed with him.

There was a lot she could tell him, but Les had warned her against it. There was nothing he could do anyway. What could anyone do? Her original plan had been to find a hiding place, somewhere she could blend in and wait—

But she couldn't do that alone, and when she was honest with herself, she was ashamed of wanting to. These people were human, they weren't merely subjects of an anthropological study. And they faced starvation or worse. But she wished she had as much confidence in Rick as Tylara had.

There was a scratching at her door. "Yes?" she called.

Caradoc came in. "We are leaving, Lady." He stood nervously at the door.

"Have you no one else to say farewells to?" she asked.

"No, Lady."

"I've told you a dozen times, my name is Gwen—"

"Aye." He hesitated. "Gwen. A lovely name. Will you wish me well?"

"Of course." She wasn't sure of what to say. This wasn't the first indication she'd had that Caradoc was interested in her—more than interested. She wondered why. She certainly wasn't pretty in her present condition, and as captain of one of the archery regiments, Caradoc could have his pick of a dozen girls.

But he seemed fascinated by Gwen and spent as much time with her as he could. He treated her like a goddess, and that was flattering—and he was a very attractive man.

She wanted to hate men. All of them. But she was lonely, and the need to have someone of her own was a physical ache. "Come back, Caradoc," she said. "Come back to me."

"I will." He hesitated, then came closer to her. "I will."

She took two steps forward into his open arms. She let him hold her, but she felt her distended belly pressing against him and she was afraid, afraid to care for anyone again, and she hated herself for wanting to.

PART SIX:

WAR LEADER

1

Most of the outbuildings and slave quarters had been burned, but the villa still stood. Rick was surprised that it remained. Despite everything he could do, it was difficult to convince the camp followers that their purpose was loot, not pillage and rapine. He had trouble enough keeping the army itself from breaking ranks and joining in, and only constant threats to abandon them thirty miles inside the imperial boundary stones kept them in line.

A hundred candles burned inside the villa, and most of his officer corps were getting drunk in the main hall. For that matter, there was plenty of wine in the smaller room where Rick assembled the senior commanders.

"They won't be fit for anything in the morning," Rick complained. "Listen to them out there."

"They'll be all right," Drumold said. " 'Tis their way of celebrating."

"They ought to be ashamed, not celebrating," Rick said.

"We won," Balquhain protested.

Tylara looked at her brother in contempt. "Won a fight you were not supposed to be in," she said. "Drove away the local militia and lost three men-at-arms doing it. Were you not told to wait for the army?"

"I do not run from a fight," Balquhain protested.

149

"The next time, you will," Rick said. "Or I'll send you back as escort for the wagon train."

"You'll not dare—"

"He dares," Drumold said. "We hae all sworn on oath to fight as Rick commands. We will keep that oath."

"I will ride with the scouts in the morning," Tylara said. "If you do not understand what Rick wants from you, I do."

Both Rick and Balquhain spoke at once. "There's no need for that—"

"There is," Tylara said. "The maps brought back today were wretched. You'll need better." She eyed Rick defiantly.

The problem was, she was right. Dozens of medieval armies were defeated because they hadn't an elementary notion of the terrain they operated in. Rick had laughed in contempt when he read how the crusade commanders hadn't even known where their own columns were, but now he was beginning to appreciate their problems. There were almost no maps, and nobody in his army thought a map was as important as any other weapon.

Nobody but Tylara. She'd had experience with maps in her western country, and she had a good eye for distance and detail. Her troops would obey her, too, which meant that a detachment she led would actually scout instead of stop at frequent intervals for loot. But dammit—

There wasn't a lot of choice. They were deep in the imperial province, and if they marched on without locating the local garrison, they'd all be killed. "Tylara will take the scouts tomorrow," Rick said. "Balquhain will stay with the heavy cavalry."

Balquhain opened his mouth to protest, but he saw his father's look and subsided.

"That's an important job," Rick said. "They'll take orders only from you or your father."

The heavy cavalrymen were a pain in the arse, and he'd be better off sending them home, but that was out of the question. The trouble was, all the armored men were aristocrats, and that meant they had silly notions about the obligation of the aristocracy to get out front and fight for their honor—which would mean that most of his officer corps would be slaughtered in the first five minutes of real combat, and that would demoralize the infantry. Somehow he'd have to keep his two hundred armored horsemen out of it until the pikes and arrows had settled the matter. "Drumold, I think you should entrust your banner to your son. We'll give the mailed knights the honor of protecting it."

Drumold nodded seriously, and Balquhain seemed satisfied. Tylara concealed a grin from her brother. Sometimes Rick thought she was the only one in the army who paid attention to his lectures on tactics.

❖   ❖   ❖

They marched in oblique order. The First Pike Regiment, a block of a thousand, was ahead and to the right. Behind and left of them was the First Archers, then the Second Pikes, his main body and two thousand strong. The Second Archers and Third Pikes, another thousand-man block, followed on the road. Rick kept the heavy cavalry force with him, just behind the First Pikes. That way he could keep an eye on them. If anyone was likely to do something stupid, it would be his armored ironheads.

The wagons and pack horses came last. They were escorted by a screen of mounted archers acting as MPs under Mason's command. It had taken some doing to convince Drumold and his subchiefs that carrying food *into* the Empire would be a good idea. There'd been shouting and sulking. By now Rick was getting very good at pretending rage. He shuddered at the alternative; the army would have to break up into foraging groups every time they wanted a meal.

Tylara's scouts fanned ahead of the column. Rick wished he could go with her, but he didn't dare. The troops looked more like an army than a mob, but they still thought they needed his magic star weapons to protect them. They had no real confidence in themselves, and that could just be fatal.

❖   ❖   ❖

Caius Marius Marselius, Caesar's Prefect of the Western Marches, was annoyed. He'd hoped to avoid trouble for two more years, after which he would retire to his estates near Rome and let someone else worry about the province. He was not surprised when a local militiaman reported an invasion of hill barbarians, but he was definitely annoyed.

He was also careful. The militia officer had seen only light cavalry, but he thought there might be a larger body of barbarians behind the cavalry screen. He'd been unable to get through to find out.

That was unusual enough to make Marselius take notice. Normally these tribesmen came in like a flood, looted whatever they could, and ran. They had not thought of security. Marselius wondered if a Roman officer had defected and was now leading the barbarians. He couldn't think of anyone, but it was possible.

"We'll have to go into the hills and teach them a lesson," he told his legates. "It's been ten years since we had an expedition beyond the borders. High time."

The senior legate looked at him curiously. Marselius smiled faintly. He knew what the man was thinking. Initiative was not encouraged in Caesar's prefects. An outstanding officer might be contemplating rebellion. Caesar needed no generals who commanded greater respect from their legions than Caesar held.

And perhaps the legate was right. Marselius knew he was no threat to Caesar. He wanted only to retire. But would Caesar believe that?

The Empire would fall to that kind of suspicion someday. Marselius was convinced of it. When prefects were afraid to carry out their plain duty—

"Whether we follow them to the hills or not, we will want to destroy these barbarians," he said. "Not merely defeat them, but kill so many that they will tremble at the very thought of Caesar. For this we will require the full legion. Send for the reservists, call up the local knights, and bring in the detachments from Caracorum and Malevenutum. We will strike when they are all assembled."

"That will give the barbarians time to gather loot. Many of the landholders will be ruined, and they will protest to Rome," the senior legate said.

"Let them. There are few patricians in the border hills. God's breath, must I live in perpetual fear of Caesar's wrath?"

The legate did not answer. He did not need to.

Four days later, Marselius listened to the reports with growing amazement. The barbarians had not stopped to loot the foothill country. They had marched straight into the province.

"By nightfall they will be at the villa of Patroclus Sempronius," the scout commander reported.

"So far?" This was ruin. Sempronius was a cousin of the Empress. Worse, the considerable town of Sentinius was just beyond. Caesar would never, never forgive the prefect who allowed a Roman city to be sacked by barbarians. They would have to be stopped, and quickly.

"How many legionaries do we have?" he asked the legate.

"Three thousand, prefect."

That would include all the regulars and a considerable number of the reservists under their local leaders. Marselius sighed with regret: he could remember when a full four thousand regulars were kept in the camps. Ten years of peace in this province had robbed it of half that number. Caesar didn't care to keep armies larger than necessary, for fear they would rebel.

"Three thousand should be more than enough," Marselius said.

The legate grinned agreement. "They are only barbarians. They have no armor and few horses. What can they do against our knights?"

"What indeed? Sound the trumpets. Before the True Sun sets, I want the legion between Sentinius and these tribesmen. We will attack them in the morning when two shadows show clearly."

❖   ❖   ❖

Rick sighed with relief when he saw Tylara return at the head of her cavalry. He still didn't like her going out on patrols, but had to admit that she was the most effective scout commander he had.

The villa where he stood was a good example. It was large and comfortable, and she'd not only waited for the advance guard before charging the thin screen of armed retainers defending the place, she'd also kept the troops from looting and burning it. Now it could be systematically stripped of its valuables. There were over a thousand bushels of wheat in the granary, and the barns held both wagons and horses to transport it.

He went down the broad steps to meet her, and helped her down from her horse. Not that she needed help, but he found he liked being close to her.

"I have seen the legion," she said. She spoke quietly, so that no one else heard.

"Where?"

"About thirty stadia."

The Romans used miles, a thousand paces of a legionary, but Tylara's people had stayed with the ancient Greek measure, about a quarter of a kilometer. "What were they doing?"

"They had dismounted and were pitching tents. I left five men to watch them. Two have crept close to the Roman camp. If the Romans begin to saddle their horses, they will bring word instantly."

I may just have fallen in love with you, Rick thought. *That is, if I didn't weeks ago.* He looked up at the suns. About an hour of daylight, and another three hours of dimmer but adequate light from the Firestealer.

"We'll fight them here," he said. "It's as good a place as any." There was a lake—not large, but big enough to stop heavy cavalry—five hundred meters to the south. It would do as an anchor for the right flank, and there was a game preserve, thickly wooded, a kilometer off to the left. Fifteen hundred meters was a pretty long line to hold with the number of troops he had, but it beat hell out of trying to form squares in open country.

"Pity they didn't come last night," Rick said. "We had a

better position between those hills. But this will do fine. Let's find your father. We'll have to get the men into position while there's still light."

The preparations didn't take long. Rick had told them over and over the importance of bivouacking in a battle position, and eventually it had sunk in. He didn't have to adjust the fronts of the regiments at all.

The First Pikes were forward and to the left, at the edge of the woods, with a foam of armed camp followers stiffened with a few archers in the woods itself. The Second Pikes, his largest force, were two hundred meters behind and three hundred meters to the right of the First Pikes. The diagonal between was ditched, and stakes were set. Each stake was driven into the ground so that it slanted forward. They were set in a checkerboard pattern, three-foot intervals between stakes, so that the First Archers could move through the thicket. Behind them was Mason with his battle rifle.

Slightly behind and all the way over to the lake was the Third Pike Regiment. This left a gap directly in front of the villa of nearly eight hundred meters between the right edge of the Second and the left edge of the Third. He filled that with the remaining archers, and in front of them he had the troops dig ditches, drag up wagons and brush, and dig a random pattern of small hoof-catching holes.

"I want lanes between those obstacles," he told the engineer officer. Lanes would funnel the enemy for the archers and would also be a path for a cavalry counterattack if the moment came for one.

The engineers were a group of slaves liberated from looted farms. They'd been promised their freedom and a share of loot in exchange for their help. Rick's offer to pay them had surprised the slaves almost as much at it surprised his own troops. Some of them had even offered to enlist, but Rick refused. During the battle, they'd be locked in their barracks. He didn't need untrained and untrustworthy men wandering around at a crucial moment.

At dark Rick threw another screen of light cavalry forward

to observe the enemy force. The other troops were allowed to fall out and make camp, leaving their weapons in place to mark their exact position on the battle line.

He rode around the encampment for an hour, stopping to talk with groups of clansmen around their watchfires. Julius Caesar had used a pickle to illustrate obscene jokes on the night before Pharsalia. How could you measure the morale value of a pickle? Rick settled for more conventional pep talk, emphasizing the surprise the Romans would get when the star weapons began knocking them off their horses.

Eventually it was done, and he could go into the villa for his own dinner. By then it was nearly midnight.

"There's one more order," he told a staff officer. "I'll hold you responsible for seeing that the cooks are up at dawn. I want hot porridge for every man in the outfit before the sun's an hour high."

❖   ❖   ❖

The man who until a few hours before had been master of the villa sat across the table and glowered at Rick and his officers.

"Caesar will have your head," he blustered.

Rick examined him curiously. The man was fat, about forty Earth years in Rick's estimation, and didn't look any more like a Roman than a heavy cavalry brigade resembled a legion. Rick wondered which group of kidnapped expeditionaries had furnished his ancestry. That was one question it would do no good to ask.

"As Yatar wills," Rick said. "But you're likely to lose yours before Caesar knows of ours."

"I am cousin to Caesar," the man protested. "Caesar will ransom me."

"We'll see. At the moment I want information. How many troops will we be facing in the morning?"

"I am Spurius Patroclus Sempronius, and I do not betray Rome," the fat man said.

"Hah!" Balquhain stood and drew his dagger. "We'll see how he likes being sent to Caesar a piece at a time."

Sempronius turned slightly green, but he set his lips in a tight line.

"No need," Rick said gently. "My scouts have told me all I really need to know." He turned back to the prisoner. "Tell me this: what keeps the slaves from revolting? There were over a hundred here."

"Three hundred. Why should they revolt? They are well treated. And Caesar's legions would crucify them."

That or a variant on the theme was the answer to just about every question. Caesar's legions kept order and Caesar's officers collected taxes. Caesar's freedmen ran the post office, and Caesar's slaves kept the city sewers in repair.

"Is there no Senate?" Rick asked.

"Certainly. I am a senator of Rome."

"Curious. When does it meet?"

"When Caesar wills it, of course."

It turned out that Caesar willed it about once every five years. The meetings were brief and did nothing more than ratify Caesar's decisions and perhaps vote Caesar a new accolade. Compared to the Assembly, though, the Senate was nearly omnipotent: the Assembly met precisely once in each reign, to proclaim its acceptance of whatever new Caesar the army had elected. Otherwise the citizens had no part in government and wanted none; they were happy enough if Caesar would leave them alone. In exchange they got peace and order and protection from bandits like Rick.

Late Empire, Rick decided. The military was more like the time of Charlemagne, but the government was definitely from the Dominate period of the Roman Empire. The army kept the citizens from making trouble, the Praetorian regiments kept the rest of the army under control, and Caesar spent most of his time worrying about how to control the Praetorian guard.

Once Rick had Sempronius talking about politics, he was able to extract a little more information. The most important was that there was a town about twelve Roman miles away.

It had a granary, and the harvest had been good this year. Now all he had to do was get through the Roman legion guarding it.

❖   ❖   ❖

Tylara turned quickly at the sound of footsteps on the roof behind her.

"I thought I told all my officers to go to bed," Rick said.

"I couldn't sleep."

"Me neither." He came over to the parapet to stand beside her. The flat roof of the villa gave a good view of the watchfires spread out across the estate. Edward III had used a windmill as a command post at Crécy. This villa would be better.

"Do you truly believe we can win?" Tylara asked.

"Tomorrow? Yes. There's no reason why we shouldn't. We've got more troops, and we've got better weapons."

"I know you have few thunderbolts for your weapons," she said.

"Gwen must have told you," Rick said. Tylara nodded. "And yet you came with us, and you haven't told your father."

"For all my life I believed that the Empire had the best soldiers in the world," she said. "But now we will beat them, and it will not be because of the weapons."

"Weapons, organization—Tylara, nothing's ever certain in war, but if I wasn't pretty sure of the result, you wouldn't be here."

"How would you send me away?"

"If necessary, tied to a led horse," Rick said.

"Do you dislike me that much?"

"You know better. You *must* know better," he said. He moved closer to her. "I don't dislike you at all."

"But you have a woman—"

"Gwen? She's not my woman."

"Her child is not yours?"

"Yatar, no! What made you think that?"

"No one wanted to ask," Tylara said. "Then—there is no one else? No one you will return to?"

He put his hands on her shoulders. "The only girl I care about is you. Didn't you know?"

"I hoped." She hesitated. "Rick, I will always love Lamil. My husband—"

"And never anyone else?"

"I already love someone else."

Custom demanded a longer mourning period, but if Rick didn't care, she didn't. When he came to her, she did not resist.

2

He was awakened at dawn, as he'd ordered, but the cavalry screen reported no signs of movement in the Roman camp. Rick sent out another scouting force and tried to return to bed; after half an hour he knew it was no use and went out to see that the troops all had a hot breakfast. Wellington had insisted on hot meals the morning of Waterloo, and always believed the biscuit and "stirabout" had as much to do with his victory as anything else.

If the Romans attacked early, the sun would be in his archers' eyes. There wasn't anything he could do about that except worry.

The camp was deathly still. It wasn't the silence of professional soldiers confident in their abilities. There were sporadic murmurs, small jokes that normally would have brought belly laughs, speculations about various women, even some attempts to cheer, but each conversation died away to silence again.

"They're scared, Cap'n," Mason said. "I can feel it."

"Me too."

"It's the waitin'," Mason said. He squinted to the east. "Almost wish they'd come and get it over with, even if it'd be better with the sun higher."

"They'll be here soon enough. Walk around a lot. Look mean and be sure they see your rifle."

Mason grinned. "Won't show 'em the bandolier, though."

"This won't be our only battle," Rick warned. "Don't shoot yourself dry." He hesitated. "If everything comes apart, I'll try to get Tylara out. The Romans will try to cut us off from the road back. If I can get to that first villa we sacked, I'll wait for you there as long as I can. You do the same."

"Right. I wouldn't worry so much, Cap'n."

"Don't you worry?"

"Don't get paid to worry. That's what officers are for."

The true sun was half high and the Firestealer three hands above the horizon when the scout messenger rode in. The legion was coming.

"All of them?" Rick asked. "How are they formed?"

"They are all together," the scout reported. "They come in two large groups. The one on their left is slightly ahead of the other one."

"And where is the lady Tylara?"

"As you commanded, she is retreating from them but keeping them in sight. She will send messengers if they divide their force."

"Excellent," Rick said. He turned to Drumold. "Sound the battle horns."

The Tamaerthon hill people were obviously of Celtic origin, and Rick had expected them to have bagpipes; but either their ancestors had been from a group that didn't use them, or the art had been lost during the centuries on Tran. Instead they employed a long, curled horn that looked something like a thin tuba. At Drumold's wave, these sounded, and the camp followers began the rattle of drums. The pikemen and archers ran to their weapons.

Rick climbed to the roof of the villa. It would be better for morale if he were with the ranks, but he couldn't afford courageous gestures. More than one battle had been lost because the commander didn't know what was happening to all his forces. The staff officers he'd chosen to keep with him didn't like being up there either, but he'd stressed the importance of communications until at least a few of them

understood how vitally he'd need messengers whose orders
would be obeyed.

His view to the east was partly obscured by low hills,
but from the vantage point of the roof he could just see
the scarlet and yellow pennants of his light cavalry. They
had stopped at the brow of the hill and were looking at
something beyond. He tried to pick out Tylara, but the
distance was too great. He felt a momentary panic. Suppose
she'd been caught by the Romans? But there was no point
in worrying about that now.

The First Pikes were moving nicely into formation, a
rectangle 125 men wide by 8 deep. The Swiss had formed
their pikemen into precise square blocks, but he had too
broad a front to cover for that. As he watched, they grounded
arms, acting nearly in unison. That way they wouldn't be
exhausted when the combat began.

What looked like a forest of pikes came up just in front
of him as the two thousand men of the Second presented
pikes. The binoculars let him see individual troopers. They
looked nervous. Well, so was he. Here came the archers to
take their places among the checkerboard of sharpened stakes
that marked their position. Their ranks were nowhere near
as geometrical as the pikemen. They weren't supposed to
be. If those heavy cavalrymen ever got among the archers
to melee in hand-to-hand fighting, the battle would be over.

He shifted back to the horizon. His light cavalry were
facing him now, and riding like hell. He raised the binoculars
in time to see the first of the enemy come over the low
hills twelve hundred meters away.

❖   ❖   ❖

The Romans trotted toward them like an armored flood.
Tylara had no difficulty getting the light cavalry force to
simulate panic. The problem would have been to hold them
once the Roman horses broke into a trot. It looked as if
nothing could stop that steel tide.

They rode hard, past the First and Second Pikes and down
the cleared lanes leading to the villa. Their horses were
lathered before they were inside their own lines. Tylara had

deliberately stayed in front, and now when she reined in, the others halted. Some of them might not have. One cavalry group—Rick called it a "platoon," a strange word—would go on south beyond the slave barracks to warn of any Roman attempt to circle the woods and attack from behind, but Rick had stressed the importance of halting first to demonstrate that they weren't *really* running away.

Once again she marveled at the details he thought of. Nothing seemed too trivial for him to worry about. Any good chieftain inspected his clan's weapons, but Rick looked at their boots and sleeping cloaks as well. Who would have thought of bringing spades? Or grindstones? Or of having special details to bring in wood for cooking fires? Without him they'd be lost. He was right to stay on the roof of the villa instead of the forefront of the clans. He wasn't afraid of battle, no matter what some of the young warriors said.

She dismounted at the villa steps. Just in front, her brother sat his horse with their father's banner, surrounded by their few armored cavalrymen. Tylara grinned to herself as she went up the stairs to the roof. These proud young men might protest that their place was at the forefront of the battle, but now that they'd seen the Romans, they didn't look so eager to charge out.

Rick was looking through his far-seeing glass. Binoculars. She'd have to remember that word. She went to the parapet to join him. His smile warmed her.

"How close did you get?" Rick asked.

"Longbow shot. They carry short bows, and we did not want to be closer."

"You're learning," Rick said. He muttered to himself in his strange language, then spoke in hers, but still more to himself than to her. "Lances and swords. No shields."

"Why have they halted?"

"Dressing ranks," Rick said. "But mostly they're hoping we'll break formation and come after them." He turned to a staff officer. "Go out to each regiment. Make certain the commanders understand that the Romans may charge and then act as if they're running away. They want us to scatter.

If we take that bait, they'll cut us down. The first man I see breaking formation without orders, I'll shoot down from here."

"I had better take that message myself," Tylara said. "The clansmen will not like to hear it."

"They've heard it before, and I'll need you here. Get moving, Duhnhaig. And come back when you've told them."

The sept chief looked curiously to Tylara. She smiled thanks and gestured him on his way. "You speak roughly to important chiefs," she told Rick when Duhnhaig was gone.

"God damn it—no. Sorry. You're right. It's my fault if we lose no matter why. That's why I need you with me. I can handle the Romans—it's our own troops I have to worry about."

There was a blare of horns from the Roman ranks. They had formed into two massive blocks, each ten ranks deep, horsemen knee to knee, their lances with pennants held high. The trumpets blared again, but there was no movement.

They were answered by the drums of the clan women, and the shriller sound of Tamaerthon war horns.

❖   ❖   ❖

Prefect Marselius cursed silently. He had hoped the barbarians would either charge him or break and run, and they weren't doing either. More and more he was certain that a Roman officer led them. He'd never heard of hill tribes standing in regular formation to wait for an attack.

Those blocks of spearmen looked remarkably steady, too. Over the centuries Rome had worked out tactics to deal with any situation. Standard practice when opposing standing spears was to come to extreme bow range and gall them with arrows until they charged, then cut them down with swords.

That wouldn't work here. He could see all too many archers formed behind those ditches and stakes, and he'd had experience with those hillmen's longbows. They outranged anything a horse archer could carry, and an exchange of archery fire would cost far more than it gained.

Standard tactics against archers was a charge with lance.

You rode as hard as you could and lost some men getting in among them; but once there, the battle was over. If they were mixed in with spearmen, as they often were, you did the same thing. If they'd planted stakes and other obstacles, several centuries would dismount and cut a path for the rest.

The tactical writers hadn't considered the situation of mixed blocks of archers and spears. Marselius had never heard of such a situation. But then he'd never heard of barbarians penetrating this deep and waiting for a battle, or of having cavalry screens that kept watch on him from camp to battlefield.

"The men grow restless," his senior legate said.

"Let them. Leave time for fear to grow among our enemies."

"We also tire the horses."

True enough. An armored man was a heavy burden, even for a war-horse. The longer they were saddled and still, the slower they'd be in the charge. "Sound trumpets," Marselius ordered. "Play false calls. Marching music."

The cornu blared out, to be answered from the barbarian camp by their own horns and drums. That, at least, was standard. The hillmen's women rattled tom-toms incessantly. It was said to be a form of supplication to their barbarous gods.

He reviewed the situation again, reconsidering his decision not to send any of his force around either the lake or the forest to fall on the tribesmen from behind. The morale effect of an attack from the rear was often devastating, but he suspected these barbarians wouldn't be shaken by it. Anyway, in that mass of irrigation ditches south of the villa, his cavalry would be worthless. It wasn't worth the cost of dividing his legion.

He could withdraw. Shadow the tribesmen, wait to catch them in the open. The legates would not care for that—it smacked of fear. And although in the open the barbarians would be the more easily defeated, more of them would also get away. No. They must be taught not to invade the Empire.

There was one other factor. The villa had not been burned.

A bold stroke now would return it intact to Sempronius's family—perhaps even rescue the patrician alive. Instead of hatred there might be gratitude from Caesar's relative.

They must attack while the horses were still fresh. There was nothing to be gained by waiting. He stood in his stirrups. "Sound the calls for a charge with lance," he ordered.

3

The steel tide broke forward into a walk, then a trot. The lances came down in unison, and the armored horsemen poured toward them, spurring to a canter. Rick felt a final twinge of fear, swallowed hard, and gained control of his nerves.

They came in a single wave four ranks deep, riding almost knee to knee, their line stretching nearly from woods to lake. "They mean to roll right over us," Rick said. He wondered what he'd do if he were the enemy commander. A hard charge carried home? That would certainly be a more effective tactic than the French used at Crécy, where they'd come in small driblets of undisciplined feudal lords. These troops were a lot better than anything Philip had with him that August day.

They were almost within extreme archery range. Rick could be certain of the exact line because he'd had it marked with stakes. The archers lifted their bows and drew back. One or two released arrows. Rick hoped their noncoms got their names. The time of release had been carefully calculated: assume heavy cavalry moves at 15 miles an hour, and time the flight of an arrow to longest range—

"Let the gulls fly!" someone called. The arrows flocked upward in a volley, arced high, and fell among the charging horsemen.

The effect was instantaneous. The lines in front of the archers lost their geometric precision and dissolved into a wave of rearing wounded horses. There were screams as horses and men felt the bite of the iron-tipped shafts.

English longbowmen could get off a flight every ten seconds. The Tamaerthon archers were just about as good. As the Roman cavalrymen—Rick still couldn't bring himself to call a formation of armored men on horseback a "Legion"—covered the final 250 yards, the Tamaerthon gulls flew three more times. Then the archers skipped back among their stakes and fired at point-blank range.

What struck the archer's line wasn't an orderly formation at all. The horsemen were moving too fast to stop when they saw the angled stakes, and tried to guide their mounts around them, but the horses got in each others' way, while wounded and riderless mounts dashed randomly among them.

Meanwhile, the First Pikes had taken the initial shock— only there wasn't one. The first rank of pikemen knelt and held their weapons butt grounded, angled at the eyes of the horses. The next three ranks held theirs high, points outthrust over the heads of the kneeling first rank. They presented a wall of pointed steel, and the horses wouldn't stand it. They swerved about, or halted, some with a shock that dismounted their riders. Not a single lance struck home among the pikemen.

"This would be the time for a charge," Rick muttered. "But I can't. They're not disciplined enough to stay in formation."

The first line of Romans dismounted to attack the pikes with swords. They were braver than their horses, and several got in among the pikemen, although most were thrust down by the heavy points. The few who managed to close slaughtered several of the front rank, but the rear files thrust forward to strike them down. The pikemen shouted triumph, and the cheer ran down the ranks.

It was all happening at once, and far too fast for anything Rick could do to influence the battle. The battle on Rick's left wing was nearly over before the Roman horse could reach the much larger block of archers and pikemen close under the villa.

As the leading wave of Roman cavalry approached the broad face of the Second Pike Regiment, the horses shied away from the steady wall of points edging to their left so that they clumped in front of the archers. The wagons and downed trees and other obstacles concentrated the enemy ever tighter as each horseman tried to go down one of the cleared lanes.

The grey gulls flew down the cleared lanes to strike down horses and riders alike. The charge came on, deeper into the pocket. The line of archers here was much thinner than that between First and Second Pikes; it had to be because there was three times the front to cover. The arrows flew less thickly, and the comparative safety of that front, compared to the solid wall of pikepoints, drew more and more of the steel-armored Romans like a magnet.

Those stopped by ditches and trees dismounted and continued forward shouting war cries.

"Now!" Tylara shouted. "Use your star weapons! Now!"

"Not yet." Rick watched the situation develop. The Romans on foot were dangerous. Their armor partly protected them from arrows. But they were also much slower, and the archers had more opportunities to shoot. The Roman wave came forward ponderously, past the wagons, around the abatis of felled trees, around and over the ditches, onward toward the archers who now had no protection but their stakes. The archers fell back involuntarily, back again—

To be stopped by backing against the heavy cavalry and Drumold's banner. They held for a moment, resolutely firing another volley of arrows point-blank at the Romans among the stakes that had been their final defense line.

"Now," Rick said. He shouted to a mounted messenger below. "Now!" He ran for the stairs, shouting for his orderlies and his messengers. It was time to get into the battle.

✧   ✧   ✧

Tylara watched the opening charge of the terrible Romans without fear. She had confidence in Rick, if not in her clansmen. When she saw the Roman wave break against archers and pikemen alike, she was certain they had won.

But the Romans pressed on. When they dismounted to charge headlong toward the archers and her father's banner behind the archery line, Tylara took fear again. Did Rick not understand that if that banner fell, half the clansmen would try to save themselves any way they could? Why did not Rick kill them with his thunder weapons?

He seemed to have forgotten that he was armed. He was far more concerned with shouting orders to messengers. Now he ran for the stairs. Tylara followed, wondering.

The din of battle filled her ears. She heard Rick shout again, but she could not understand him. Just below, not thirty yards from the steps of the villa, there was desperate fighting, with the Romans marching forward into the hail of arrows. The archers retreated, still in an orderly line, but here and there a man broke and ran—

The Romans had to be stopped. Her light-cavalry escort stood near the villa. It would not be much use against armored men, even armored men on foot. But her brother's heavier-armed men might be thrown in now—Rick was running there, and his orderly was holding a horse for him. Was Rick going to lead them himself against the Romans?

That was Rick's affair. The light cavalry was hers. She shouted to them to dismount and led them forward to stiffen the retreating line of archers. The archers let them through gladly, and she rushed forward swinging her battle-axe. She knew she was not skilled with it, but the only way to be certain the others would attack was to lead them herself.

A Roman thrust at her with his lance. She parried with the axe, stepped inside his reach, brought the axe around to cleave at him. It struck his helmet but did not cut through, and while the man was staggered by the blow, an archer ran forward and struck the Roman again with the mallet used to place stakes. The armored man fell.

Other Romans advanced. Many of the archers had no

more arrows, and although a few drew swords and stood resolutely, others melted back. They would all run soon—

The Roman line halted. There were screams and shouts, and the Romans faced about, bewildered—

The Third Pike Regiment had faced left and charged the Romans. They formed an irresistible battering ram of steel points, and they pressed onward, catching the Romans from the side and from behind.

There were more shouts. The rear ranks of Second Pikes had also joined the battle, wheeling to form a block thirty men square and bearing down on the Romans, mounted and dismounted alike.

Now the Romans thought of nothing but retreat. Those still on horseback tried to get back out through the narrow lanes between the ditches, while those afoot tried desperately both to catch their horses and avoid the pikes coming from either side. Another volley of arrows fired point-blank struck among the Romans caught in the pocket.

They were still dangerous. A Roman charged at Tylara and she swung her axe furiously, missing him but causing him to flinch away. Then the pikemen came on again, and the Roman threw down his sword and fell at her knees.

Tylara turned from the battle to look for Rick, just in time to see him lead the heavy cavalry off to the right.

❖   ❖   ❖

Rick shouted orders as he ran. "Third Pikes to face left and charge." He saw that messenger off and called to another. "Second battalion of Second Pikes form square, face right, and charge." *Now I hope to God all that drilling we did during the summer has an effect. We've got them! By God, we've got them.*

There was one weak point. When Third Pikes moved into the battle, they'd leave a gap between them and the lake, while what used to be their front would become their fully exposed right flank. A charge there or through the gap would be disastrous.

It wasn't likely. The Romans hadn't kept back a reserve. *Poor tactics. It was always worthwhile keeping a reserve.*

Without reserves you couldn't exploit the enemy's mistakes, and victory generally went to the side that made the fewest errors—

He found his horse and threw himself into the saddle, waving to the heavy cavalrymen to follow. He cursed when he saw Drumold and his son leading. He didn't want the banner exposed. But then he saw why. The others hadn't moved, but now reluctantly followed their chief and banner. Of course. They wanted to get in on the fight, and here Rick was leading them away from it. Drumold had worked a miracle in holding them as it was.

Okay, the banner came too. Now he didn't dare commit this reserve until he was certain of victory. He wished he could see what was happening out in front of First Pikes. That charge had shattered them, and it would take damned good work to re-form for another—but the Romans had shown they were steady, and he had no right to assume their commander was a fool.

They rounded the right—now the rear—of Third Pikes, shouting battle cries to reassure the infantry. He didn't want them panicked by hearing strange hoofbeats behind them.

Out in front, things were quiet for a moment. The right wing of the Roman army had pulled back and was milling around. There'd be a little more time before they could get into any formation for another charge.

First Pikes were standing at ease, looking curiously back toward the main battle. Balquhain raised the clan banner high. A cheer ran up and down the ranks.

The archers linking First and Second had returned to their stakes, and a few more were out in front of them stripping bodies and making sure what they stripped were bodies. There didn't seem to be any way to stop that.

Inside the pocket, the slaughter continued. The escape lanes were piled with bodies, and some enterprising officer of the Second had pushed a knot of pikemen into each one. The pikemen stood behind heaps of dead and faced the villa, preventing anyone from escaping. The Romans inside that caldron were pressed so close together that they couldn't

use their weapons. They'd be tiring now, too. That was the
trouble with armor. The protection it provided came at a
high cost.

Ha. The Roman right wing had got itself into formation.
Rick used the binoculars to pick out their commander's scarlet
cloak and gold bracelets. The man stood in his stirrups to
study the battle. It was obvious that he didn't know where
to charge. The best place—Third Pike's flank—was covered
by Rick's heavy cavalrymen; hit Third and the Romans would
expose *their* flank to a cavalry charge. Meanwhile the Roman
commander was losing half his army down in the pocket.

Aha. He was going to have another go at the junction
between Second Pikes and the archers linking First and
Second. If they got through there, they'd cut Rick's forces
in two, and they'd have an excellent chance to crush his
main force as well as relieve the pressure on the troops
caught in the caldron. It was good tactics, but stupid. If
they couldn't break the archers with their first charge, why
think they could do it now when the horses were getting
winded?

But what else could he do? Pouring men into the caldron
would be worse than useless. What would I do if—

"We stand like cowards!" Dughuilas, chief of the largest
of the subclans, drew his sword. "I will not have it said that
I watched this battle without taking part."

Oh, God damn it. That's all I need. "Hold!" Rick shouted.
Half the cavalrymen had drawn weapons, and even Drumold
was looking anxious. "We protect our men here. If we leave
this place, the Romans will strike—"

No good. They weren't listening. Rick drew his Mark IV
.45 automatic and aimed it just past Dughuilas' left ear.
He fired.

The clan leader winced. At four feet, the muzzle blast
would be enough to take off hide. "Another step forward
and I strike you from the saddle," Rick said. "You and any
other who desert."

"Desert? We want to fight!" someone shouted.

"You'll get the chance to fight. Hah! They're going to try

it." He pointed. The Roman line swept forward again, this time in a thick column, aimed like an arrow between First and Second Pikes.

Again three flights of arrows struck among them before they could reach the stakes. This time they pressed forward, heedless of losses, walking the horses into the staked area now hastily abandoned by the archers—

It was the last of the Roman reserve. Rick spurred forward, riding hard toward the First Pike regiment. He had no thought that the others would follow him, and they didn't; they made straight for the Romans. Well, that would be all right now. The important thing was to get First Pikes to face right oblique rear and charge. They'd finish the Romans a lot more thoroughly than these ironheads.

But at least the chiefs would get a chance to fight.

They do, I don't, Rick thought. Not that I particularly want to. But this battle's all over except the cleaning up, and I haven't fired a shot.

Then he grinned when he remembered that he had fired exactly once.

4

The battle was ended. Wherever Rick went, the men raised cheers. Tamaerthon casualties were light, and the Romans were totally defeated. The triumph was complete.

But then he felt the elation drain away with the adrenaline that had sustained him. In the military history books, the battle ends with the victory. The chesspieces are swept into the box, and all is quiet.

But there was no quiet. There were the screams of pain, from horses and men, mingled with the shouts of triumph and joy from the victors. An archer sat stupidly as he watched the blood flow from an arm severed above the elbow. A Roman warrior writhed in pain as pikemen stripped off his armor and cursed him for bleeding on their loot. And everywhere the horses and centaurs screamed and shied away from blood.

The centaurs were the worst. Worse, somehow, than the dying humans, far worse than the horses. The beasts tried to use their ill-developed hands to pluck out arrows or stop the flow of blood. They were not intelligent enough to understand what had happened (in a million years, would they have evolved good hands and high intelligence?), but they were sentient enough to be aware. Like dogs, they howled and whimpered and begged their human masters for help that couldn't be given. Thank God, Rick thought; thank God the Romans used few of them.

175

And thank God this is done. With luck we won't have to do it again. I can be through with war. The battles in Africa weren't so bad. The helicopters came and took the wounded away. You didn't have to look at what you'd done.

He had no more time to brood. There were a million details to attend to at once. Stop the slaughter and let the Romans surrender: the aristocratic airs of Rick's heavy cavalrymen helped there. It was beneath their dignity to kill an enemy who couldn't defend himself. Some of them were even intelligent enough to realize that if your enemies thought they'd be killed anyway, they'd fight on after the battle was lost.

Slaves directed by Mason and his MP's stripped the dead and disarmed the captured. That couldn't be trusted to the clan warriors. And Rick had to convince the chiefs, and they had to convince the archers and pikemen, that the loot would be divided fairly. The idea that a battle was won by all and all should share in the spoils was new to the hillmen.

Cavalry screens had to be sent to keep contact with the Romans who had escaped and to watch for any new Roman units. Arrows had to be recovered from the battlefield and distributed. Midwives and priests to examine the wounded. Prisoners with deep punctures in chest or abdomen had to be killed mercifully—there wasn't anything else you could do for them. Other kinds of wounds to be cauterized, or washed and bound up—thank God they hadn't come up with the insane theory of bleeding a wounded man!

And that's something I can do now, Rick thought. I can teach medical science. I don't know much, but I can teach the germ theory of disease, and aseptic practices, and get some of the acolytes interested in anatomy and dissection. But how do we develop penicillin? Maybe we can't. Sulfa drugs? I don't know anything about them, either. No technology. No chemistry theory, no experimentalists, no scientific method. No surgeons, and I don't' know enough, but I can make a start. I can teach them how to learn, and maybe one day a perforated gut won't be a death sentence.

Grooms and camp followers had to be sent to collect

the captured horses. Let the centaurs go—those not mortally wounded. The hill clans weren't used to them and wouldn't keep them. Send more MP's to see that no one stole horses or ran away with loot. And total up the butcher's bill.

Medieval armies left that to heralds. After Agincourt the French heralds had inspected the battlefield and worked with the English heralds to collect the names of the dead and captured. That useful organization hadn't developed on Tran. Rick had tried to foresee the problems of victory and organize for them, but even so he had to be everywhere at once.

And everywhere he went, men stopped what they were doing to cheer him. He could feel pride in that. He'd won the battle, and it was worth winning. Without the grain, the hill tribes were doomed. And the cheers were important, too, if he were to have any control over them. Men want to cheer a commander who wins victories for them. But he wished they'd get on with the work and let him hide in the villa. It was a splendid victory, but he didn't want to see the battlefield any longer.

◇   ◇   ◇

Tylara came into the villa leading a prisoner. "I have found the Roman commander," she said.

He'd been stripped of his armor and gold bracelets, but she'd let him keep his red cloak. Even with that, it was difficult for Rick to recognize him as the haughty officer he'd seen organizing the final charge.

Rick invited him to sit and sent for wine. The Roman seemed surprised. He studied Rick's face carefully and listened to his speech, then shook his head. "You are no Roman."

"Of course not," Rick said.

"I had thought these bar—these hillmen must have been led by an officer trained by Rome."

Rick smiled faintly. In a way, that was true, but hardly the way this man thought. "Lord Rick Galloway, war chief of the host of Tamaerthon," Rick said. *Pretentious*, he thought. Pretentious, but necessary. Perhaps he could use this man. Words cost very little. "I have long admired Roman ways," Rick said. "Your men fought well, as did you."

"Ah. I am Caius Marius Marselius, Prefect of the Western Marches."

"Prefect. In the Rome I knew, a prefect was both military and civil governor. Is that your office?"

"Yes." A gillie brought goblets of wine, and the Roman officer drank thirstily. "Thank you," he said to Rick.

Rick studied the Roman officer. "Head bloody but unbowed," he thought. A proud man holding his head up after defeat. But he knows he's beaten, and maybe he's sensible.

"You can prevent a great slaughter," Rick said. "We have come for grain and loot. Now that we've beaten your legion, there is nothing to prevent us from sacking the town of Sentinius. I would rather not do that. If you will arrange for the wealth of the town and the contents of the granaries to be loaded on wagons and brought to me, only officers to inspect the granary will enter the city. If you do not, we will take the town by storm, and there will be no controlling the men and the camp followers."

The Roman's eyes narrowed. "You ask for tribute from Caesar?"

Damn. Of course he'll see it that way. "No. I demand what is mine by conquest. I will have all of the grain and much of the wealth. That is certain. The only uncertainty is whether or not the people of Sentinius and the city itself will survive the experience. Do you truly believe the citizens can oppose me now that their legion is destroyed?"

The Roman officer pursed his lips in thought. He took a deep breath and said, "No. The citizens would be killed to no purpose. How am I to arrange this?"

"You will be free to go. My cavalry will watch the city gates. If by sunset tomorrow there are no wagons of grain, then we will do as we will with Sentinius." Rick paused. Might as well sweeten the pot. "In addition, I will release your soldiers and whatever equipment we cannot carry with us the day we cross Caesar's borders to return to our mountains." Rick shrugged. "What use are they to me? We are not foolish enough to wait for a ransom which would likely be escorted by five legions."

Marselius seemed puzzled. "Now I am certain that you are not a barbarian," he said. "Who are you?"

"That is no concern of yours."

"Perhaps not. What assurance have I that you will not sack the city no matter what we do?"

"You have the word of a Tamaerthon lord," Tylara said coldly.

"I have seen you shouting at your officers to make them spare captives," Marselius said. "You are no barbarian." He seemed to take comfort from that. "Very well, I agree. But may I ask, why this concern with grain? In the past, the hill tribes have raided for other wealth—"

"I remind you that I also demand some of the more usual loot," Rick said. "Small valuables. Trinkets. Goblets. Cloak pins and ornaments. Jewelry. I do not doubt that your citizens will keep their most valuable objects, but make certain that they send out enough gaudy luxuries to please my clansmen. As to why we are concerned with grain, if you care to return— as my guest—after the loot is transferred, I will tell you. It is a story worth knowing."

❖   ❖   ❖

The last of the wagons rolled westward. They were an impressive sight; over a thousand wagons loaded with wheat and barley and oats and a grain that Rick had never seen before which grew on a plant resembling a giant sunflower, and produced a seed that more resembled rice than anything else. Other wagons were loaded with onions, spinach and other vegetables needed for winter nutrition. Fifty were loaded with heavy valuables—furniture and bolts of cloth and iron implements. The light-weight loot— rings and ornaments and personal arms—had been distributed to the army. Interspersed with the wagons were flocks and herds driven by camp followers and liberated slaves.

An impressive sight. Drumold had never seen its like.

Everyone was certain there was food enough for all, enough to last through two winters—

And they were utterly wrong.

❖   ❖   ❖

Columns of pikemen and archers guarded the wagon train, and the light cavalry screens were well out to the flanks and forward to warn of any Roman attempt to recapture the loot of Sentinius. Rick took a position among Mason's mounted archers in the rear guard.

He shifted uncomfortably in the saddle, not caring for the weight of the Roman mail he wore. It itched. He'd rather do without armor, but that wasn't possible. He needed the armor and a personal bodyguard of freedmen loyal to no clan chief—and Mason at his back whenever possible. That wasn't because he was worried about the enemy; the problem was that he might be assassinated by his own officers.

The army was loyal enough. He'd won a complete victory with trivial casualties: a score of pikemen killed when the Romans managed to close with the first rank, another score of archers and pikemen cut down in the desperate fighting that closed the day, and nearly thirty heavy cavalrymen who hadn't sense enough to let the pikemen and archers do the work and had to go riding in to fight in personal combat with the defeated Roman heavies. Most of the armored men were related, and the survivors blamed Rick for their losses; if he had led the armored charge himself instead of riding to bring the pikemen in, they would not have lost sons and brothers . . .

They also resented losing the opportunity to sack a Roman city.

"Let them," he'd told Tylara and Drumold. "If we turn those lads loose in Sentinius, they won't be fit to fight for a ten-day. We'd be helpless against any kind of Roman attack. Don't forget that a full thousand Romans got away—more than enough to kill us all if we scatter. I would rather stay in a strong position and let the Romans bring the loot to us."

"We have defeated the Roman legion," Balquhain said. "They can bring in no other for a ten-day. The chiefs know this, and they say that we can use that time to loot the province. There would be much wealth."

"To what purpose?" Rick demanded. "We have taken more grain and loot than we have wagons to carry it in. It will take a ten-day and more to transport what we have back to the passes, and we will be fortunate to get it all into the Garioch before the snows begin. Seizing more wouldn't help us, only harm the Romans—and when the Demon Sun is closest, we may have need of them as friends."

"Caesar will never befriend us," Drumold said.

"Perhaps not, but only a fool gives his enemies reason to hate him, and I am no fool."

"No one says you are," Balquhain protested.

"Then let them do this my way, as they have sworn." And let me go back to the hills without a useless battle. I don't suppose it's possible to live the rest of my life without another fight like this. It takes a quart of wheat to feed a full-grown man for a day. The fifty thousand bushels of wheat we've taken can't possibly last us two winters. But there's no more to do this year, and for that I'm grateful. Glory's a heady drink, but the bar bill's damned high.

The chiefs had accepted the decision, but they had another complaint, too. Rick had distributed the loot among the soldiers rather than giving it to the chiefs to parcel out. They felt he was trying to undermine their authority.

They were right. He'd bought the loyalty of the common soldiers and noncoms, but incurred the hatred of many of the officers. The result was that he had to wear armor and endure the itch. Considering what he'd got for it, Rick thought the price worth paying.

❖   ❖   ❖

The cavalry escorted the Roman prefect into the camp on the third night of the march. Freshly shaved and in clean clothing, he looked very different from the last time Rick had seen him—but he'd wisely refrained from wearing jewelry. His sword had been bound into its scabbard so that it couldn't be drawn, but they had let him keep it.

"I had not thought to see you again," Rick said. "I had

even thought those troops you've kept ten miles south of me might be planning an attack."

"If your information is that good, you also know I have fewer than two thousand men," Marselius said. "I have come to see if you will honor your word and release my legionaries. Also I wished to hear this curious story you said it would be worth much to know."

"Then you will not be disappointed," Rick said. "But will Caesar not have your head? Surely he will say you have not done all you could to punish us for invading his realm."

"Caesar will have my head no matter what I do," Marselius said. "He will not deal lightly with a prefect who allowed barbarians—your pardon, but that is what he will consider you—to escape unharmed with the loot of a Roman city." He shrugged and lifted a goblet of wine in salute. "But Rome will not be well served by wasting the balance of my troops. Your cavalry scouts would give ample warning of my approach, and if we could not face your longbows and longer spears before, how can we now? I have never seen weapons like those spears. You call them pikes?"

"Yes."

"An interesting weapon," Marselius said. "I have not read of its like. Although there are stories of a time when Romans fought on foot and carried throwing spears, the records say nothing of these pikes." The Roman governor eyed Rick curiously. "In our earlier meeting, you spoke of 'the Rome you knew,' as if you were not certain it was the same as our Rome. Do you know of Roman history, then?"

"More than you know," Rick said. "Rome was once a nation of free men. Its citizens were its army, and a Roman citizen did not bow to any man."

"Are you then a Republican?" Marselius asked.

"You know of the Republic?" Rick asked.

"There are tales. In books, mostly. Caesar does not encourage Romans to read those books, but I have seen copies. Livius, and Claudius Nero Caesar, and—"

"The history written by the Emperor Claudius! It survives here?"

"Yes—"

"I would pay nearly anything for a copy," Rick said.

"It is written in an ancient language few can read—"

"I have an officer who reads Latin." I'd forgotten where I am, Rick thought. A treasure like that. On Earth, Claudius's histories were lost centuries ago. I wonder what other lost documents they have in this new Rome. "Do you know that the Emperor Claudius lived on another world?" Rick asked. "That your city of Rome is but a copy, and there stands on another world lit by another sun the original city of the Tiber?"

"How do you know of this?" Marselius demanded. "I have always suspected, but the priests say it is not true, for God created but one world and anoints but one true king, who is Caesar—" he hesitated. "Christ came but once, and to but one world. The priests are certain of it. But I have never been certain that world was ours."

"It was not," Rick said. He wondered how much he should tell the prefect. If the Romans immediately began intensive farming of all their land, they could store up enough food to save part of their population. Otherwise nearly all would die.

There was no point in telling him about starships and the *Shalnuksis*. That still left a lot. "I come from a land far to the south and so far west that one could sail for weeks before reaching it," Rick said. "There we have many old documents, and there we know that the stories of the worlds are true. If you wish a sign, look to the skies. The Demon Star comes close, and soon there will be fire and flood and famine in the land."

The Roman's eyes narrowed. "I have heard such tales," he said. "And I have heard another, that you come from farther away than the other side of the world."

Now who's been talking? Rick spread his hands. "The old legends are true," he said. "As to the other story, I do not gainsay it, but I make no such claim. Now listen and I will tell you of the times to come. They are times to make brave men fear."

PART SEVEN:

SCHOLARS

1

Snow lay deep in the passes of Tamaerthon. Rick could hear the winds from the north scream past the walls of his lodge.

There were no palaces in Tamaerthon. Drumold's lodge home, over a hundred feet long and half that wide, with walls of earth and stone ten feet thick, was the largest structure the hill country boasted. When the army returned from the raid on the Empire, the tribesmen built a lodge for Rick within the stone fortress circle and close by Drumold's. It was nearly as large as the chief's, which meant that the great hall was nearly impossible to heat, and Rick spent most of his time in the smaller room he had built to use as an office. It had whitewashed walls he could write on with charcoal.

He had intended to work there, but he found that very difficult. There was no glass. The best they had for windows was thin, oiled parchment; there was no good light even in daytime. He began to understand why the Northmen had slept late and spent their evenings at drinking bouts and listening to bards recite. What else could they do?

He desperately needed to plan for spring, but that was difficult. No one in Tar Tageral was skilled at making parchment, and the ink was terrible. He could make notes by scrawling on the whitewashed walls with charcoal, or using his ballpoint pen to write on a precious page of his notebook. But when pen and notebook were gone, there would be no others.

At first he'd thought it would be easy to bring technology to Tran. Now he knew better. He had to concentrate on tools; in fact, tools to make tools, and often that meant going back to first principles. Wire, for example. He knew that ancient jewelers had made small quantities of wire by painstakingly hammering it. About the time gunpowder was invented, the Venetians discovered the art of drawing wire through holes in an iron plate. The craftsman sat on a swing powered by a water wheel and seized the wire with tongs, letting his weight on the swing aid the work. But how thick a plate? How do you drill holes in iron? And where do you get the copper bar stock to make wire from?

And steel. Knowing that steel was iron with just the right amount of carbon was all very well, but how much is the right amount? And how do you experiment if you can't operate a forge and you don't want the smiths to think you a fool?

There were dozens of similar problems, and they gave him a headache. For relaxation, he invented the English custom of tea parties. Of course they didn't have tea here, but they had a plant whose boiled leaves made a caffeine drink. Rick was getting used to the somewhat bitter flavor— and teatime was a good way to spend an afternoon. He was drunk in the evenings more often than he liked.

Sometimes he would invite twenty or thirty people; sometimes none but Gwen, if she cared to join him. He was not unhappy if she chose to stay in her rooms at the far end of the great hall from his "office." She had grown increasingly moody and uncommunicative as her time approached, and her gloom and that of the weather in combination were more than enough to depress him.

But each afternoon he would have tea in his great hall. Any diversion was welcome.

❖   ❖   ❖

Corporal Mason brushed snow from his sheepskin greatcoat and dashed for the hearth fire. He warmed his hands thankfully before turning to the others. "Cap'n, its *cold* out there," he said.

Tylara laughed. "This is a mild winter. The Firestealer has plunged into the True Sun, but the ice in the middle of the lochs is barely thick enough to walk on."

"Thank God I wasn't here for a bad winter," Mason said.

"Each winter will be milder," Gwen said. "And each summer hotter." She clutched her teacup close to her swollen belly and stared into the fire.

"Aye," Tylara said. "The Demon Star is visible a full hour after sunrise, though both suns are in the sky."

"I've lost track of how many Earth days we've been here," Gwen said. She patted her swollen belly. "About eight months, obviously. We've missed Christmas."

"It's probably local Christmastide for the Romans," Rick said. "Or is it? I don't remember when the Catholic church officially adopted Winterset as the day for Christmas. Anyway, we can have our own."

"We'll have to share," Gwen said. "Yanulf is making preparations for his own ceremony . . . I suppose to ensure that spring will come."

"No," Tylara said. "We have long known that spring will come whether we coax the Firestealer out of the True Sun or no. But should we not give thanks for the signs that winter will end?"

Mason shivered exaggeratedly. "God knows that's something to be thankful for," he said. He took a seat near the fire. "Be glad when spring's here."

"Not half as much as I will," Rick said. He grinned at Tylara.

Her answering smile was warm. "We always celebrate the return of spring. This year will be double joyful."

"Even for your father?" Rick teased.

She laughed. "It is only his way, to complain that the dowry will impoverish him. He will drink as much at our wedding as any three others."

Rick looked curiously at Gwen. Caradoc, who had been invaluable during the battle and now was commander of the archer company that was Rick's personal guard, was often in Rick's great hall. Usually he had business there, but sometimes what he wanted to discuss was trivial. He always managed to say a few words to Gwen before he left.

Would the spring ceremony be a double wedding? Officially, Gwen was the widow of an Earth soldier; the story provided an acceptable explanation of her condition. Only peasant women had illegitimate children. Since no one knew precisely when by local time Gwen's husband had been "killed," it was decided that her period of mourning would end at the same time as Tylara's.

"Spring's a long time away," Rick said. "Too long. For now, let's have an old-fashioned Christmas. No turkey here, but we can have a goose—"

A distant trumpet sounded.

"That's the lads down in the lower village," Mason said. "Reckon I'd better go see what it's about."

"You don't have to go out in that cold," Rick said. "That wasn't an alarm—"

"It's all right, Cap'n," Mason said. "I'm glad of something useful to do. I've been getting cabin fever." He got up and put on his heavy coat. The wind blew flurries of snow into the great hall when he went out.

❖   ❖   ❖

The letter was on thick parchment. It was brought to Rick in his office.

The Roman had spoken the same language as Tylara, and she had told Rick that there was one universal tongue from the Five Kingdoms to Rustengo. But the letter was written in Latin—Rick could read enough of it to know that. He sent for Gwen and handed her the parchment. "Can you read that?"

"Just barely. I had three years in high school." She sat near the fire and read laboriously.

" 'From Caius Marius Marselius, onetime Prefect of the West, to Lord Rick, war leader of the tribes of Tamaerthon, greetings. Peace be with you and your house. This letter is sent by the hands of Lucius, my freedman and friend, who brings you—' I think that's 'gifts'—'and a message which I hope—' I don't know that verb. It's future tense. From the content I'd guess it was 'will heed.' Anyway. He says, 'Lucius has power to speak for me.' It's signed with a lot of flourishes." She handed Rick the parchment.

He looked at it curiously. "No way to tell if it's genuine. But I suppose it is. Who'd fake it?" He nodded to his freedman attendant, a young NCO who'd escaped from a Roman slave barracks and fled to the hills. "Send their leader in, and see that the others are given food and drink and a fire. They are my guests."

"Sir!" Jamiy stamped to attention, did an about-face, and left the room.

Gwen giggled. Rick looked wryly at her.

"Well, it's funny, that's all," she said.

"I tend to agree," Rick said. "Blame Mason. He's the one who's been teaching them military manners—mostly learned from watching old British Army movies, I think. It amuses him." And he thought, it's not really so funny. There's a point to military ceremonial. Under the circumstances, I'm not so sure Mason's wrong. We'll probably have to fight again. Even if I manage to wriggle out of it, I'll need disciplined forces.

The visitor was wrapped in woolen clothing so that only his nose and eyes showed. When he took off his scarves— three of them, counting the one wrapped around his face— and the hooded cloak and the thick gloves, Rick saw that he was quite elderly and very thin. His beard and long hair were nearly white, and he had almost no teeth.

Dentistry, Rick thought. Have to invent that from scratch. Thank God my teeth are in good shape, but that won't last. If I live long enough, I'll lose them all. Dentistry's another benefit of civilization you take for granted until you haven't got it.

"Were you able to read my master's letter?" the elderly man asked.

"Yes. What is your message?"

"Do you object if I sit? My bones are old, and the cold has made them brittle."

"Please do." Rick indicated a chair near the fireplace. "The matter must be urgent, to bring you here at Winterset."

Lucius sat heavily and huddled forward for warmth. "It is that. But first—" He reached down to a leather case he carried and took out a thick roll of parchment. He held that near the fire to warm it until it would unroll slightly, then held it out to Rick. "Marselius thought you might prize this," he said.

Rick took it curiously. The letters were handprinted in a block form and easily recognized. He read slowly. "Ego Tiberius Claudius Drusus Nero Germanicus—" He broke off, staring. "Is this truly a copy of the great history by the Emperor Claudius?"

"To the best of my knowledge," Lucius said. "I have no reason to doubt it. You are pleased with the gift, then?"

"I am indeed," Rick said. He frowned. What was this going to cost? "I am pleased that Marselius remembered my interest."

"He has written down every word you spoke," Lucius said. "I know, for he dictated them to me."

"May I see?" Gwen asked.

Rick was reluctant to let the parchment scroll out of his hands. He knew that was silly. He couldn't read it, and he'd need her help. He gave it to Gwen and watched to see that she didn't damage it, but she held it as tenderly as she might hold a baby.

"There are other documents," Lucius said. "One seems to be the story of how a group of soldiers came to this world from another."

"Where are these documents?" Rick demanded.

"Prefect Marselius has them," Lucius said. "They, too, could be gifts for you."

"Your friend is generous," Rick said.

"What does he want in exchange?" Gwen asked.

Rick frowned at her, but Lucius didn't seem upset. "Your friendship," Lucius said. "And an alliance."

"Alliance?"

"Perhaps I should begin with what has happened since you left." Lucius shifted in his chair.

"Jamiy," Rick shouted. "Tea, please."

"Sir."

"So what has happened?" Rick asked.

"The legions of the western provinces have proclaimed Marselius as Caesar," Lucius said. "I see this does not surprise you, and indeed it was inevitable if Marselius did not wish to be recalled to Rome and executed. The soldiers you released from captivity had no more pleasant expectation, and Marselius was popular with the other troops as well— and they could see the Demon Star. They have heard the tales. We all have. They believed Marselius when he told them what he had learned from you of the times of trouble to come. Few of the province, citizen or soldier, believe that our present Caesar will know what to do—or indeed care.

"Naturally, Marselius first sent for his family. His son and grandchildren were on the family estate near Rome. I was tutor to the household, as I have been for thirty years. For the past year, I have been working in the libraries of the friends of Marselius and his son. The letter that ordered young Publius—I call him young Publius, although he is a man older than you, my lord—the letter that ordered young Publius to join his father also instructed me to take many documents including that history by Claudius." Lucius sighed. "I fear we have betrayed many trusts, but Marselius assures me that the parchments will be replaced for all those who survive the coming times."

Jamiy brought in a pot of tea and three stone cups. As he put the tray down, Rick studied Gwen. She didn't seem overjoyed by the news of the documents. Rick wished he could think of a good reason to have her leave. I could simply order her out, he thought. I don't have to be polite to anyone—well, except Tylara and her father.

What is she hiding from me? "Jamiy."

"Sir."

"Tell Major Mason that our new guests have brought important documents, and that I would like him to see that they are given to no one but me. No matter who might ask for them, they come to me and no one else. Is this understood?"

"Sir." Jamiy stamped to attention.

"Excellent. Dismissed. Lucius, your story is fascinating. But has Marselius a chance? Will not Caesar bring the other legions against him?"

"Certainly he will try," Lucius said. "But neither Caesar nor the army likes winter campaigns. They will wait for spring. By spring Marselius will have a surprise for Caesar." He grinned toothlessly. "Marselius has freed many slaves, and is training them to make and use those long spears you call 'pikes.' He has studied your methods well, and is also training crossbowmen since only your hill clans use the longbow."

"A surprise for Caesar indeed—"

"A surprise for you," Gwen said. "What advantage will you have now?"

"You need none," Lucius said. "Marselius offers alliance with you."

"A trap to get you back onto the plains," Gwen said.

Rick switched to English to say, "Gwen, teach your grandmother to suck eggs. And please stop interrupting. I want to know everything I can about the situation, and you are not helping."

"I'm sorry," she said. "I—I seem to be scared all the time lately. I don't want—I'll shut up, Rick. And I am sorry."

"We know that you have no reason to trust Marselius," Lucius said. "But he does not expect you to send your soldiers to help him. What he wishes is assurance that you will not raid the western provinces. We will pay you well for that. Marselius intends to plant many of the parklands and game preserves in grain. He will build storage places in the high hills. We will keep much, but there will be enough to send you more than you could take by raiding the Empire."

"Do you have caves to store it in?" Gwen asked.

"Few, Lady." Lucius looked thoughtful. "The older

documents all stress the importance of caves as the only safe place when the fire and the deadly rains fall. There are caves in the northern hills, and others near Rome. Perhaps we can take those. But there is no chance at all if we must fight your hill tribes as well."

It can work, Rick thought. For that matter, I could do more. Once Marselius is involved in a civil war, I could join him. The army would follow me, and with allies in the Empire, I could take Rome itself. A civilized place, with real potential. Who could stop me? "And he went forth conquering, and to conquer."

William took all of England with less going for him, and the English were better for it. Well, better in the long run. They didn't see it that way at the time. "So stark a man," the chronicles say of him. "So very stern was he, and hot, that no man durst do anything against his will." But even his enemies said that a man could cross England with his bosom full of gold. I could govern better than Caesar . . .

No, I'm no conqueror, and the face of battle is not a lovely sight. I'd rather be a teacher—and we don't have to fight anymore. "It is not my decision alone," Rick said. "But I will counsel Drumold to accept this offer. And to make another. There is land in the hills below our mountains. The Romans do little with it because they have better. Yet we have crofters with no land at all, and our best is no better than those hills. Let us work that land in peace, and it may be that we will have gifts for Marselius in exchange for the gifts he offers."

"Rick, you can't turn down tribute," Gwen said in English.

"I don't intend to," Rick answered. "But trade's a lot more stabilizing than tribute." He turned to Lucius. "There will be many details, but I believe we can agree. With the Demon Star coming near, there will be slaughter and death enough. We need not add more."

2

Rick used charcoal to add another equation to the list on his whitewashed wall. He wished he had been a better physics student. He couldn't remember the basic equations of harmonic motion, and he wasn't sure he had derived them correctly. "Newton was one smart cookie," he muttered to himself.

The wall was covered with equations and notes and memoranda. One whole section listed things urgently needed, such as paper, and better lamps, and an adequate supply of pens and ink—all of which would be needed so that he could copy out a table of logarithms from his pocket calculator before its batteries failed. Another held the best data he had been able to obtain on crop yields. Next to that were diagrams of plow designs and crop-rotation schemes.

There were endless details. The work would never be finished; but it was more satisfying work than building the army had been. The raid had bought time, but now he could do something lasting. Tamaerthon could become a center of learning, a place whose security rested on something more solid than military power. If only he had decent light to work by . . .

When he heard the knock at his door, he turned with relief. The work was satisfying, but conversation was a welcome diversion.

Caradoc stood uncertainly in the doorway. "Come in," Rick invited. "There's good wine in the flask on the table."

"Thank you." Caradoc poured a cup of wine and looked curiously at Rick's charcoaled equations and the diagrams of the Tran system. Rick knew that Gwen had been teaching Caradoc to read, and the archer commander had shown a lot of interest in Rick's work in the past. Today, though, he said nothing.

Rick frowned. "Some problem, Captain? Speak up, man."

"I am concerned for the lady Gwen," Caradoc said. "She sits and stares at the fire, and wants no one with her. It cannot be good that she wishes always to be alone."

"Don't let her be. Stay with her."

"Lord, I try, but she has an evil temper."

"That she does." Lately she had taken to throwing things. Rick had long since given up trying to talk to her. He looked at his chalked calendar. Tylara had grown increasingly moody as well. Certainly the long winter had a lot to do with that, but she seemed to be brooding over something else as well— something she wouldn't discuss. I'm surrounded by unhappy women, he thought. Just when things are going so well.

Whatever Tylara's problem, though, there was a simple explanation for Gwen's moods. "Her time comes near," Rick said. "I do not have personal experience, but I am told that all women are hateful for their last days before a child is born. Especially a first child."

And, he thought, it would be particularly tough for Gwen. She didn't even know when the baby would come. The local day on Tran was slightly more than 21 hours long, and the gestation period seemed to have stabilized at 290 local days, as opposed to 270 on Earth; but would that be true for Gwen? No one knew. Straight mathematics; multiply 270 by 24 and divide by 21, and you'd get 300 days. How much of human physiology responded to hours passed, and how much to the day-night cycle? And was Earth's moon involved? Women's menstrual cycles seemed to coincide with Luna, but Tran's double moons were small and much closer than Earth's. Did they have an influence?

"You care for Gwen, don't you?" Rick asked.

"Yes, lord. And before the raid, I believed she cared for me. Now I do not know."

"She mourns her husband," Rick said. "But you are right. She is too much alone. I'll speak with her about it."

❖   ❖   ❖

"Your boyfriend's worried about you," Rick said.

Gwen sat close to the fire. She looked up without smiling. "Oh, leave me alone!"

"For God's sake, Gwen, snap out of it!"

"Why?"

"Do you think your problems are unique?" Rick demanded.

"Yes."

"Okay, I put my foot in it that time," Rick said. "Look, I've talked with the midwives. And Yanulf. They think everything's normal—"

"The medical experts," Gwen sneered.

"Well, they've delivered a lot of babies," Rick said.

"Sure. And lost a lot of mothers. Rick, I'm scared out of my mind!"

"Sure you are," Rick said. "Mind if I sit down?"

"Suit yourself."

"Thanks. Look, I've probably started a population explosion here, but I've taught them the beginnings of the germ theory of disease," Rick said.

"You couldn't have. I've tried," Gwen said.

"You didn't go about it the right way. I told them diseases were caused by little tiny devils, and that blessed soap and boiled holy water would drive them away. They can accept that." He looked thoughtful. "You know, I may be right about a population explosion. It happened that way on Earth."

Before the end of the nineteenth century, women often died of "childbed fever." But then came Ignaz Semmelweis with his theory that childbed fever was caused by physicians' dirty hands. His colleagues forced him to resign for saying it was their fault, but though he ended his days in a madhouse eventually enough of them believed him—after that most women lived to raise their children and have more. "There's no way we won't change things here," Rick said. "It isn't easy, but I'm trying to look ahead. Maybe we can avoid some of the problems we had on Earth."

"Maybe we can't."

"Look, dammit, snap out of it," Rick said. "You're working yourself into a depression. Keep it up and you'll get to me, too."

"I'm sorry," Gwen said. "I really am. But it all seems so futile."

"Why? Because we can't go home? We can make a home here," Rick said. "And—dammit, Gwen, we're more useful here than we ever were back on Earth. There wasn't much chance that anything we'd do there would change history, but we can here. We've already changed political history. We've got peace with the Empire and land to farm. Even if Marselius loses, we can hold those border hills for long enough to get in a harvest. With the new plows I've got the smiths working on, we'll triple the yields. We've helped these people already, and there's a lot more we can do!

"Sure, I've got an ambiguous status. The bards are trying to make up ballads about the raid, and they keep running into the fact that I never fought anybody. They can't figure out if I'm a war leader or a mere wizard. But whatever I am, everyone wants to learn from us.

"Gwen, we can start a university! Well, we start with grade school. But we can found a learning center that will *really* change this world. Look at what we can teach! Just the idea of scientific method and experimental science will bring on a revolution. And mathematics. We're not genius level, but we know more about geometry and algebra than was known on Earth through most of history. Medicine. Dental hygiene. Physics. Even electricity. I'm not up to transistors, but I can make batteries and vacuum tubes and—what the hell's the matter with you? You look like you've seen a ghost."

"Rick, for God's sake—you haven't built radios, have you?"

"Not yet. I'm still having trouble getting wire. But—"

"Don't! Please, please don't." Her voice held genuine panic.

"I see," Rick said. He stood and went to her, then took

both her hands in his. "Don't you think it's time you told me about it?" he asked. "For God's sake, Gwen, what did Les tell you, and why can't you tell me?"

Tears welled in her eyes. "We're safe now," she said. "Just don't change anything. Oh, Rick, I'm scared—"

"I know you are. But I don't know why. Gwen, please. Please tell me."

She buried her face in her hands and wouldn't talk anymore.

❖   ❖   ❖

Three days later a messenger arrived from the west. Drumold summoned his counselors to his great hall to hear the news.

The messenger was a young clansman who was proud of his mission. He said greetings to Drumold, then spoke to Tylara. "Six days ago there came to Tar Kartos a dozen lords and knights of Drantos. They had traveled in great haste and could go no farther. One lord asked if the Lady Tylara lived. All were overjoyed to learn you are safe in your father's hall. They then asked my chief to send a messenger to you, and I left that night. They asked me to greet you as Great Lady, Eqetassa of Chelm, and to say they regret they cannot come to you. They beg you to come to them."

"Eqetassa of Chelm? But I have been driven from that land," Tylara said. "Who are they?"

For answer the messenger held out a signet ring.

"Camithon? But I saw him die," Tylara said. "He was thrown from the battlements."

"A trick to bring you to them," Drumold muttered. "Sarakos hates you yet."

The messenger looked pained. "Do you say that Clan Ebolos aids enemies of Mac Clallan Muir?" he demanded.

"No, no," Drumold protested. "But I do not understand what they want of my daughter."

"Nor I," the messenger said. "But Calad my chief listened long to their story. Then he bade me speak these words: 'I have learned that which is of great importance to all the

clans of Tamaerthon. I beg that Mac Clallan Muir and the
Lady Eqetassa come to Tar Kartos with all haste.' "

"In this winter?" Drumold demanded. "Nay, it will wait
until the snow is gone from the passes."

"My chief says not."

"Father, you may wait," Tylara said. "But I have never
heard that Calad is easily alarmed, or that he does not know
how deep the snow lies in the passes. As for me—do you
return now?" she asked the messenger.

"As soon as I am dismissed," he said.

"Then tell your chief that the dowager Eqetassa of Chelm
will arrive as quickly as she is able."

"Tylara, is this wise?" Rick asked.

"What has wisdom to do with it? Sarakos may sit in my
council hall, but they are my people yet."

Damnation, Rick thought. Of course she'll go. "I'll get
things ready," he said. "We can leave in the morning."

"I had hoped you would come with me," Tylara said. For
the first time in several days, she smiled at him.

Drumold sighed. "Tell Calad your chief that Mac Clallan
Muir will join him within a ten-day, and that the Lady
Eqetassa will accompany him."

❖   ❖   ❖

Tar Kartos was at the western edge of the mountainous
highlands that formed Tamaerthon, and over the centuries
had been built into a strongly walled town. After five days'
travel across the frozen lochs, Rick was glad to reach the
somber fortress.

Calad, chief of Clan Ebolos, was nominally subordinate
to Drumold as Mac Clallan Muir, but that was a point no
one wanted to stress too hard. When Drumold's party was
invited into Calad's council hall, Drumold was content to
take a place opposite Calad and leave the question of which
end of the table was head and which foot for someone else
to worry over.

Besides Calad and his advisors there were half a dozen
knights and bheromen of Drantos. Before they could be
presented, Tylara ran up to their leader—an elderly soldier

whose craggy face held a long ugly scar. "Camithon!" she
cried. "I could not believe, even though I hold your ring
and heard them describe you. I saw you thrown from the
battlements of Castle Dravan."

"Nay, Lady, I was not thrown. Before they could do that,
I broke free of them and jumped. Would I not know the
places where the moat is closest to the walls? Once away
from Dravan, I had aid from the countryside until I could
join Protector Dorion and the young Wanax. . . . You must
not know, then: I am Lord Protector of Drantos."

"Protector—"

"Aye. Dorion was killed in the battle with Sarakos. To
say this is to say little. He was torn to shreds by thunder
weapons. Aye, at my side, and we nearly a league from the
battle."

"Mortars," Rick said.

Camithon looked at him curiously.

"Lord Rick is our war leader. He knows of these weapons,"
Drumold explained.

"Where is the Wanax Ganton?" Tylara asked.

"The lad has caught the fever," Camithon said. "He rests
in this castle." The elderly soldier paused. "We have come
as beggars," he said. "To beg Tamaerthon aid against Sarakos.
Yet, in truth, we come as more than beggars. We bring news
I think you will not find unwelcome."

"It had best be welcome news," Drumold growled. "I
am nearly frozen. What news have you that could not wait
for you to come to us?"

"Hear him out," Calad said. "I did not lightly send for
you. Protector, tell Mac Clallan Muir of the war in Drantos."

"After Castle Dravan fell, I fled to the army of the
Protector Dorion," Camithon said. "We caught Sarakos
in an unfavorable situation and thought to destroy him in
a great battle. I do not know who would have won that
day, but suddenly our knights were cut down like wheat
before the scythe. Sarakos had made alliance with men
from the stars who hold evil weapons." He paused to study
Drumold's expression. "You say nothing to this?"

"We know already," Drumold said.

"Strange," Camithon mused. "Yet this makes the telling easier. After Sarakos and his allies had beaten us, we fled to the mountains where we thought to fight on. Sarakos made our task the easier, for his armies ravaged the land. He turned out every bheroman in Drantos to replace them with his favorites. They so enslaved the commons that all, great and humble, were ready to join us. We fought no great battles—we knew we could not win such. But we harassed the land, burned the crops, killed his messengers, struck down his new knights and bheromen when they took possession of their villages. Sarakos has known no peace in Drantos. Many of his horses have starved or been eaten. Even so, many of his soldiers are dead of hunger and the plague, and many more have fled. He will lose more before spring, for the snows have closed the road to the Five Kingdoms, and we have destroyed the harvests in Drantos.

"It was after winter came that we heard of your great victory over the Roman legions. I have once before seen what Tamaerthon archers can do in battle, and it came to me that with the forces I hold and can gather, and with the aid of some thousands of your archers, we can drive Sarakos from Drantos and restore the lady Tylara to her dower lands. This I have come to ask."

Drumold leaned close to Rick. "What think you of this?"

"Lord Camithon," Rick said, "have you forgotten the star men and their weapons?"

"No," Camithon said. "This is the welcome news I bring. The star men have divided. Many have fled from Sarakos. Fewer than a dozen remain. Surely a dozen men will not frighten you who have bested the Romans."

"How do you know the star men have divided?" Rick demanded.

Camithon smiled grimly. "I have brought a present for Mac Clallan Muir and his daughter." He turned to an officer. "Bring in the prisoner."

The officer left and returned moments later with a man dressed in peasant woolen trousers and thick jacket. He had a scraggly beard that hadn't been shaved or trimmed for weeks, and his hands were shackled together with iron bracelets riveted to a foot-long chain.

He stood sullenly, looking defiantly at the council table, until he saw Rick. He stared a moment, then shouted, "Captain! For God's sake, Captain, help me!"

It was Private Warner.

✧   ✧   ✧

Despite the blazing fire, Rick's quarters were cold. And not just the chilly air, Rick thought. He could feel the chill radiating from where Tylara sat by the hearth.

"I had thought you would be pleased," she said. "Are not your enemies my enemies? Sarakos can be killed, and I can rid myself of this burning hatred for him—"

"We don't know that," Rick said. "Tylara—Tylara, every time I think of what Sarakos did to you, I get sick. I hate him as much as you do. I love you!"

"You do not seem to."

"More than you know," Rick said. "It is my wish to make Tamaerthon strong without endless war. Should we risk all that for revenge?"

Before she could answer, there was a knock at the door. "Come in," Rick called with relief.

Warner had been shaved and given better clothes. He was almost pathetically grateful when Jamiy brought him in. "Thank God you're here, Captain. Thank God—"

"Have a seat," Rick invited. "Jamiy, pour him a cup of wine."

Warner sat gratefully. He chugged the wine, and Rick poured his cup full again. "Take it easy," he said. "Before you get drunk, I want to know your story." He laughed. "You know, it wasn't a week ago I was wishing I had you around. I was trying to derive some of Newton's equations. Think you can remember college physics?"

"Yes, sir," Warner said. "Uh—ballistics?"

"Maybe," Rick said. "But mostly just general science." He switched to the local Tran dialect. "Warner, this is the lady Tylara. We'd both like to hear your story."

"Yes, sir. But could I have some more wine first?" Warner drank eagerly. "Where should I begin?"

"We know Parsons made an alliance with Sarakos," Rick said. "And that you helped him win the battle against the Drantos army. What happened after that?"

"At first it was pretty good," Warner said. "Captain, I can tell this better in English."

"Go ahead. I'll translate for Tylara."

"Yes, sir. Well, like I said, at first it was pretty good. We'd won, and we owned the country. Parsons gave each one of us a couple of local girls. It was a little funny owning slaves, but that's the way things are here. We had women and jewels and lots of good food and pretty good wine, and it was like Parsons said it would be. We lived like kings. Even out in the field we had servants. We took over the best houses for quarters, and we didn't have to fight much—just when the locals ran into something they couldn't handle. Then we'd come up with the machine guns and the mortars.

"Everything was fine for a couple of months, but then it all came apart. Guerilla war. Captain, it was like Vietnam, only worse, because we didn't have any choppers or trucks or anything. We had to ride horses, and by the time we got anywhere, the charlies had gone off into the hills. We weren't safe anywhere outside castles. Ride through the woods and you never knew but what an arrow or a crossbow bolt would kill you.

"It just never stopped, and it didn't look like it was ever going to get any better, either. Those people hated us, and we couldn't kill *all* of them. And it got kind of hungry, too, even for us—and we had more to eat than the poor bastards with us. And Parsons! He got so mean, you couldn't get near him. Claimed it was all our fault—we weren't disciplined enough—but he'd fix that. So one day a bunch of us got fed up and rode off."

"How many?" Rick asked.

"Twenty-two," Warner said. "Gengrich and I organized it. We went south, to the city-state territory. We needed some way to make a living, so we arranged to hire out to

the city republic of Kleistinos. They fed us and our wives—
most of us brought one or both of the girls we'd been living
with—and we didn't have to fight, either. Come spring we
were supposed to escort a big caravan south, and that sure
sounded like easier work than what Parsons had us doing."

"So how did you end up here?"

Warner looked sheepish. "I got drunk, passed out in a
tavern, and woke up with those handcuff things. The local
tavernkeeper sold me to the Drantos rebels."

"I see. Excuse me, I'd better tell Tylara what's going on."
Rick summarized Warner's story.

"They are not rebels," Tylara said coldly when Rick
finished. "They are fighting for their homes against bandits."

"Yes, Lady," Warner said. "If you say so—"

"She *did* say so," Rick said. He changed to English to
say, "I'd be very careful, were I you. She's got a sharp temper
and a sharper dagger." He poured himself a cup of wine.
"What weapons did Gengrich take with him?"

"One of the mortars," Warner said. "And our rifles and
pistols, of course."

"So André has one mortar and the recoilless. How many
mortar bombs?"

"I'd guess a dozen," Warner said.

"The star men are greatly weakened," Tylara said. "And
Sarakos has lost much of his army."

"They're not as strong as they were," Warner agreed.
"Captain, are you planning on fighting them?"

"I don't know."

Tylara looked at him coldly.

"Sweetheart, you don't understand," Rick said. "They think
because we handled the Romans so easily, Parsons can't
be that tough. They just don't know. One mortar shell in
the right place, and I don't have a pike regiment, I have a
disorganized mob. And Yatar knows what machine guns
would do to my archers—"

Tylara got up and went to the door. "Jamiy," she said.
She pointed to Warner. "Take him to his quarters."

"He's to be well treated, but he is not to escape," Rick

said. "Warner, I really am glad to see you. If we all survive, you're going to be a professor in the only university on Tran."

"I'd like that," Warner said. "It's got to be better than fighting for a living."

Rick waited until Jamiy and Warner had left, then turned to Tylara with a sigh. "All right, darling. Let's have it out."

3

Her cold look changed to one of unhappiness. "I do not like to quarrel with you," she said.

"God knows I don't enjoy it much either—"

"Please. Let me finish. All winter my father and I have waited for you to speak formally to him of our future."

"I was waiting to be sure you wanted me to," Rick said. "And I wasn't sure when would be the right time—"

"I had hoped you wanted me."

"I do. God knows I do. I love you," Rick said.

"As I love you. More than you know. Our customs are not yours. Never in our memory has a woman married before she was avenged, yet—yet I was willing to do so. Rick, your ways are strange. You are not like my husband was. You are a warrior, but you do not wish to fight. I have seen men insult you, and yet you did nothing, though lesser words demand blood—"

"Is that what you want? Should I collect heads?" The Tamaerthon clansmen no longer kept the heads of their enemies as trophies, but there were many legends of heroes who had.

"Hush," she said. "No. You should not. I have come to understand that although killing gives you no pleasure, you are no weakling. And I have seen you in the great battle, and again when you have spoken of the school you wish to

208

build. I know which pleases you more. I have heard you tell of the things you wish to teach, and how this will help everyone—the clans of Tamaerthon and all the others on this world. There is much about you I do not understand, but there is much I do know, and I have come to love you. Not as I loved Lamil. That was nearly unendurable—no, do not look away, and do not be sad. I was no more eager for my wedding night with Lamil than I am to have you possess me. Between us there is more than Lamil and I ever had. Lamil was handsome, but he was frivolous. He had no daemon driving him as you do. Nor did I, then, but I have since learned what duty is, and no less a daemon rides me now. You and I, we may belong to each other, but we also have ambition. Not for wealth, but for something greater."

He came to her and put his hands on her shoulders. "Then why are we standing like this—"

She removed his hands gently and stepped away. Her face held concern and sadness. "Please. This must be said. Rick, when I believed Sarakos secure in Drantos, I swallowed my hatred for him though it burned like fire. I had thought you must feel the same, that the man who, who—*gods!* that a man who had done that to me should live!"

"You can't know," Rick said. "God, sweetheart, you can't know—"

"I dream of flaying him," Tylara said. "Yet, because of what we believe you will do for Tamaerthon—aye, for all the world—I have lived with the knowledge that Sarakos would never be punished. As did my father and my brother. We agreed—you are important to Tamaerthon, and we have no hold on you. There is no reason for you to stay in Tamaerthon—none save what I hope you feel for me—yet we need you. And so I have not died trying to avenge myself. As much as I hate Sarakos, I have grown to love you more. Once I lived only to kill him. Now I have you."

"But now you want me to kill Sarakos for you."

"Now it is possible," she said.

"No. What's changed?" Rick asked. "André Parsons has

fewer men, but he still has more than enough weapons to destroy us, and without the pikemen, Tamaerthon is doomed. Do you trust Marselius? I do as long as he is afraid of my pike regiments, but not longer. And we may yet have to fight Caesar if Marselius fails."

"Are you certain nothing has changed, my husband-to-be?" Tylara asked. "The star men are divided. Sarakos has lost half his army. Is this nothing?"

"Is it enough?"

"I do not know. These are things you know," Tylara said: "But this I do know. Chelm is mine. Lamil left no other heir. You have heard how it fares with the people there. They die. There is endless war. The Time approaches. Do I not have a duty to them? And do you not have a greater one?"

"Me? I've never been there—"

"You brought the star men here," Tylara said. "Now they are as wolves in the land. Have you no responsibility for this?" Tears welled in her eyes. "My love. My father feels as I do. If you truly believe that nothing can be done to rid the land of these evil men, then we will send Camithon on his way without aid. But I beg you, think on it."

She would have to say that. My responsibility. I brought them here. I didn't want to, and I—what the hell's the point in quibbling? I brought them. But damn it— "My university will be more important than you know," Rick said. "We can change this world. Should we risk all that merely to kill Sarakos?"

"My love, I know there is no other like you," Tylara said. There was no banter in her voice at all. "But can not the lady Gwen and the man Warner teach much of what you could?"

There went my last argument, Rick thought. Oh, damn it. "Yes. They can," he said. God help me, she's right. And nobody else can stop Parsons and Sarakos. Can I? Sarakos is no problem. His medium and heavy cavalry don't sound as effective as the Roman heavy troopers, and my pikemen have a lot more confidence now. But I still need massed formations, and Parsons has the mortar and at least a dozen riflemen—more than enough to scatter the pikes for Sarakos's heavies—

Skirmishing archers could take Parsons, if we could get him on a decent killing ground. But he's too damn smart to be caught that way. He'll always have enough local cavalry with him to keep the archers at a distance. So how to get the Earth troops separated from the rest of the army—

"You have a plan," she said. "I have seen that look before."

"Something Warner said. Tylara, even if everything works properly, a lot of people are going to be killed—"

"More than will die if we do nothing?"

"No. Not nearly so many." He sighed and took her in his arms. "I could have had my pick of a hundred women," he said. "I could *have* a hundred women. So of course I have to be in love with you." He kissed her. They stood close for a long time.

Then she pushed him gently away. "In spring," she said. "And for now—we must send food for Camithon's army before he loses more men and beasts to hunger."

"Yes." And a thousand other details. Summon the western clansmen and start drilling them in the new tactics. More pikes and arrows. Baggage and grain carts. Politics. Keeping the clans working together was hard enough; now they'd have Protector Camithon and the boy king to worry about as well.

And more details yet. Patrols to seal the passes and keep secret as long as possible the fact that Tamaerthon was arming for war. A second iron curtain so that when spies inevitably found that the clans were mobilizing they still wouldn't be able to report that they were drilling with pikes. And inside that the greatest secret of all.

"Why do you smile?" Tylara asked.

"It would take long to explain," Rick said. How could he tell her he'd thought of calling his inner circle "The Manhattan Project"? But of course he couldn't use that name. It would signal Parsons as clearly as would a report that someone in Tamaerthon was gathering tons of manure and sulfur.

They'd need a secure area to leach saltpeter from manure. His scholarship wasn't good enough to make sulfa drugs or penicillin, but something simple like that would be no problem at all. Saltpeter 75 percent, charcoal 15 percent, sulfur 10 percent: fifteen to three to two, a formula tested in war's caldron for centuries. And they'd need a gristmill with no metal parts in which to grind it.

And there'd be a thousand more details. The business of war. They sing ballads about heroes, but the details are what win campaigns.

Or lose them.

PART EIGHT:

JANISSARIES

1

Gwen's delivery had been difficult. The baby was large and she was small. She was many hours in difficult labor, and afterwards was laid up for weeks. She remembered few details. One vividly stayed in her mind: the moment when Yanulf laid her baby on her breast. That couldn't have been more than a few seconds after the boy was born.

She didn't remember telling Yanulf that the boy was to be called "Les," but she didn't regret that. Someday she'd be able to tell Les of his father and give him the message the pilot had left for his child.

It took a long time to regain strength. For weeks she could only nurse her son once a day. Fortunately two other children had been born a few days before Les, both to robust clanswomen with milk to spare. Later Gwen wondered if this had not been the origin of the ancient custom of godparents; without other women's aid, Les would have died.

Gradually she became aware of life outside her lodge. At first she took little interest beyond a feeling of bitterness that Rick and Mason had not returned from Tar Kartos and had not allowed Caradoc to return either. She had one letter from Rick, telling her that the university could begin the next summer, if the peace with Marselius held. She was delighted. Everything seemed to be going well.

Then she found that many of the young men were gone.

All of the officers and noncoms of Rick's new model army had been summoned to Tar Kartos, as were the smiths. When she tried to find out why, she learned nothing. None of the women knew why their men had been sent to the western mountains. A few thought there would be another raid when the ice had melted in the lochs and passes, but no one was certain. There was no way to find out. For the first time since she'd come to Tran, Gwen was afraid that she'd lost control of the situation.

The suns stood at an angle of thirty degrees and the snows had melted in the lower passes before Yanulf was allowed to visit Tar Kartos. He returned to tell her in great secrecy that Rick planned war to restore Chelm to Tylara.

"Aye, Lady," he said. "They tell me I will be able to return to Castle Dravan before Midsummer's Day. Even as we speak, the fiery axe runs through the Garioch."

Gwen was horrified. This was the ruin of all her plans. "But—this is madness! He makes war on the star men?"

"Aye. No one knows what the lord Rick intends, but it is said that he has a plan to destroy both the star men and Sarakos. I do know that he has every cart in the land carrying manure to a place near Tar Kartos where he has built a water mill."

Manure. "And he also gathers brimstone?"

Yanulf looked surprised. "Aye. Manure and brimstone. But I do not know what magic he can make with those."

"I do," Gwen said. Gunpowder. "Every cart in the land" was probably an exaggeration, but it still meant that Rick was making a lot of black powder. Why had he decided on war, black powder against machine guns? "Yanulf, I must speak with him," Gwen said.

"It would not be wise," the priest answered. "You have yet to regain your strength. Besides the army marches as soon as the clans reach Tar Hastigar. You might not arrive before the war begins."

"Then it will be even more important that I speak with him."

"Your fear shows clearly," Yanulf said. "Do you not believe

that the lord Rick will be able to defeat the star men? Drumold believes so—"

"I do not know," Gwen said. What can Rick be planning? He doesn't take foolish chances. He must believe he can do it. And if he does— "But there is much that he must know before he goes to battle. We must go to him."

Yanulf studied her carefully. "This is important to you."

"It is important to everyone on this world," Gwen said. "On this world, and on other worlds as well."

"Can you not send him a message?"

"None that he would believe," Gwen said. "Nor dare I tell anyone what must be said. It would be more unwise to write it. No, I must go myself, and quickly."

"I believe you," Yanulf said. "I will arrange what I can. But we will not travel swiftly, my lady, for you would not survive a swift journey. And we will require nursemaids for your child, and soldiers to escort you. This will take time."

"We have so little time," Gwen said.

"I will do what I can."

❖   ❖   ❖

"It would be better if we waited," Camithon said. "The spring rains are barely over, and the mud will be thick. We will not be able to travel swiftly."

There were murmurs of assent from around the council table. Rick was pleased to see that Drumold and Balquhain said nothing, but waited for Rick to speak. "Neither will Sarakos," Rick said. "But more than that; we will not have sufficient food to wait longer and still carry supplies with us. Mason has trained the new troops well."

"I'd like more time with them," Mason said. "But I think they'll be steady enough."

"Thus we gain little by delay," Rick said. He pointed to the map on the council table. "At noon on the day after tomorrow we march. We'll take the direct route along the road. At dawn tomorrow I want the scouts out ahead to make certain that news of our passage does not get to Drantos ahead of us. Now there are other details." He unrolled several parchments, and bowed to the boy seated at the end of the table.

"Majesty, these are decrees," Rick said. "The most important proclaims a general amnesty for all acts prior to this spring and guarantees that each man will inherit from his father. When we reach the borders of Drantos, these will be sent throughout the land as quickly as possible."

"You ask me to forgive the traitors who rose against my father," the boy said. His voice rose. "Never!"

"You must," Rick said patiently. "How else can we arouse the countryside against Sarakos? Think upon it, Majesty. Would you rather sit on your father's throne, or look at your kingdom from exile?"

"If every man inherits from his father," Calad said, "how do you propose to reward our clansmen and allies?"

"Sarakos has created vacant places enough," Rick said. "Lands without heirs, for those who would be bheromen of Drantos rather than clansmen of Tamaerthon. One of these documents gives Mac Clallan Muir the right to dispose of the ownerless lands in two counties. Another gives the lady Tylara the same rights within Chelm."

"My lord," the boy said, "the price of your aid comes high."

Rick said nothing. After a moment, Camithon said, "It is not so high as might be. We came to Tamaerthon as beggars, and we leave with hopes of victory. Sign, lad. You will not see a better bargain."

Rick took the parchments to the end of the table. In the past weeks he had come to like the young king. The boy was intelligent enough to bow to the inevitable.

"What are these other parchments?" Ganton asked.

"One is a treaty of alliance between Tamaerthon and Drantos," Rick said. "It contains provision for the Roman Empire to join the alliance if Caesar wishes." And getting both Camithon and Drumold to agree to that had taken many nights of arguing; nights that Rick would rather have spent planning the battle. Eventually the growing Demon Star had convinced them more than any arguments Rick could make. When the invading star got closer, the lands to the south would be too hot to live in. They could expect hordes of refugees, an influx they couldn't possibly accept. And the refugees would come armed—a wandering of the tribes such as had happened in Julius Caesar's time. It would take a strong alliance to force them to settle elsewhere.

"Another document states that you will live in the household of the lady Tylara during your minority," Rick said.

Ganton smiled. "Oh, I'd like that. She's nice," he said. He looked up at Camithon. "Since the Lord Protector agrees, we consent," he said formally. He took the pen and scrawled his name on each parchment.

One less thing to worry about, Rick thought. At least we've made a start on the mess I'll face after we win.

If we win.

✧   ✧   ✧

Gwen arrived at Tar Kartos to find the fortress town nearly empty except for Caradoc and a company of mounted archers.

"The lord Rick received the message that you were coming," he said. "He could not wait, but asked me to remain to greet you. He left this for you." The archer commander handed her a parchment.

Gwen unrolled it. "Gwen," it said. "I've already had Camithon send marching orders to the holdout forces in Drantos. This operation takes careful timing, and I've got to move now if we're going to link up with them. I can't wait for you.

"If you're still in a hurry to talk to me, Caradoc will escort you. You'll be taking your chances. I intend to make a fight of it as soon as I can, so you might be coming into a battle. I think we'll win, but nothing's certain in war.

"My advice is to stay in Tamaerthon. Even if we lose, they're unlikely to annihilate us. There'll be enough force left to hold Tamaerthon no matter what. The university is more important than the war. I've sent Larry Warner back

to the Garioch. He wasn't much of a soldier, but he ought
to be pretty good as a professor. If I don't come back, you'll
have all of my share of the plunder from the raid, and that
ought to be enough to get a school going.

"I almost left orders to have them keep you in Tar Kartos,
but I'm just scared enough of what you know that I want
to leave that choice up to you. I hope you decide to stay."
The parchment was unsigned.

She looked up to Caradoc. "How long will it take to catch
up to them?"

"They left nine days ago," he said. "And they intended
hard marching. We can travel faster than they, but I doubt
we will reach them in much less than a ten-day."

Just possible, she thought. Yes. I may get him to call off
this war before it's too late.

I may not get there in time, either. "I will come with you
as soon as I have arranged quarters here for the nursemaids
and my baby," Gwen said. "We must find Rick before he
battles the star men."

❖   ❖   ❖

They reached the rear guard of Rick's force seven days
later. It took another day to pass through to the front. The
countryside was wooded and hilly, and the single road was
clogged with baggage carts and camp followers. Toward
evening they reached an area where the countryside opened
out and the road ran through broad fields. The army had
deployed in battle array across a front three miles wide.
Before they could reach the forward edge of the front, they
were stopped at a roadblock. Despite Gwen's shouts and
Caradoc's rank, they were firmly escorted back to a
headquarters pavilion a kilometer behind the lines.

The headquarters was occupied by orderlies and staff
officers. Messengers came and went in obvious preparation
for a major battle on the next day. No one seemed to know
why Rick had taken the light cavalry and several heavily
laden wagons three kilometers farther up the road to the
only village in the area.

Just before evening, Gwen heard shouting and then saw

several groups of heavy cavalrymen ride northwest up the road. The sun was setting when she heard them returning. They were followed by the mounted archers at full gallop and, a few minutes later, by Rick and his personal guardsmen.

He paused to send messengers off with orders, then came into the pavilion. Gwen would not have recognized him if she hadn't heard him talking. He was dressed in chain mail and the scarlet cloak Marselius had sent as a gift. His helmet was the typical bullet shape with nasal guard worn by heavy cavalrymen, and he wore steel shoes and greaves rather than boots. As he came in, Jamiy helped him remove his helmet and gorget, but he kept the rest of the armor on. He sat at the table across from Gwen. "They told me you were here," he said. "If you'll excuse my saying it, you couldn't have come at a worse time."

"Why?"

"Because I've a battle to plan," he said. "Before dawn tomorrow, which means there are a million details tonight. If you've got something to say, Gwen, make it quick. I want you a good way toward Tamaerthon before the fighting starts."

"Your concern touches me."

"What's that supposed to mean? You could have stayed in Tar Kartos. I wish you had. I don't intend to lose tomorrow, but if I do, I'm counting on you to start the university. I still think that's the most important thing we can do for this planet."

"The most important thing you can do is to call off this war," Gwen said.

"Are you ready to tell me the truth at last?" Rick asked. "That calls for a celebration." He turned to the door. "Jamiy, a flask of wine, please. And ask the lady Tylara to join us when she arrives."

"Sir. I think I hear her patrol coming now."

"Good. All right, Gwen, why is this so important, and why haven't you told me before?"

"It wasn't my secret," Gwen said. "Why couldn't you leave things alone? Everything was going so well. We had a perfect place to hide, and enough to eat. Parsons would grow those stupid drugs—"

"That's debatable," Rick said.

She looked up in alarm. "Why?"

"Parsons and Sarakos don't have much of a hold on this country. They'll be doing well to feed their army, much less grow a couple of thousand acres of madweed." He shrugged. "It doesn't matter anyway. With any luck, Parsons and Sarakos will both be dead by morning."

"How?"

Rick grinned without humor. "I selected this place pretty carefully. Took real timing to reach it just about the time that Parsons would. We've got a nice muddy field out there— better suited to my infantry than Sarakos's cavalry. Ideal for a battle. Of course there are other places like that, but this one has a special feature. There's only one village for thirty kilometers up the road ahead."

"I don't understand—"

"Swampy fields. One village. We held it last night and most of today, but we let Sarakos chase us out of it this afternoon. We had to run fast. Didn't get a chance to burn it down. Warner says Parsons and his people don't like sleeping in fields. Guess where they'll make their headquarters tonight—"

"What are you planning?" Gwen demanded.

Rick looked at his watch. "The hardest part was the fusing," he said. "Took me weeks to come up with a slow match that burned reliably, and I still can't time it too close. Making twelve barrels of gunpowder wasn't so difficult, and it was no trick at all to bury it in the village. An hour or so before dawn, André Parsons is going to get one hell of a surprise."

"You're going to kill them all? And destroy all their equipment?"

"I certainly hope so. I wish there were another way, but I can't think of one. I can't even parley with them. If André knows he's fighting me and not just locals, he'll be a lot more suspicious. Were in hell is that wine?" He shouted for his orderly.

"You don't look very pleased," he said. "I thought you

lived in terror that Parsons would find us and report to the *Shalnuksis*. Now you won't have to worry."

"Oh, boy!" she said. "And I was trying to be careful. I didn't expect you to be able to win—"

"Thanks for the confidence."

"Rick, this isn't a game! If you win—when you win— will you be able to grow the *surinomaz* for the aliens?"

What is this? Rick wondered. He had noticed her alarm when he told her Parsons might not be able to grow the crops for the aliens. Now this.

Could I manage it? Probably. I've got enough allies, and I can talk Camithon and the king into it provided we can import enough grain. But I can think of at least one damn good reason not to deal with the aliens at all. Why is she worried about *surinomaz*? And how can I make her tell me what she knows?

He shrugged. "Without the equipment Parsons has? Not easily. Madweed isn't a popular crop here, and taking that much good land out of grain cultivation wouldn't be simple. But Gwen, I've been listening to those legends about the dangers of dealing with the sky gods."

Jamiy came in with wine and pewter cups. "The lady Tylara has returned safely," he said. "She will come when she has spoken with her brother." The orderly hesitated. "I do not think she was pleased to learn that the lady Gwen is here."

Rick laughed. "I don't expect she was," he said. "Thank you." He filled the cups. "Look, what's got you scared?"

"I don't even know where to begin."

"Maybe I can suggest something," Rick said. "I've given this a bit of thought, too. Try this. The rogue sun comes at six-hundred-year intervals, and that's the only time the *Shalnuksis* have any interest in Tran. That's roughly 1400 A.D., 800 A.D., 200 A.D., 400 B.C., 1000 B.C., and 1600 B.C. The languages are Indo-European and you've several times mentioned similarities to Mycenae and Crete. That's 1600 B.C. or a little later; the rogue's period isn't a full six hundred years. All right so far?"

She nodded. "It's the earliest I'm sure of. Archaeologists

on Earth have violent arguments about the languages of the Mediterranean in that time period—"

"They'd love to know what we know," Rick said. "All right. The 1000 B.C. expedition blends in with that. Maybe that's when they brought the Celts. Then or 400 B.C. There's no question about 200 A.D. —that's Imperial Rome about the time of Septimius Severus, and we've even got Lucius's parchments. Then about the time of Charlemagne they brought in a group, and there's plenty of evidence for that. Charlemagne was crowned Holy Roman Emperor on Christmas Day in 800 A.D., and they must have picked up some of his heavy cavalrymen not long before. That brings us to 1400 or so. There's not one single trace of that visit. Why not?"

Gwen didn't say anything. Rick leaned forward to throw a block of peat onto the small hearth fire.

"We know they didn't skip that time," Rick said. "You told me you'd studied Tran languages of six hundred years ago. But nobody knows anything about longbow tactics, so they couldn't have brought English or Scots or Welsh. Maybe French. The French didn't learn anything from Crécy. Only nobody ever heard of the Swiss pike, either. Nobody knows how to make plate armor, but they were using it in Europe in 1400. So who did they bring? There's no sign of mixed races. No Orientals or blacks or Indians.

"And 1400 is well into the age of gunpowder, but they never heard of it here. Is that reasonable? And it's not just weapons. Magna Carta in 1215. Nobody ever heard of it. Thomas Aquinas, Roger Bacon, Malatesta, all thirteenth century. By 1400 a whole slew of geniuses had lived, and nobody's ever heard of them. Not even Lucius, who's spent his life digging in old documents; or Yanulf, who's got epic poems so old there's even a version of Homer. The 1400 expedition vanished without a trace.

"What happened, Gwen? Did somebody kill the lot of them?"

She looked up unhappily. "Les thought so. For about the same reasons you just gave. Why hasn't there been any progress on Tran? You can't blame it *all* on the unstable climate," she said. "But he didn't know. There weren't any records in the computer."

"But that was why you didn't want electricity. Or anything else. You weren't all that worried about Parsons, it's the *Shalnuksis* who've got you scared."

"Of course. But if Parsons knew where we were, he'd tell them." She took a deep breath. "Rick, have you guessed the rest of it? Secret caves. Fire from the sky. And those epic poems about the bad luck that comes from dealing with the evil sky gods. They bring wondrous gifts but take them back again. Fire will fall from the sky, and the only safe place is in deep caves. And there's another I don't think you heard—about a taboo place where nothing grows, and a lake with a glass bottom—"

Rick nodded gravely. "They don't do things by halves, do they? Atom bombs—"

"I don't *know*. But even without knowing about Yanulf's epics, Les thought it likely. That's why he wanted me to run away. Hide as far from Parsons as possible."

"And why you didn't warn me that Parsons was going to mutiny," Rick said. "So you'd have someone to go with."

"Yes. Rick, I'm sorry."

"Sure. But I don't understand why you didn't tell me all this before."

"Because I didn't know what you'd do. Rick, I'm sorry I've kept you in the dark, but after all, we've done pretty well. We have a safe refuge, enough to eat, a place for a university—I thought of starting one before you did, but it seemed better to let it be your idea. Everything was going fine. Why should I complicate matters by telling you about problems you couldn't do anything about? And I was afraid you'd want to warn Parsons. After all, they were once your men—"

"I probably would have. I'd do it now if I weren't about to kill them anyway." He drained his wine cup and cursed. "If I'd known before, maybe this war wouldn't have to be. André can't have any love for Sarakos."

"You still don't understand," Gwen said. "You have to warn him now. Rick, no matter who wins tomorrow, we've got to be certain the victor has enough power to be *sure* of growing *surinomaz*."

"The hell we do. You've just told me that dealing with the *Shalnuksis* isn't very smart. So we just vanish. Hide in the caves when they show up. Let them whistle for their drugs."

"It's not that simple," Gwen said. "Rick, you said your university would be important to the people of Tran. You seemed to care."

"Sure, I'd like to accomplish something worthwhile," Rick said.

"That *surinomaz* crop is more important than your university," Gwen said. "And to far more people than just those on Tran. It's important to the whole human race."

2

Rick refilled his wine cup. "I think you'd better explain that last statement," he said carefully. "You've told me often enough that this *surinomaz* crop isn't worth *that* much to the *Shalnuksis*. How can it be important to the whole human race?"

"It's a long story," Gwen said.

Rick looked at his watch. "We've got between four and six hours before the gunpowder blows. That ought to be long enough. Only this time tell me the whole story. I'm tired of trying to operate in the dark."

"You haven't done too badly," Gwen said. "All right. If the *Shalnuksis* send a ship and find out there's not been a harvest and won't ever be one, they won't send another. But if they think there'll be good harvests, they'll arrange for ships to come every year the crop will be good. Eventually they'll have to send Les."

"Jesus Christ. Gwen, are you still in love with that S.O.B?"

"I don't know. Sometimes I am. Not that it matters." She spoke defiantly. "Don't look at me like that. I know what you're thinking, and it's wrong. Rick, he didn't just throw me out. I could have gone with him."

"Why didn't you?"

"Because they wouldn't have let our baby live."

"They? Who? And why not?"

"The Confederacy. They breed their human servants. Even if they'd let my baby be born, they wouldn't have let me raise it. All their human children grow up in a school."

"Gwen, what the hell are you talking about? Breed humans?"

"For loyalty," Gwen said. "But sometimes they breed in 'wild' humans from Earth to give the strain initiative. Les had a wild grandmother, and they won't allow more wild genes in his line. Rick, I know it sounds fantastic."

"Fantastic. That's a good word," Rick said. "How long has this been going on?"

"At least five thousand years."

Five thousand years. "And you believe that?"

"Yes. Everything I saw in the ship's data banks is consistent with it. And look how long they've been coming to Tran."

"But five thousand years? Gwen, all that time, and they've never made an official visit to any government on Earth. All that time they've been dealing with us without contact—"

"They can't and they won't," Gwen said. "They don't allow barbarians in their confederacy. They have a stable union of nearly a hundred races. Most of those never did have periods of unlimited growth. When they run into an aggressively unstable race, there's usually a war. They've exterminated some races they decided were hopelessly barbaric. As a result, they've achieved what human philosophers always wanted but no one really believes we'll ever have: universal peace and order and stability."

"If they're so damned peace-loving, why have they kept raiding Tran? Why drop atom bombs on their last expedition?"

"The *Shalnuksis* aren't peace-loving," Gwen said. "They just don't have any choices in the matter. They're a long-lived race, and Tran is a—Les called it a family business. The *Shalnuksis* don't want Tran industrialized, and the Confederacy doesn't know about Tran."

"There was a police inspector. Agzaral. He knew all about it," Rick said.

"Agzaral and some of the other humans know. They're keeping it secret from their government."

Why wouldn't there be corruption in a bureaucracy five thousand years old? "And your friend Les is helping them keep it a secret?"

"Yes." Gwen fought tears. "Rick, it's not what you think. It's so hard to explain! Have you ever heard of janissaries?"

"Sure. Slave soldiers of the Ottoman Empire. Administrators, too. They pretty well ran the empire for the Turks. Taken in childhood as tribute from Christian subjects and brought up in schools, lived in barracks and forbidden to marry—God almighty! Gwen, what are you driving at?"

"What you've guessed. Humans aren't members of the Confederacy, but human soldiers and policemen and administrators like Inspector Agzaral enforce the Confederacy policies. That's why Earth has a special status—not taken into the Confederacy and not interfered with. They need a strain of wild humans to mix in with their tame janissaries."

"Slave soldiers. Bred for loyalty, and raised in creches— Gwen, do you believe all this?"

"Yes. Why would Les make it up? Why would he say he was a slave?" she demanded. "He was crying when he told me. He said he felt like a dog attacking his master, like a traitor—"

"If they're that loyal, why *was* he betraying them? All because of you?"

"No. Oh, maybe partly," Gwen said. "But that's not the real reason. Rick, he said it was important that the Confederacy never learn about Tran because—he said the Confederacy's governing council is worried, now that humans on Earth are going into space. Some of the Council wants to knock Earth back to the Stone Age. Agzaral thinks that may have happened once already. Don't you see, the humans are being torn apart! They're bred for loyalty to the Confederacy, but they're humans, too. They don't know what to do or who to trust."

"Does this council truly expect human soldiers to bomb Earth?" Rick asked.

"The Confederacy Council doesn't know who to trust either," Gwen said. "But there are humans who argue it's the best thing. That wild humans simply can't be allowed to get loose with their crazy ideas about unlimited growth and continuous progress. They've enforced the peace for thousands of years, and that's more important to them than a planet they've never lived on. But other humans want to save Earth. The Council doesn't know what to do, and neither do Agzaral and his people.

"Some of the janissaries—I may as well call them that," she said. "Some of the janissaries want the Confederacy to force Earth into membership. It would mean that the Confederacy Council would interfere in Earth's government. Humans would have to accept the Council's policies. Stability. Limited growth. The end of what we think of as progress."

"I see," Rick said. "They call it 'stability.' But there's another word for a society that hasn't changed in thousands of years. Stagnant. Or decadent.'"

"That's almost exactly what Les said. His group wants to do more than just save Earth from destruction. They want— Rick, it sounds trite, but they want humanity left free."

"But where does Tran come in?" Rick asked.

"If they do bomb Earth, or even if they just make Earth into another decadent member of the Confederacy, humans on Tran will still be free. With any luck, one of Agzaral's people—probably Les himself—will be sent here to collect the drugs. Only this time he won't be leaving on such short notice. They can bring translations of their textbooks. Scientific equipment. And they've got the kind of bureaucracy you'd expect after five thousand years of stasis. Agzaral thinks they might even be able to lose a ship in the recordkeeping and send it here after the *Shalnuksis* have gone away."

"Except that the *Shalnuksis* will be doing their best to kill off anyone who could help Tran progress beyond the Iron Age—"

"Yes. They will. They'll almost certainly bomb the groups they've been trading with. But they might trust that mission to Les or one of his friends. They don't like long journeys to out-of-the-way places. That's one chance, anyway. And another is to hide. They won't kill everyone on Tran. They can't afford to, because they'll want to do some more drug trading six hundred years from now."

Rick shook his head. "They've got the stars. Why do they traffic in drugs?"

"You don't understand real decadence," Gwen said. "Who are the heavy drug users on Earth? It's not the poor and downtrodden who have big parties with bowls of cocaine."

"And I suppose the *Shalnuksis* make a lot of—what? Money? Do they have money? Anyway, the drug trade profits them."

"It must," Gwen said. "But I wonder if they do it for profits at all. It must be a game to them. Excitement." She thought for a moment. "Take the Mafia as an example. Surely the top dons are fabulously rich already. They could retire, go legitimate, but they don't. It must be like that for the *Shalnuksis*."

"So if we don't grow the drugs, your friends won't have any legitimate reason to come here."

"Yes. And the first ship here may bomb the planet before we've had time to prepare—"

"And this is why you were hiding?"

"Yes. It was all we could think of to do. Les didn't have much time to talk to me. He was afraid the ship was bugged. He had to whisper everything to me in bed. He didn't want to leave me here, but I wouldn't let his damned machine abort my baby, and there wasn't another choice. He told me to run away and hide and stay a long way away from where they'd be growing *surinomaz*. When we heard Parsons plotting to throw you out, we thought I'd have a better chance if I stayed with you. Les even told me to marry you. Maybe I would have, too, if you hadn't met your raven-haired beauty—"

Rick didn't know what to say to that. Would he have found Gwen attractive if he hadn't met Tylara? It hardly mattered, and it was too late to worry about, anyway.

It was too late to worry about anything. He looked at his

watch. Five and a half hours at most. And a battle to be fought in the morning. The battle didn't seem so important now. What was? Assume what Gwen said was true. What should he do about it?

"I wish you'd told me earlier," Rick said. "This makes—it makes everything we've done rather trivial."

"Not really. You've done rather well."

"I've survived. Look, we don't need André's military equipment. I presume that you've got communications gear. You'd have to, if you expect Les to find you again."

She nodded. "I have a transceiver. He told me when to listen, and not to answer unless I hear a certain code phrase."

"So. I guess I can grow the damned crops for the *Shalnuksis*. Maybe we can even work it so they don't kill too many people with their bloody bombs. Tylara says the caves under Castle Dravan are even deeper than those in the Garioch. But it's pure dumb luck we can do what's needed because you wouldn't tell me enough to let me make an intelligent plan."

"I wish I had," Gwen said. "But I didn't really trust your abilities. We—Les and I—thought Parsons was right: that you were too inexperienced, that Parsons would have a much better chance.

"But Rick, it wasn't blind luck. Sure, all you were working for was survival, but you're an ethical man. I don't think it's luck at all. Ethical actions may be the best survival tactics after all. I wish I'd acted that way. Instead I trusted Parsons, knowing he'd use brutal tactics—and he failed completely. I wish we'd warned you about the mutiny and told you everything we knew."

"So do I."

He thought about what she'd said. Had he acted ethically? Not always. He had tried, and that had to count for something.

Ethics as the best survival policy, even without complete information? He wasn't sure he could accept that as a general proposition, even though it had worked here and now and this time. The most you could say for sure is that if you did the ethical thing and you did survive, you'd have an easier time living with yourself.

Which, he thought, brings up another point. He sighed and turned toward the door. "Jamiy."

"Sir." The orderly came into the pavilion.

"We took one of Sarakos's officers prisoner this afternoon," Rick said. "Bring him to me, and bring me parchment, pen, and ink."

"Yes, sir."

"Why do you want him?" Gwen asked.

"Ethics. You said that the most practical action is the ethical one. I'm not sure I believe that, but I am sure I've got no business sitting here waiting for a bomb to go off under a dozen men I brought to this planet."

Her eyes widened. "What are you going to do?"

"What I should have done in the first place," Rick said. "I'm going to send a letter to André Parsons and offer to parley."

3

"Man, are ye daft?" Drumold demanded. "We hae won, and you would throw it away." He looked sideways at Rick. "I had thought you loyal—"

"They are his countrymen," Tylara said. "As is Gwen. We are not."

"You know better," Rick said angrily. "Aye. They are my countrymen. I brought them here, as Tylara reminded me. And if bringing them made me responsible to the people they oppressed am I less responsible to my own men?" And then, bitterly: "You are in no danger. Dughuilas never tires of saying that I have never fought in a battle. You do not need me."

"If you are offended by Dughuilas' words, I will have his head brought to you," Drumold said. "Och, talk sense. You know full well your value to us. As do we. Wi'out your direction we fight as we did before you came, as a mob. 'Tis your craft that bested the Romans. If we have not often enough told you that we know your value, I tell you now. Do not be offended by hasty words spoken wi'out thought. I do not doubt your loyalty, and well can I understand that you wish to save your countrymen. But think of the risk!"

"I have," Rick said. "It's mostly to me. I've planned the battle for you. The catapults and ballista are in place, and their officers know how to use them as well as I do. You know what weapons Parsons has—if they survive. I have not told him of the gunpowder buried beneath the village, and it's likely he'll go back there if our talk fails to convince him."

"I do not care for this at all," Drumold said.

"Nor I." Tylara pointed to Gwen. "What has she said to take away your senses?"

"I didn't want him to do this!" Gwen protested.

"It would take too long to explain," Rick said. "But I tell you this. If I am killed tonight or tomorrow, the only way you'll live through the Time is to listen to Gwen and do as she tells you." He looked at his watch. "It's time to go. I told Parsons I'd meet him and Elliot and one other on the road midway between the lines. Mason—"

"No sir."

"Eh?"

"I said, 'No, sir.' This is a volunteer job, Cap'n, and I'm not volunteering."

"I see. Maybe that's wise of you. All right, I'll go alone."

"I do not think I should permit you to go at all." Drumold said.

"I doubt you can stop me," Rick said. He held his hand near the holstered Mark IV .45. "I don't doubt you could kill me, but that seems a strange way to save my life."

Drumold stood aside.

"That's all then," Rick said. "I'll be back in an hour."

✧　　✧　　✧

All was quiet at the forward outpost. Rick stared out into the darkness. Tran's outer moon gave very little light, and he could see nothing on the road ahead. He heard footsteps behind him and turned to see Mason.

"I'd feel better if you were coming along," Rick said. "But you're right. You're needed more here. If I don't come back, take charge of the catapults. A dozen of them firing grenades ought to knock out Parsons' machine gun."

"Yeah. Maybe. Cap'n, I'd like it a lot if you didn't do this, but I know you have to. I don't believe you can talk sense to Parsons, but I hope I'm wrong. He's got some pretty good men with him. Elliot, McCleve, Campbell—"

"That's the way I see it," Rick said. "Okay, here I go."

He was startled by another voice behind him. "Wait," Tylara said. "I am coming with you."

Like hell you are. He stopped and turned. "No."

"Yes. You have said there is no danger to you. If there is none to you, there is less to me."

"You won't even understand what we're saying," Rick protested. "We will speak in English—"

"Yet I am going," Tylara said. "Do you think I wish to live twice widowed but not yet a bride?" She smiled softly. "And I give you the same reply you gave my father. You cannot stop me without killing me, and that is a strange way to protect my life."

Oh, bloody hell. And she means it, too. "All right. Let's go."

❖   ❖   ❖

There were footsteps on the road ahead. Rick halted. "André?" he called.

"Yes. Hello, Rick."

There was no mistaking that bantering voice. "Who's with you?"

"Sergeant Elliot and Corporal Bisso," Parsons said.

"Let me hear them."

"It's us, Captain," Elliot's voice called from the darkness. "Nobody else."

"And who is with you?" Parsons asked.

"Tylara do Tamaerthon," Tylara replied.

Now where did she learn enough English to know when to answer? Rick wondered. Mason?

"You have brought a woman?" Parsons asked.

"Sure, André. This is a flag-of-truce meeting. I didn't think I needed bodyguards."

The low laughter came back. "Still naïve, my young friend. Well, this time you were correct. I have brought no more than you have heard. Do we now stand and shout in the darkness?"

"No. There's a hill about a hundred yards to the left. It's bare on top. We'll go up there and sit. I've brought a dark lantern."

"So have I. Well, let us get to it, then."

They reached the top of the knoll together. Rick pulled back the dark shutter from his candle lantern. He could see Parsons grin as he sat down.

"I must say I am completely surprised," Parsons said. "I suppose I should have suspected when I heard that hill tribesmen had won a great victory over the Roman legions, but I did not." He took a flask from his belt. "Wine?"

"Later—"

Parsons' laugh was a low, mocking sound. "Ah. Me first." He tilted up the flask and drank. "Are you certain you will not join me?"

"I have my own," Rick said. "I was about to offer you some. Share mine?"

"Perhaps it is better if we each keep our own," Parsons said. "That way there is no suspicion." His voice hardened and took on a more serious note. "Why have you asked me to meet you? Do you wish to surrender your army?"

"No. I came to tell you things you don't know. First thing; have you listened to the local legends? About caves, and fire from the sky?"

"No."

"I thought not. But you do know about the caves."

"I know there are caves beneath many of the castles," Parsons said. "They are important in the local religions. My friend Sarakos was very unhappy that he could think of no way to enter those under one of his castles. He would like me to help him cope with the ammonia, but I have better things to do."

"You'd better learn about the caves," Rick said. "That's one reason I wanted to talk to you. If I lose this battle tomorrow—"

Parsons laughed.

"I said if, and I meant if," Rick said. "We'll get to that

later. But if you win, you'll need to know about the caves. You'll need them for fallout shelters."

"I fear you make little sense—"

"Listen." Rick told him of his deductions about the fate of the 1400 expedition, and Gwen's suspicions. He was careful to be certain that Elliot heard the story as well as Parsons.

"Interesting. I do thank you," Parsons said. He sounded very thoughtful.

"Of course that may not matter to you," Rick said. "I understand you won't be able to raise the *surinomaz* for the *Shalnuksis*." He laughed. "You said I didn't have enough experience to accomplish the mission, but I seem to have a bigger and better army than you do. And there's no guerrilla war where I live. So who's so damned efficient now?"

"That is unkind of you," Parsons said.

"My apologies. But you see, that *surinomaz* crop is more important than you know. A lot more."

"How do you know this?"

"Gwen. Remember her? The pilot's girlfriend. She found out a lot about the people who brought us here. There's a lot going on up there." He pointed to the bright stars and their strange constellations.

"You have not told me why this *surinomaz* is important."

"I don't know that I can trust you," Rick said. "It involves a lot of people. Including some back on Earth. But assume I'm lying. It's still important to *you*. Without that crop, you won't be getting any juicy trade goods from the *Shalnuksis*. In fact, André, just what *are* you accomplishing with your superior skills and experience?"

"Is there any point to this conversation?" Parsons demanded.

"Certainly. I hope to persuade you to join us," Rick said. Parsons laughed.

"Why not?" Rick asked. "Together we can grow those crops and trade with the *Shalnuksis*. We might even be able to capture a starship and get the hell off this planet! If we work together.

"Or we can go on fighting, and no matter who wins we

both lose. You aren't going to grow that crop. Sarakos can't even feed his army! The people here will never stop fighting as long as he's here. But you must know already that we've been welcomed as liberators. My alliance is with the legitimate king, and I've got most of the nobility as well. I can get crops planted and harvested. You can't.

"Come over to our side, and you'll have an honored place. Wealth and influence, and you won't have to fight all the time. We both win. Fight me, and we both lose."

"So," Parsons said. "You are persuasive, if over-confident. And yet I wonder. I have been thinking since I received your letter, what is it that you can do? Gunpowder? Muskets? I think you have not had enough time. Hand grenades? Undoubtedly, and catapult bombs as well. Tell me, what range do you get with them?"

"Enough. And I have a lot of them," Rick said. "André, for God's sake, let's end this damned war here and now. Can't you see it's better if we work together?"

"I see that you are the cause of my troubles," Parsons said. "The guerrilla war—"

"That was spontaneous," Rick said.

"I do not believe you. Without you the resistance will collapse, and in the morning we will destroy this barbarous army of yours." He smiled thinly. "What makes you think I will share power with you and your hill clans?"

"You share with Sarakos—"

"For the moment. I need him. But that will not be forever."

"André, you've gone crazy," Rick said. "What do you want?"

"What I said I wanted before we left the Moon," Parsons said. "To be a king. And I do not think you can offer that. Rick, you are a fool. Without you, your cause collapses. I will have your army as well as my own." His hand darted under his jacket.

It seemed to Rick that everything moved in slow motion. Parsons' hand reached his pistol, and Rick threw himself violently aside, his hand scrabbling for his own weapon.

Then there was a shout. "No! Damn it, no!" Elliot's shout startled Parsons so that he fumbled his draw, but Rick was still too slow. He had the .45 in his hand, and the safety off, but before he could swing it around to point at Parsons, André's own weapon was lining up with Rick's head—

There were three shots very close up. Rick's ears rang with the muzzle blast. He heard shouting, but it was incomprehensible through the ringing in his ears. Gradually he realized that he was still alive, and that he felt no shock or pain.

André Parsons fell heavily. His face held a look of total surprise. "My honorable young friend—" he gasped. Whatever else he was going to say never got out.

"Take it easy," Sergeant Elliot was saying in the Tran dialect. "We surrender." Elliot held his empty hands high, and after a moment Bisso did the same.

"What happened?" Rick asked. "Who—"

"I tried to stop him myself," Elliot said. "I already made one mistake about you, Captain. I didn't want to let Colonel Parsons make another. But he was too fast. I didn't even draw. It was your girlfriend there." He pointed to Tylara. She sat motionless, still holding Mason's pistol in both hands in the approved military grip. One of the baggy sleeves of her cloak was charred, and wisps of smoke rose from where she had shot through it.

✧   ✧   ✧

Mason came up the hill moments later. "You all right?" he asked.

"Yes—" Rick's ears still rang. Tylara had been no more than a foot behind him when she fired. His head was clearing, but it seemed to be a long time doing it. Tylara seemed dazed as well. And now here was Mason. "Where did you come from?" Rick demanded.

"Out there," Mason said. "I did a little scouting in case Parsons brought a sniper. Nobody around just at the moment, but after those shots there will be. We'd better get going. How you doing, Sarge?"

"Just what is going on?" Rick asked.

"Hell, Cap'n, I wasn't going to let you come out here by yourself," Mason said. "Figured I'd be more use out where they couldn't see me. Only you had to pick a place I couldn't get close enough to! Good thing Tylara thought of borrowing my pistol. She's been taking lessons dry-firing that thing for weeks now. Cap'n, we really had better get going."

"All right." He got up and felt himself swaying until Elliot steadied him with a hand on his shoulder. "Tylara—"

She got up slowly. She kept the pistol in her hand, but she was careful not to point it at anyone. "I had not known," she said softly. "I did not intend to—shoot—but once."

"They'll do that," Mason said. "Come on, I hear people comin' from both directions. You move out—I'll hang back and discourage visitors." He patted the H&K battle rifle affectionately.

"What now, Elliot?" Rick asked.

"We'll accept your offer," Elliot said. "If it's still open."

"It's open," Rick said. "But it won't be for long." He looked at his watch. "You have no more than two hours to get back to the village and bring any men who want to come. Bisso will stay with me."

"Yes, sir," Elliot said. "Two hours." He stood awkwardly for a moment, obviously fumbling for words. "I'm not much for apologies," he said. "I thought I was doing the right thing back when we first landed. Now—"

"You don't have to apologize," Rick said. "Just get back with the men. Leave equipment if you have to, but bring the men and what you can carry. Two hours."

"Yes, sir. Two hours."

Forty minutes after Elliot brought a dozen men and the light machine gun to Rick's pavilion, the gunpowder exploded.

EPILOGUE

Tylara looked down from the battlements of Castle Dravan with satisfaction. The last remnants of Sarakos's siege works had been removed, leveled over. They were gone without trace. Dravan stood strong again.

It would need to be. Sarakos was dead—had that been his body in the silken robes? The gunpowder bomb had obliter–ated the face. Whoever that was, Sarakos had died; and with neither king nor star men to lead them, his armies had dissolved at a touch from Rick's pikemen and archers. Drantos was free, but there were rumors of war from the north, and more than rumors of invasions from displaced tribes to the south.

The Demon Star stood brightly above the horizon, visible even at high noon. She thought she could already feel its warmth. The Time was coming, and there were myriads of details for the attention of the Eqeta and Eqetassa of Chelm. She turned away from the battlements to where Rick and Gwen stood, and she smiled faintly. Rick was sending Gwen away. She need no longer fear what her husband might feel for his countrywoman.

❖   ❖   ❖

"They can't expect a crop for another year," Gwen said. "The invader star won't be bright enough. Are you sure you won't need me here?"

Rick shook his head. "I'll manage. Tylara doesn't like having you around anyway—"

"I've noticed."

"But the main thing is to start the university as soon as possible. You'll have Warner and Campbell, and I'll send you McCleve as soon as he's finished his work on a tetanus inoculation."

The medical sergeant had already developed a smallpox vaccination, and was teaching anatomy to some of Yanulf's acolytes. That knowledge would soon be spread too far for the *Shalnuksis* to eradicate even with atom bombs.

"I wish you didn't have to stay here," Gwen said. "Not—Tylara has nothing to be jealous of. But there's so much to do."

"I'll come by for visits," Rick said. "I want to keep an eye on Marselius. He's keeping the peace so far, but you never know. I confess I envy you. A tranquil university life looks pretty tempting compared to what we'll have to do here."

More detail. Fields to be cleared for the *surinomaz*. Careful planning of the cultivation area so that the population could quickly take refuge in caves. The caves to be stocked with food, and more fields to be plowed with the newly designed plowshares. And always the threat of wars—

Tylara came to join them. Rick took her hand and stood close to her. Living with her was like having a dozen wives: one moment she could command armies, but in the next she would be shy and seem helpless. At the moment she wore armor and looked very much the warrior aristocrat.

They'd been married two months, and he understood her less now than he had when they first met. There was only one certainty: he couldn't imagine living without her.

Well, one other certainty. Gwen's leaving couldn't hurt. The Chinese ideograph for "trouble" was a stick drawing of two women under one roof, and the last months had shown the truth of that.

"Before you go, there's something I've been meaning to ask you," Rick said to Gwen. "You might not want to tell me. You once mentioned that Les had a message for his child. I'd like to hear it."

"All right," Gwen said. "It wasn't long. He said he wanted his child to know this much: to know that his father believes that the human race has a greater destiny than to be the slave soldiers of a so-called civilization preening itself over remaining unchanged for five thousand years." She looked up at the Demon Star. "I hope he was right."

"Damned right he was," Rick said. "Even if Les can't come back with his textbooks and a ship. All we need is time, and we'll have that. We'll have six hundred years. It didn't take Earth half that long to go from the steam engine to the space shuttle. We'll do it in a generation because we start with more."

Gwen nodded agreement. "A lot more. And we know starships are possible."

"Yes. That does help. You go start your university, and I'll deal with the *Shalnuksis*. One way or another, your child will inherit the stars."

"Our children," Tylara said.

EXPERIENCE THE BEST-SELLING WORLDS OF
JERRY POURNELLE

Chronicles of the CoDominium

High Justice ◆ 69877-X ◆ $4.99 ☐

King David's Spaceship ◆ 72068-6 ◆ $4.95 ☐

Prince of Mercenaries ◆ 69811-7 ◆ $5.99 ☐

Go Tell the Spartans ◆ 72061-9 ◆ $5.99 ☐
(with S.M. Stirling)

Prince of Sparta ◆ 72158-5 ◆ $4.99 ☐
(with S.M. Stirling)

Other Works

Exiles to Glory ◆ 72199-2 ◆ $4.99 ☐

Birth of Fire ◆ 65649-X ◆ $4.99 ☐

The Children's Hour ◆ 72089-9 ◆ $4.99 ☐
(with S.M. Stirling) A Novel of the Man-Kzin Wars

Created by Jerry Pournelle

Death's Head Rebellion: War World II ☐
72027-9 ◆ $4.99

Sauron Dominion: War World III ◆ 72072-4 ◆ $4.95 ☐

Invasion: War World IV ◆ 87616-3 ◆ $5.99 ☐

CoDominium: Revolt on War World ☐
72126-7 ◆ $5.99

Blood Feuds ◆ 72150-X ◆ $5.99 ☐

Blood Vengeance ◆ 72201-8 ◆ $5.99 ☐

If not available through your local bookstore, send this coupon and a check or money order for the cover price(s) to Baen Books, Dept. BA, P.O. Box 1403, Riverdale, NY 10471. Delivery can take up to ten weeks.

NAME: _____

ADDRESS: _____

_____

I have enclosed a check or money order for $ _____

LARRY NIVEN'S KNOWN SPACE IS AFLAME WITH WAR!

Once upon a time, in the very earliest days of interplanetary exploration, an unarmed human vessel was set upon by a warship from the planet Kzin—home of the fiercest warriors in Known Space. This was a fatal mistake for the Kzin; they learned the hard way that the reason humanity had decided to study war no more was that humans were so very, very good at it. Thus began the Man-Kzin wars.

Alpa Plasma Center